100 Stories for

100 Stories for Haiti

an anthology

Bridge House

British Library Cataloguing in Publication Data

A Record of this Publication is available from the British Library

ISBN 978-1-907335-03-7

This edition published 2010 by Bridge House Publishing
Manchester, England

DEDICATION

I started this book alone. Worried, nervous, and quite frankly, scared out of my wits that the idea would fail. The people listed on the following page pitched in without a thought to themselves. This book is dedicated to them, the hundreds of writers who sent their stories, and to all those who helped make it happen. And if you're reading these words, if you bought a copy of this book, it is also dedicated to you.

Proceeds from the sale of this book go to helping the victims of the Haiti earthquake. To find out more about the *100 Stories for Haiti* project, please visit
http://www.100storiesforhaiti.org.

Greg McQueen, founder, The 100 Stories for Haiti Book Project.

EDITORS

Viccy Adams, Elizabeth Cake, Tony Cook, Tammi Dallaston, Nick Daws, Jane Dixon-Smith, Mark Gallacher, Danny Gillan, Elaine Gowran, Dayna Hester, Jayne Howarth, Louise Jordan, Claudine Lazar, Katherine Lubar, Lorraine Mace, Naomi Mackay, Hannah Moss, Anne KG Murphy, David Robinson, James Skinner, Caroline Sutton, Marie Teather, Maureen Vincent-Northam.

SPECIAL THANKS

Amy Burns, Mark Coker, Jo Chipchase, Tony Cook, Dorothy Distefano, Nick Harkaway, Sarah Lewis-Hammond, Mai McQueen, and the *Bridge House* publishing team: Debz Hobbs-Wyatt, Gill James, Martin James, Nicola Rouch, Ollie Wright

Contents

Introduction

By Nick Harkaway

If you didn't actually look at the images, it was because you knew what you'd see: a pall of smoke or dust; hands under bricks; smudged, stunned faces in flapping hospital tents; overloaded doctors from a hundred countries; and wailing, desperate people clawing at the camera lens or running after a truck they hoped might have food on it.

We all knew what the Haiti Earthquake was as soon as we heard it had happened. And we knew, too, that at some point there would be a story about how the money we put into those tins on shop counters wasn't making it to the front line or wasn't being spent right, and we gave anyway because you'd have to be an ogre not to hope.

I have friends in Haiti. Every time my email chimed I thought I'd be getting one of those ghastly, toneless letters saying: 'I have to tell you that so-and-so did not survive.' By chance, they're all okay, at least so far. I say 'so far' because, although the earth is still again, the crisis continues, as it will for months and – if we stop paying attention – for years.

This, then, is the moment when we demonstrate that we are actually the people we want to be: the lucky, wealthy nations with skills and power and heart. This is when we try to see past the accusations of one doctor that too much time was spent looking for survivors and too little on saving those already found. This is where we acknowledge the relief effort is not perfect but nonetheless we have a job to do.

This is the moment when we keep giving.

Of course, while giving is, according to a recent scientific study, more pleasurable and healthy than receiving, it can become a bit burdensome after a while – especially if you can't see the real time effects of your gifts. That's where this book comes in. The writers and publishers will do the actual giving, and you just have to buy some really great stories which you would, of course, have rushed to buy anyway because of the sheer weight of unrefined awesome contained within these covers.

This is an eclectic collection. It's a bundle of literary odds and ends tied up with string and sent, shoved under the seat of an old four wheel drive truck and squeezed between tins of peaches in syrup and bags of unfashionable clothes, to where it's needed. As I write this, I have no idea what the stories in it will be, or by whom they will be written. I had a message in my Inbox one morning: Nick, will you do this? Yes. Of course. I'm a writer: I can't go flying off to Haiti and make a difference. The absolute best I could achieve over there is to get in the way. So how can I help? Like this.

Open the book. Pick a page. There's nowhere to start and nowhere to finish. 100 stories, in a crate, bound for Port-au-Prince, because we're writers, and this is all we know how to do. When you've finished the book, if you can find one story, one page, one line in it which was worth reading again, join up: get someone else to buy it.

Enjoy the book. And thank you for helping us to do more than just wish there was something we could do.

All-Or-Nothing Day

By Nick Harkaway

They say that Marlon Agonistes was the greatest gangster the world has ever known. They say he robbed the Special Express and carried off early sketches of the Mona Lisa; that he stole the nails from the cross and the trident from the devil's paw; that he beat down Iron Roy Branden and made love to Giant Jean. They say that – when he died – every gunhand and soldier, every rickshawman and scurryboy, every footpad, skulldugger, lightfinger, long con and short con, matchfixer and pimp, every dealer, doper, dandy and dastard, every wrecker, smuggler, inside man, shill, car thief, chequebouncer and murderer, every single one, in other words, of the notable and notorious professional crooks in all the five cities, felt a sharp and undeniable pain in his chest, and a sense of overwhelming sorrow.

Marlon Agonistes was a titan. He had flashing eyes and broad shoulders, a generous middle and wide, cruel lips, and he sat behind a table at Robbie Tresko's café in a fancy suit.

Marlon Agonistes was the keeper of the keys; he solved problems in a town which was just a towering stack – nothing but – and people came to him with everything. My marriage is over; I can't afford the rent; this guy's roughing me up; my daughter's afraid to walk home at night; my manager's making eyes at me. And all these problems were fixable. Everything could go away. Departing wives at his request would stay another month and try again, and wicked bosses kept their hands to themselves; bullies disappeared for ever. Even solid citizens would come to him, because the borough was so broken an honest joe was as busted as a crook. Marlon Agonistes understood. He inhabited the most fundamental tenet of the gangster's creed: he lived reciprocity. So when the bulls came down, wild blue lights and howling affront, Marlon Agonistes was invisible. No door was closed to him, no house lacked concealment for Papa Marlon. He was the last priest of the church of us, a one-man revolution.

When he knocked over Lombard & Raye, and the take was twenty million, the gutters of the borough ran with gold. Trust funds appeared for children's education, lost uncles left fortunes to deserving widows, and debts long written off were paid in full. Businesses foreclosed by banks stuffed full of public money were resurrected, refinanced. This wasn't just profit, this was restitution; half for Marlon and his boys, and half for the borough. Not forty per cent, the so-high tax legitimate businessmen paid their legitimate accountants to avoid, but the full fifty, every time and without complaint. The numbers appeared on a board at Tresko's, beside the specials. Pie for a fiver, fish and chips six twenty, library for the Tolpuddle School two hundred and ten thousand, plus ten grand for the Widow Liskard to go to Egypt in fine imperial style.

Marlon Agonistes was our king, keeping peace and doing justice, taxing and disbursing, making war. He was the city, with all its quirky generosity and sudden rage. From his cream and brown brogues to his solid gut and vast belt buckle to his diamond tie pin he was regal, and on his head was a crowning mass of hair.

The hair was where he kept his magic, they said. It was all in the hair. His eyes could transfix you, his hands could bend steel, he could eat and drink like a starved Italian and fight like an Irish rover, but it was that mahogany thatch of fire and shadow on his pate which made all the difference. Marlon Agonistes had the hair of the Medusa. It lay across his face when he was angry, made his wrath more terrible because it was only partly glimpsed. When Marlon was joshing you, his forehead was high and clear and he rocked like Father Christmas in his grotto, but come the moment for serious talk, his hair knew it, tumbled down and over, blocked one eye like a pirate's patch and cast sharp shadows over his cheeks. Beware, the hair whispered. Beware. There are no second chances in this room. No light forgivenesses.

There was a memorial garden in Latimer, and a park in Trenchard, and people said if you touched the earth in either place, you could feel the exothermic heat of decomposing fools and thugs who'd been slow to show respect. You'd never find

13

mention of anyone done in by Marlon Agonistes. They vanished whole-cloth. People forgot them, pictures faded, registers and records went away. The only trace was those little fingers of warmth on an icy day, reaching up through the soil and preserving the roses, even in winter.

They say he killed a multitude, an actual myriad with his bare hands, but no one can remember who they were.

Marlon Agonistes ruled the borough and the five cities for a decade, and he aged not at all. His hair was mahogany when he arrived, and mahogany it remained until the day it all came to an end.

It came to an end because of evolution.

Marlon Agonistes was an evolutionary force. His peculiar brand of wickedness built civic responsibility, formed good habits. He wouldn't stand badness; legal or the other kind, he wouldn't have it. You don't take that lady's house, he snarled at Arger Fitz the bailiff. You don't take it because it's wrong. He vanished the Cockleshell Men from docklands after Finny Albright was found, and faced down Boss Laughlin in the winter of '27. That badness which comes from not paying attention, not caring who your life might touch, that was his special hate. He right about wiped it out all together, and folks got smart, got brave and educated under his law. Out of the smoking ashes of City Hall – it turned out Mayor Klintock was importing slaves from Haiti by way of Tendry Docks, and the face of Marlon Agonistes was entirely covered by his hair that day – grew the New Assembly; from the borough council came a candidate named Bostonia Kite, fresh-faced and new-minted with letters after her name.

'Seems to me we're old enough now,' Bostonia Kite said. 'Seems to me we're past the point we need a cold, hard fellow as a monarch in a backstreet bar. Seems to me it's time we had some law.'

A lot of the professionals in the borough wanted Marlon Agonistes to warn her off, but he wouldn't hear of it. She won with eighty one percent.

They say Marlon Agonistes died the following morning. They say it, and everyone knows it's true, because of that great stab of pain they all remember and the soft, lingering sorrow of growing up and being a solid citizen which came upon them, after. Knifemen became barbers and pickpockets became puppeteers. They say that one shared moment of pain and the shadow of extinction was enough for everyone to cross the street to the sunny side, and stay there. So I never tell what I saw at mile marker fifteen, the evening Bostonia Kite won the election.

The marker's out past Tayton and by the Ledbury farm, and the hills are rich with corn and grapes. The smell of loam rises out of the ground with the mist. I go there when I need to. I'm not city born, and sometimes the purples and the oranges and greys of streetlamp life are more than I can carry, and the circular skyline of house and tower and brick is too tight across my back. I go where the city fades and the world is in a different palette, and I sit. There's a hedge with a hollow stone on top, and Old Man Ledbury doesn't mind if I perch on it and eat a beef sandwich and drink beer. Sometimes we talk about things. Most times we don't.

But this evening, with the sun low and the west all red, and water in the deep breaths, Old Man Ledbury was somewhere else doing Ledbury things, and I sat watching the cows and the mile marker and the cars going by, and I was quiet inside.

So quiet, I was, that the man who came over the hill didn't see me. He was a big guy, wide in the shoulder and the gut, but he moved with a light step, like a dancer. He carried in one hand a canvas sack, and in the other a spotted handkerchief looped to make a bag. He was so joyful and so careless, I didn't know him until the light caught his great mahogany mop and for a moment he was still, and then I saw Marlon Agonistes, the greatest gangster of the world, and I saw him smile like a great, shaggy dog lolling its tongue at a plate of steak. He cast around, and found a bit of branch by the hedge, and bent to pick it up.

The sun went down that minute, the way it can outside the city, in a sudden rush. The sky turned gold and green, and it lit him up like a spotlight or the finger of God so I could barely see.

But it seemed to me then, and it seems now, that he reached up to his titan's head, and rolled his shoulders like a man shedding a mighty weight, and took off his hair, and laid it in the sack by the side of the road. It seemed to me that he shrugged out of his gangster's suit, and put on jeans, and left the whole great terror of himself behind. It seemed that he wandered away with a bundle of life in a chequered handkerchief on a stick, and that, three hundred yards later, a venerable Rolls Royce automobile, its maroon sides scarred by vast and improbable battles, stalled beside him as it slowed to pick him up.

They say that Marlon Agonistes died as he lived, in a great conflagration and convulsion, and that with him died the time of thuggery and sorrow in the five cities. They say no one in the borough missed him and they tell stories of the titan days, the all-or-nothing days he lived through. They say that, bit by bit, the park in Trenchard and the memorial garden in Latimer grew cold, and old sins went back into the Earth.

But this is my truth: that when the car stopped at mile marker fifteen, the big man who had been Marlon Agonistes was embraced by the laughing, regal fellow who was its occupant, and together, with much unnecessary debate and discussion, they restarted the stalled vehicle and went on their way into the coming dusk.

About Time

By Mo Fanning

Cake. She has to have cake. For an entire week, Anna managed to walk past the window of Truly Scrumptious, averting her eyes.

Last night, she had two bowls of cabbage soup and a bifidus yoghurt. Then later, infused with Zen-like smugness, she ran a hot bath and lit candles. Surrounded by expensive foam, she congratulated herself on a week of self-control.

At 3 am, she woke, went downstairs, and poured a whole bag of oven chips onto a baking tray.

*   *   *

'Morning Anna,' Glenda said, looking up from arranging éclairs on a tray. 'Haven't seen you all week. Have you been away? Anywhere nice?'

She shook her head. Words were the least of her concerns. She wanted one of the blueberry muffins piled up behind the glass.

'We've got some lovely carrot cake. Baked it myself.' Glenda wiped her hands and placed the éclairs on the counter within reach. Anna could smell the bitter dark chocolate topping.

'I'll take a plain scone,' she forced herself to say.

Glenda's face said it all. 'Just a scone?'

'Just a scone.'

'But you'll have clotted cream and jam? Strawberry jam.'

'I'm on a diet,' Anna said.

Glenda's face changed. 'You? On a diet?' She didn't add 'you don't need to lose weight'. Her face said 'about time.'

'I'm trying to slim down for my holiday.'

'Well, each to their own.' Glenda put the single miserable-looking scone into a brown-paper bag. 'As long as you're doing it for you, not for some bloke.'

'As if.'

Anna managed a smile.

*   *   *

Later that morning, Anna sees him across the room. He's leaning over Lesley Fowler's desk. Skinny Lesley. She's doing that giggly thing she does when there's a good-looking bloke within flirting distance. He looks up, smiles at Anna and does a goofy wave. She does the same back. He mimes drinking. She nods. So they've made a date.

Except it isn't a date. Ben is her best friend.

'Lunch orders.'

Anna looks up to find Lesley smiling. 'I've got some left-overs,' she lies.

'Suit yourself. I'm going to Bert's.'

Anna pictures apple pie. Oozing pastry, dusted with cinnamon. Bert's do the best pie in town. Everyone knows it.

'Get me a salad,' she says.

'Just a salad?'

'Plain green, no dressing.'

'Are you on a diet?'

'Sort of. Not really. Well, a bit. Just watching my carb intake.'

There's that look again. 'About time.'

*   *   *

At five, Anna switches off her computer, shrugs on her jacket and goes to find Ben. Together they head for the next door pub. He orders bitter. She has lager. Pints. They find a table in the corner and collapse into soft leather armchairs.

'I'm thinking of asking Lesley out,' Ben says.

'Oh?'

'Am I batting out of my league?'

Out of his league? Is Ben mad? He's tall, slim with matinee idol looks.

'You're probably too good for her,' she says, taking a slug of her drink.

'What makes you say that?'

'Lesley's a nice person,' Anna lies, 'and I really like her.' She'll go to hell for adding one untruth to another.

'But?'

'But nothing. Ask her out. You two look good together.'

Ben downs what's left of his drink and goes to the bar. Anna watches him, wondering where it all went wrong. First day in the job, he was appointed her mentor. He showed her round and took her to lunch, insisting she order whatever she wanted, and laughing when she suggested two deserts over a main course. Two weeks later he'd asked her for a drink, then took her to dinner. For a while, it looked like they might become an item. But instead, they drifted into friendship. Meeting up after work to laugh and gossip.

'I got you some nuts,' Ben says as he sits down.

'Oh right. Thanks, but I'm trying to lose weight.'

She studies his face, waiting for the 'about time' look.

'Why?' he asks.

'Why what?'

'Why are you trying to lose weight? Is there a man involved?'

Anna folds her arms. 'Why can't I do something for myself? Why does it always have to be for someone else? Why does everyone assume I'm doing it for a man?'

Ben's face changes. 'Sorry.' He looks away and mutters something.

'What?'

He shakes his head.

'Go on. Tell me what you just said.'

'OK.' Ben takes a deep breath. 'What I hate about you is that you never tell people the truth. You say what you think they want to hear. You spend half your life tip-toeing around when the worst thing that could ever happen is that someone doesn't like you.'

'Wow,' Anna whistles. 'Where did this all come from?'

He's not done. All the time he's addressing the floor, not looking her in the eyes. 'And all that would be fine, if just for once, you'd stop thinking about what others want and…'

'And what?'

'Do what you want. Put yourself first.'

'I am doing what I want. I'm losing weight for me.'

'But I like you as you are.'

'Bully for you. Shame everyone else sees this big fat lump.'

Ben looks up. 'Is that what you think?'

Anna nods.

Here it is, she thinks. The 'about time' face.

The kiss, when it happens, takes them both by surprise.

*   *   *

The next morning, their eyes open at almost the same time.

'Did you mean what you said?' she asked.

He nodded. 'About time,' he'd said. 'About time.'

Amplified Distance

By Siân Harris

I wish I didn't think about you when I walk past the war memorial. It feels like tempting fate, and I'm suddenly desperate for there to be a penny on the floor that I can pocket, or for two joyful magpies to fly across the green – just something, anything that might cancel out my gloomy thoughts and keep you lucky. I know you'd laugh at me – Load of superstitious bollocks Jen, since when have you been so daft? – and really, I think that you're right, but it comforts me to think that I can store up good fortune for you. It comforts me to think that I could keep you safe.

That was always my job, remember? I held your hand across the street, stopped you talking to strangers. You used to have this little yellow duffle coat with a big hood – you thought it made you look like a fireman – and I swear I lost count of the times I had to grab onto that hood and pull you clear of the road, or next door's pitbull, or the duckpond in the park. I wish it could still be that easy to hold you back.

The thing is, looking back on it all, I could only look after you as long as you let me. I might have been the bossy one, making the most of the eleven minutes I had in the world before you arrived, but you were always stubborn, always so much stronger than me. So either you were humouring me, or – and I think this is more likely, really – you were relying on me. You knew that I'd step in, you knew that I'd never let you get hurt. I'll not be telling you this theory, I know just what you'd have to say: Oh aye Jen? Been reading psychology books at college again, have we? But it keeps me awake sometimes, thinking about how we used to be, and how far you've gone since then.

I saw Katy Dean by here last week – remember her? I worked with her last summer, in the café. Thick as a brick, and that's being generous. She's the one who, when I told her I had a twin brother, asked if we were identical. Anyway, she was waiting for her bus, and we chatted for a bit. She asked how you were getting on, and I gave the usual patter about how brave you're being, how proud we all are. And then, of course, she put on that 'concerned' voice they all assume sooner or later, and she asked me if I thought that I would you know, feel something, if anything happened – not that it will – but you two are ever so close, aren't you...

Thankfully, her bus came then, because I was just about ready to snap. Close? We're not close. We're nearly four thousand miles apart. Daft cow. I was still fuming about it by the time I got home, and I had to slip quickly through the kitchen, keeping my head down, so I could get to my bedroom without anyone asking me what was wrong. They're nice enough, my flatmates, but we don't have a lot to say to each other, and it's been a bit tense round there lately. All my fault, of course. I got into a stupid argument with Sophie's new boyfriend. He's a politics student, you know the type: roll-up in one hand, Big Book of Anarchism for Beginners in the other. He said his piece and I said mine, and then I played you like a trump card, the ace up my sleeve. It was a cheap move, and I can't tell you how much I regret it. Not least because I'm going to have to pick at least a fiver in pennies up off the street before I feel like I've atoned to Lady Luck.

The strange thing is, for all that I don't like thinking about you here – with the memorial benches and the battered wreaths, and old St George up there, forever slaying that poor dragon – despite all that, this is still the place I think of you most often. I walk around the square, like we used to do together, back when you were going through your emo phase and nicking all my eyeliner: Don't be so tight Jen, I've only used a little bit. Nobody looking at you in those days would ever believe how things turned out. It can only have been four years or so back. It feels like a lifetime.

Anyway, I walk, and I smoke, and I read the benches, and I think about you and us and I keep my eyes peeled for even the smallest sign that luck is still on your side, that you're going to be alright. So really, I should have been delighted when I was cutting through the square this morning, hurrying to make it on time for my lecture, and some bastard seagull chose that moment to shit all down the sleeve of my new jacket.

I know what Katy Dean and her kind mean when they ask me if I'll you know, feel something. They want to know if I'll feel the repercussions of a bullet to your spine, or if I'll find myself passing out the very second that your foot plants down in a minefield. I don't know if I will, and I hope that I never find out. But today, when I was standing there, on the verge of total hysterics, I knew that you'd be laughing. Four thousand miles away or not, I felt that all right. And I don't know if you felt it back, but eventually, I joined in.

And the First Note Sang

By Catriona Gunn

When Tom – who played the harp – went to get the morning paper, he found a note of music wrapped up inside it. He took the note out carefully and gave it to his sister Lizzie. She put it with the note of music that had been humming by the kettle. Then she gave both the notes to their cat Mouse who took them outside on her whiskers and added them to the note she had found sitting on the doorstep. The three notes were picked up by a bird and added to the note that had been sitting on the end of the branch of a music tree. Da-di-dah-dah. The four notes fell on top of a young man going to the station to catch a train.

'Well, well,' he said to himself and began to hum the notes. He added a note that he had been keeping in his pocket. On the train he gave the notes to a pretty girl. She smiled and added a note from her little red bag. Then she gave all the notes to a fat little baby in a pram. He played with them for a little while and then blew them into the air with the note that had been caught under his fat little chin. The notes were caught by a boy in school uniform. He added the note that had fallen off his football boots and gave them to a beautiful woman in a sari. She handed them gently on to the old man sitting next to her. He could just hear the notes dancing across his fingers the way they had when he had once played the violin. He added the note that was still sitting on his right thumb and gave them to a school girl who smoothed them gently and added the note from her pencil case. She gave them to her teacher.

And on and on it went. The note that Tom had found joined the note that Lizzie had found and the note that Mouse had found and the note that the bird had found and the young man and the pretty girl and the fat little baby and the boy and the beautiful woman and the old man and the school and the teacher and on and on and on. They were like a great, untidy necklace of sound.

They went across the ocean and the mountains and the desert and rivers and lakes and a glacier and little mounds and deep gullies. They were caught by people with blue eyes, brown eyes, grey eyes, green eyes, dark eyes and bright eyes. 'Just a note' they said to themselves, 'I'll add to these other notes and pass it on.'

The notes bounced and jumped and danced and twirled. They ran up and down and curled in and out, over and under. Sometimes they stood on one another, sometimes they would laugh and sometimes they would take a rest.

Eventually they made their way back to Tom who looked at all the notes and said, 'I think I can sort this out.'

He sat down and tuned the harp and sorted all the notes into the right places and then he started to play. The notes jiggled and jumped, bounced and twirled and danced. Lizzie started to dance and the cat started to dance and the bird started to do a little swooping dance and the man began to give a bouncy little walk onto the station platform where the pretty girl gave a little skip, the baby jiggled in the pram, the boy gave a little jump and the beautiful woman swayed to the tune. The old man smiled and tapped his fingers and the school gave a hop and the teacher clapped her hands and it went on and on and on and on. People began to dance over the ocean, over the mountains and the desert and rivers and lakes and the glacier and the little mounds and the deep gullies.

Tom smiled to himself and the first note sang.

Anna and Nineteen

By Claudia Boers

Nineteen's heart leapt as Anna passed by the veranda where he sat working.

The tailor kept his head bent. He fed cloth through the machine evenly and pumped the foot pedal rhythmically so she would not notice him watching her slow progress down the street. Her withered leg left a trail of smooth arcs in the red dust behind her. They reminded Nineteen of a sequence of beautiful crescent moons.

She carried a crutch fashioned from the same hardwood that the villagers used to pound cassava roots. Nineteen thought it made her distinctive, but he could tell that the crutch and her bad leg made Anna self-conscious. Ever since she lost the use of her leg she'd seemed sadder than a weeping bird. People told her she was lucky to be alive but this made no difference.

The villagers said the snake bit her because her father, a fisherman, killed one of the giant coconut crabs on Rolas Island. Legend has it that anyone who kills one of these crabs will be haunted by the crab's spirit. Anna's snakebite was not the only bad thing that happened to Cheia and his family since he killed the crab. Nineteen hoped his intentions would change the family's luck and give them reason to celebrate.

He examined the seam he had deftly finished, despite his missing index finger – that was why he was called Nineteen. He understood what it was to want to hide a flaw.

The bright fabric was soft and cool in his hands. The villagers would think the dress's full length and many layers extravagant. They would say it was impractical but he didn't care. All that mattered was that when she wore it, Anna would be able to hold her head high and feel like a queen.

Apple Pie and Sunshine

By Mary Walkden

'You here, Miss Emma?'

I knew before I pushed the back door open she would be there, she was always there. I rested my hand on the boy's small shoulder, encouraged him through the door. His eyes were wide with wonder, fright.

She beamed at me from the stove, stirring... always stirring. 'Sheriff!' It was always the same, and not just for me. She made you feel like you were the most important person in the world, that you were special. 'Come on in. Let me get you a coffee.' She poured, but I could see her eyes peeking over her glasses, taking in my new little partner. 'I have some wonderful cold fresh milk. Perhaps your new assistant would like some?' She already had a glass out of the cupboard. I chuckled.

I sat down at her table, not the one the paying guests used, but the one she had for herself and the friends who would drop by. I had spent many an hour in this room, couldn't get enough of it. It always smelled like apple pie and sunshine.

With a flick of my boot, I pushed out the chair at the end of the table, nodded for the boy to sit. Emma had his drink right there for him, just like my coffee was waiting for me – steaming and sweet; she knew just how I liked it. A plate of fresh cinnamon buns followed. I noticed she set it in the middle of the table, then gently nudged it closer to the boy.

'Miss Emma, this here is Jimmy Bradley.'

Emma sat down across from Jimmy, poured herself a glass of milk and smiled. 'I'm pleased to meet you Jimmy. You helping the Sheriff today?'

The boy shook his head slow, exaggerated. 'No, ma'am. I don't know nothing about sheriffing.' Emma took a drink from her milk, smiled her milk-moustache smile at him. Jimmy giggled.

27

'Jimmy's dad sent him up here from the city when Jimmy's ma took ill. He was staying with his Grandma, Hildy Matthews, but she also took sick. You know Hildy?'

Emma nodded but her attention was on the boy, on his frayed cuffs, his dirty face. He was only about five, had been in the door not even five minutes and he had Emma wrapped round his little finger.

'Doc put Hildy in the hospital, wasn't sure what to do about this young pup. I thought maybe he could get a meal and a cleaning here, Emma. I think he's gone without while his grandma was sick.'

Emma walked her fingers across the table, closer to the boy, a spider stealing a cookie. He laughed. Her finger tips reached his hand, running over each little dimple. 'Why, I would be delighted to have Jimmy stay here. There's a bedroom right beside mine that would be perfect for him.'

I knew about the bedroom. It had been used for this sort of thing many times before. The doc would find some kid needing a roof and a meal, he would bring 'em to me, and I would leave 'em with Emma while I found them a home. Most of 'em, boys and girls came back again and again to see Emma. None of 'em ever forgot her.

'Thank you, Miss Emma.' Jimmy gave her a shy smile. For her, his words were a whisper from an angel's lips.

'I got some of his clothes outside. I'll bring 'em in.'

I stood, headed to the door. When I looked back, she was lost in the child's face, beaming at him, loving him with all her heart already. When I came back in, she was discussing that evening's menu with the boy, learning what he liked, what he hadn't ever tried before. He seemed content with the stew she had simmering in a big pot on the stove.

'Here you go, Boy. Run put this in your room. Do it smart and make sure you keep neat.'

Jimmy took his case. It was almost as big as he was. He started dragging it out of the kitchen.

'Up the stairs, dear, first door on the left. Do you know your left?' Emma asked. The boy held up his left hand. 'I knew you were a smart one, Jimmy. When you get done putting your things away, come back down and help me make some buns, then I will show you around the garden.'

There was a shuffle, a clump, again and again as the boy heaved that trunk up each step. 'There are some toys up in that room, Sheriff, some little puzzles Fred made.' I knew that too. The toys up there were legendary, many brought by previous occupants of the room, thankful for what they found and wanting to help make a hard day better for the next child. 'He'll be fine here. No worries.'

I knew the boy was in the best of hands. I reached into my pocket, took out my wallet to give her some money for the boy's keep. She couldn't be expected to just take them in but I knew what her reaction would be. 'You put that money away. He's small. The room was empty and he won't eat much. He's just a little boy.' She winked at me. 'You're money isn't any good around this house.'

I put my cup in the sink, nodded and tipped my hat to the lady. Like all the others before and all who were yet to come here, Jimmy would be just fine. Like all the others before and all who were yet to come here, I was already dreading the day I would come and take him away. For a spell in a young life, though, it was a little piece of heaven, a little sliver of apple pie and sunshine.

The Archaeologist

By Andy Parrott

My grandfather forgot things in the home. He would set the kettle to boil for my grandmother and then return to his study, leaving the water until it was cold again.

'He's useless,' she would say.

This was the man who had held clods of earth in his fists while wearing a white jacket, hat and steel-capped boots. He had separated the features of the earth, as if opening the mouth of a giant, and pulled out treasures. Each object had been heading towards nothingness, sucked down and consumed, fading, then gone. He put them in cabinets.

In company – Grandma's friends – he smiled and nodded and held his blinks for long enough to suggest that inside his mind something had closed to them, though he didn't mean it to. Grandma would try to encourage him.

'Didn't you know someone who worked for them?' she'd sometimes ask, or 'You were saying that just that the other day, weren't you?'

In response, he would tortoise himself further into his shirt collar with a quiet 'No'.

Once, though, during a lull in conversation, he brought a bone from his pocket, held it above the centre of the table and said, 'I think he was a pilgrim.'

Grandma pulled the plate of biscuits away from the foreign object.

'This was far from his home,' said Granddad. 'He must have loved something to travel all this way.' The bone shook in his hand. He placed it back in his pocket, and looked at Grandma.

When her friends had gone she said, 'You did well.' She smiled as she said it and they kissed.

Attachments

By Jack O'Donnell

I always wanted a big plate of mince and tatties to myself. Not a brother or sister grabbing at my ankles, with snotty noses and arses to be wiped. Looking up like baby starlings at dinner time and crying 'Me, Me', their little faces, more than their words, saying: give me a bit.

But they'd already been fed. So I just gave them a taste of my favourite dinner. But in no time at all they'd be sitting round me, holding their mouths open, hoping for another spoonful. Even Bryan, who was now a big boy and at school, would sit at my feet with his mouth open, mimicking the wee ones.

Our Stephen. Da' might have called him feckless. If there was a way of doing something right and a way of doing something wrong, he was sure to confuse one with the other and end up bleating: 'it wasnae my fault.' But he wasn't such a fool. His grey eyes were set like an owl. He crouched over his plate, the food steaming hot, the smell wafting up. There weren't enough knives or forks, so like me, he used a spoon. There was no real way of telling because it was a blur as it went from the banging on the plate to his hinged mouth which snapped open and shut. His arm was out, curled protectively around his world. He swayed, deaf as the Auchenshuggle bus driver to cries of 'I've missed my stop', as little hands grabbed at him and fell away.

Then it was time for the wee one's bed. We had to tuck them into each other, for there wasn't an ingle-nook of space and only Ma and Da had known a bed to themselves. But a full belly, the heat, and the flickering shadows of the range were enough to bring out many a yawn. The potato peelings had went into the soup, which was always on the go but it was as thin as the hair on Da's head. The hearth glistened and the big kettle was not far off the boil but we'd used up the last of the tea leaves and would need to use them again. Ma clasped and unclasped her hands for there was nothing to be done and morning would come soon enough, bidden or unbidden.

There was porridge in the morning but the milk had been on the turn the last two days. Da stashed it beside the kitchen window for later. Only he and the flies could stomach it. Ma kept me off from school to watch the wee ones because it was our turn for the washing. I didn't mind. But Ma said I'd be finished soon enough, so I should enjoy it when I was there. And when she said it, her thin face looked younger, as if she was a schoolgirl herself, and her eyes looked less harried. But then the glint was gone and my old Ma came back and asked, 'Have you got the washing?'

I'd already bundled everything we had into a big bed sheet. It wasn't hard. We'd missed the washhouse the week before and we hadn't added anything, so it was still tied up in the same bundle. It bumped against my one leg and little Lorna's pressed against the other as we came down the tenement stairs.

Ma was already in the washhouse with the other wee ones. She had the cold-water tap running in the first of the big sinks, ready to sluice away the worst of the dirt. She had the big bar of soap sitting beside the washing-boards. Her hands ran up and down the smooth round buttons of her blouse, down into the pocket of her pinny and back again. They were feverish jerking hands.

'A cannae find the penny,' she said. 'A cannae find the penny'.

Something of her words sank into little Lorna and fanned out so that the wee ones started their caterwauling, one after the other.

'What about the jug on top of the cupboard?' I said.

Ma's placid face looked back at me. The days of having silver stashed away were long gone. 'Lets get the wee ones back up the stairs,' she said, 'and go in and tell Mrs Morrison that she can have a shot of the washroom. There's no point in wasting it. We can wait another week.'

'We could use the cold water,' I said.

'There's no drying in cold water,' said Ma.

'There must be something we can do,' I said.

Ma's look said there was, but she was quiet. It was up to me.

Mrs Blake was the only one in the tenement building that had an iron knocker on her door. It was in the shape of some poor animal with its mouth open which was appropriate for Mrs Blake never let an opportunity pass to tell you what she thought.

Mrs Blake stood careful guard at her door. It was rumoured that she'd lots of knick-knacks that needed constant dusting and a leather armchair in front of her grate that nobody else had ever sat in but her.

Her thin lips told me everything I needed to know. She remembered back to when God had flung the Archangels out of heaven and every brown penny was recast as proof that it was wasted on what? That's what she wanted to know. She didn't begrudge it. The greatest kindness she could offer was by not helping and not asking for help.

I trudged back down the stairs. The long day stretched ahead, running endlessly on, hemming me in, like the backcourt walls. A bit of newspaper fluttered down and up again, in the wind, like a butterfly. I put one hand up to shade me from the sun, following its gentle path, one way and then the other, until it landed at my feet.

'Did you get the penny lass?' Ma asked.

I tried to keep my face from pulling up into a grin, but couldn't. I showed her the white pound note I'd found. I'd have mince and tatties now until it was coming out of my ears.

Authority

By Katy Darby

This is a story.

I am the author, and narrator, and protagonist. (I'm not the hero though, that's too gender-specific).

This is the story, told in chronological order, of my life. What happens next?

Well, in the incidents that occur throughout the plot, my character will be revealed, sometimes through dialogue ('Won't somebody rescue that kitten?'), sometimes through action (I rescue a kitten). I undergo trials. I suffer tribulations. The kitten scratches me but I am unhurt for it is a symbolic kitten representing my compassion. I discover new things about myself and others. Eventually, I succeed or fail (tragically) to reach my goal and the story is over.

The end.

The nature of my ending reflects and reinforces the nature of my beginning and defines the tone of the story as a whole. You can't know what a story is about until it's finished. That's just common sense.

But here's another side of the story: I'm the protagonist, you're the reader. You're entertained or bored by my antics. You form a picture in your mind of me. You imagine my accent, my facial expressions, although you've never seen me in the flesh, only in your head. If your mental picture of me and the author's mental picture were stuck together side by side in an album, they might resemble one another like siblings or look completely different. But your picture is correct and so is mine. We're both right. How is that?

Alright, how about this, the same story, from a different angle: we are the authors (though I'm still the protagonist, which is a relief). Wherever I go, you go too. You infer what I imply; you read in that at which I merely hint. You create text from my subtext and here's the trick: even if you're wrong, you're right, because the reader is the customer and the customer is always right. But I, as the writer, am the ultimate authority, aren't I? Isn't that what 'author' means?

One last try:

This is a story. You are the protagonist, and narrator, and author. This is the story, told in chronological order, of your life. What happens next?

The Baby

By Rachel Shukert

From the moment Joel made up his mind to start acting like a baby, his life changed for the better.

All the tedious grown-up worries – the mortgage, the dentist's bills, the ever-present possibility of genital cancer or nuclear annihilation – which had once held such a primary place in his thoughts had vanished, usurped by a kind of benign, colourful fog that lifted only when some elemental need reared its head. Once met, the fog rolled easily in again. When he was hungry, he ate. When he was tired he slept, and when he wasn't, he laid awake. If he needed to relieve himself, he did, regardless of whether he was in the middle of something important or indeed, poised over a toilet. This last in particular he had scarcely dared to do even a few weeks ago, and when he had, he was briefly plagued by a sharp sense of something he thought purged from his emotional repertoire, something very close to shame. But now it came naturally as riding a bicycle, Joel thought, as his wife softly deposited him on the brushed rubber sheet she had laid over their mattress and peppered his bottom lovingly with a liberal coating of talc. Some things you don't forget.

For the first time since he learned to walk, he felt truly free.

Tess, Joel's wife, had entertained serious doubts when her husband announced his intention to return to infancy, but even she admitted that she had adjusted better than anyone could have hoped. True, this wasn't exactly how she had imagined things ending up when they said their marriage vows, but it definitely had its advantages. Gone were her husband's foul and unpredictable moods, the resentful insinuations anytime she happened to so much as mention another man (Jeremy? Who's Jeremy? I've never heard of any Jeremy.) She shuddered visibly when she remembered how he used to berate her for neglecting to collect his dry-cleaning or send in the check for the cable bill. And while Joel's reversion to the anal stage of his sexual development left

36

conventional intimacy out of the question, this too bothered her less than she expected. For Tess, sex had begun to seem a bit like the Second World War: excellent fodder for books and films, but not something anyone in their right mind wanted to experience again personally. Suddenly, she felt a sudden rush of affection for her husband, prone and pink and helpless on his rubber mat.

'You're my good baby,' Tess cooed, giving Joel's freshly powdered buttocks a playful spank. 'You're my good baby boy.'

'Goo goo gag a goo,' Joel replied. He rarely bothered to form English words anymore. If he had, they would go something like this: 'I know! I know! Being a baby is the best!'

One day, Tess wheeled Joel through the park in his stroller, a second-hand wheelchair festooned with pale ribbons to make it look less geriatric. Joel couldn't help but notice all the people of his chronological age walking around, looking miserable. While Joel was cool in his knit onesie, they sweated in heavy suits and neckties. While Joel happily wiggled his bare toes in the sun, theirs were pinched in high-heeled shoes.

They shouted into mobile phones; their faces were pinched in worry. For the first time in a long time, Joel felt sad.

'Goo goo gag a gag goo goo,' Joel said to Tess when they returned home. 'Goo goo goo a gag gag glurgly goo.' In English, what he meant was: 'I've been given a gift. I've stumbled across the secret to happiness, and it's my duty to share that gift with the world.'

'You want to teach other people to be babies,' said Tess.

'Goo ga,' said Joel. 'That's right.'

With Tess's help, Joel crayoned several notices for the seminar he planned to give. 'Be Yourself,' read the notices. 'Be a Baby.' Tess took him all over the town to post them, and in his push to bring the masses around to his way of living, Joel's fingers seemed to recover their dexterity. English words suddenly sprang to his lips. Once or twice, he even stood up from his ribbon-bedecked chair and walked a step or two on his own. It seemed to Tess that soon he might not need her anymore at all.

'You're still my lovely baby,' Tess said, smoothing Joel's hair back from his face. Tenderly, she circled the small smooth bald spot at the crown of his head. 'You're my darling baby boy.'

'Hurry up,' said Joel. 'I don't want this to take all day.'

Joel's seminar was an extraordinary success. The studio Tess had rented at the community centre couldn't hold them all. They spilled out into the hallways and into the parking lot. Tess watched the enormous babies strip off their confining clothes. They cavorted and mewled. A pair of fashionable women played rolly-ball in a corner. A distinguished former law professor investigated the contents of his steaming diaper with a beatific smile.

'You must be so proud,' an old woman in a yellowed christening bonnet said to Tess. 'Your husband is a visionary. He's our baby now.'

'He's my baby,' whispered Tess.

On the drive home, Joel was brimming with plans. He'd get a celebrity spokesperson, build centres all over the world. His new way to live would be bigger than Scientology, bigger than the Mormons.

'I love you,' said Tess.

'You haven't listened to a word I've said,' complained Joel. 'And you wouldn't understand anyway. Now draw me a bath.'

Tess went upstairs to the bathroom. She opened the taps, checking the water again and again with her elbow. She poured baby oil into the tub and filled it with Joel's favourite toys. She carried him into the bathroom and undressed him. She smoothed his hair and kissed his sweet bald spot.

'You're my little boy,' Tess said. 'My darling baby boy.'

Then she held him under the water until he was still.

Back to the Land

By Nicola Taylor

It was like coming home.

The white cottage nestled into the hill, its back turned against the prevailing westerlies, its face to the glory of the sunrise over the loch. And I felt I wanted to nestle there too.

While mother was organised and fussed over by the bustling neighbours, stopping her attempts to hand round sandwiches and cut cakes, I walked up the brae, the wind whipping my hair from my eyes, and thought about grandfather.

* * *

'Hair like bracken in autumn,' he'd said. 'Eyes the green of a rain-washed glen. Born to wear the plaid.'

Mother had snorted then. 'Aye, she's a throwback, right enough.'

'Like a weedy trout,' giggled little brother, casting imaginary flies in the living room.

'The croft's for her when I go,' he'd said.

'Over my dead body,' spat mother. 'I escaped for the sake of my children – they'll not be dragged back to the bogs and the busybodies.'

'Over mine,' he'd corrected her gently.

* * *

That was years ago, on the one occasion he'd visited. He took me on his knee and told me about grandmother. 'She had your hair, your eyes.' He told me how he cried when she died. 'Of a broken heart,' he said. 'My bonny Mary. She was never the same after your mother left.'

'My bonny Mary,' he always called her, as tenderly at the end as when they'd first met.

'Don't go filling the girl's head with such melodramatic nonsense,' said mother. 'It was pneumonia that killed her – and no wonder. She worked herself to death, tending sheep and cutting peats all her life in the damp and the cold.'

*   *   *

He returned to the croft soon after. 'Can't stand that smoke in my lungs,' he'd complained as he breathed in the city air. Him who'd smoked twenty a day for all those years.

'Send her up to visit me,' he'd implored mother as I waved goodbye.

'When can I go?' I asked.

'You wouldn't like it,' was all she said as she hustled me indoors.

*   *   *

Now at last I was here. In time to pay my respects – too late to respect his wish. Now at last he was lying beside his bonny Mary once more. Home again. In the midst of life we are in death.

At last I was here. And everything mother had said was right. The wind blew strong and cold, the rain fell solidly, there was mist on the hill, nothing to see but green and grey, hills and sky and sea. But such greens, such greys they were – and then the clouds lifted. The sun beamed down like a nursery drawing, every ray distinct, and the shock of the change made me feel like a child again. It was like opening my eyes on the first day of the holidays, the first sight of the sea from the car, the first breath of air when we ran down to the shore.

The warmth drew the coconut scent from the gorse, suddenly blooming into gold. I crushed bog myrtle between my fingers and breathed in the cinnamon air. A pair of wagtails swooped and soared playing catch amongst a patch of bog cotton, fleecy heads nodding as the wind dropped.

*   *   *

'In the midst of life we are...' I whispered to the sky, my hand resting gently on my swollen belly. There was one last wish I could respect. 'Aye, I'll make the croft my home. For your sake, grandfather.' Under my hand, a nestling fluttered. 'And for yours, my child.'

The Beautiful Game

By Jean Blackwell

I've never been the sporty type, so it came as a real surprise to me when I started going out with a footballer. We met at a distant cousin's wedding. David was the best man. He looked so dashing and handsome in his morning suit that I was smitten right away. Sandra, the chief bridesmaid, obviously thought so too, because every time she passed me, her eyes narrowed and if looks could kill, I'd be a dead duck.

Sandra's place name had originally been set beside David's, but he'd changed it over so that we could sit together at the reception. Which left her sitting next to a portly man whose only interest appeared to be how much food he could stuff into himself. She could hardly contain her fury.

David had a beautiful smile that lit up his face and mine, too. Soon he was telling me how in need of spectacles all referees were, only pausing to give me a sweet apologetic grin before standing up to deliver a witty, off-the-cuff speech that had us all in stitches. When he sat down again, he topped up my glass with more champagne and carried on talking as if there'd been no interruption at all.

From then on we saw each other regularly and I didn't mind that nearly all our dates were spent attending football matches or training sessions. I even began to enjoy some of them. Far from being just a bunch of men kicking a ball up and down the pitch, which is how I'd always thought of football before, I started to appreciate some of the finer points that made up the beautiful game.

After a while, I did yearn to do other things, like going to the movies, or a concert or the theatre. David was great company, though, so it seemed like a small price to pay. He encouraged me to dress well and look good. I even stopped being a couch potato and started going to the gym three times a week. I felt so proud to be by his side, especially when we went to football functions and dinners and I could bask in all the glory when the trophies and medals were presented.

Sandra, the chief bridesmaid, also attended nearly all of these celebrations. We never spoke, as she was obviously still miffed. Her brother played in the same team as David and they were great friends. Suddenly, though Sandra stopped coming, which was strange because, in a funny sort of way, I missed her. Her brother didn't say anything and I didn't like to ask.

We went to a lot of parties, but, for me, the novelty was beginning to wane. The men always stood around drinking and talking about their latest match, while we girls sat eyeing each other up to see who was wearing what and who looked the best. In our own way, we were just as competitive as the men. After a while it began to feel like routine. We mixed with the same people and went to the same places. I started to think that I was just another trophy myself.

Then, as fate would have it, some kids from a local children's home were invited to a training session and I was asked to join in. I bought some designer trainers, which Sandra's brother had to lace up for me, and a green tracksuit that matched the colour of my eyes.

Sandra's brother was in charge, as the coach. He started by demonstrating how to kick the ball properly, and we all practised doing that. I began to understand how the players felt, as the physical contact with the ball felt somehow pleasurable. After some more training, we were all divided up into teams and I went into goal.

Soon I was ducking and diving, stretching and bending, as the ball flew into the net fast and furiously. For once, I forgot about how I looked and just enjoyed mucking about with the kids. Even when I conceded a goal, they just shouted out – unlucky! It felt great to be part of the camaraderie of the team, especially when we won 3-1.

My euphoria didn't last long. Before, I'd managed to change, David roared up in his silver convertible and stared at me aghast. I had forgotten that we were having lunch at the manager's house. David was furious. I must admit that when I saw myself in the changing room mirror I did look a sight. My face was red and sweaty, streaked with dirt from when I'd flung myself down on the ground to make a spectacular save. I'd sat and listened to numerous success stories from David, but he wasn't in the least bit interested in hearing mine.

'We're going to be late,' was all he could say, as it was obvious that we were going to have to stop by the flat, while I showered and changed and did some emergency repair work to my nails. He didn't say another word to me all day, whereas I had to smile and be polite while they talked football through the entire meal.

Sandra had also been at the training sessions with the kids, although our paths hadn't crossed. So I was stunned when she turned up on the doorstep one evening soon afterwards. She had a proposition for me, one that I couldn't resist. I just prayed that David wouldn't be too upset when he read the note I left him.

Dinner in oven. Be back about 8 o'clock. Gone training with the Bradwell Ladies football team.

Betsy Fudge & the Big Silence

By Maureen Vincent-Northam

Well okay, so I talk a little.

Fact is, I totally have to tell all my friends everything about my life. There is SO much interesting stuff they absolutely need to know. For example, how I am an almost-mega-famous-actress and also how my little brother invented pizza-flavoured ice-cream (do NOT ask).

Oh, all right. I admit it. I do find it close to impossible to keep it totally zipped, even when Miss Wiley says: 'HUSH! Betsy Fudge, this is QUIET time'.

But it's not like I chatter non-stop.

So it is totally unfair when know-it-all Neville Nugent tells everyone I could win prizes for yakety-yakking. He also says I could never win a bean for keeping silent. I'll bet you anything that is what put The Idea into Miss Wiley's head.

'We are having a Big Silence on Monday,' she announced ever so casually. 'The winner will be the pupil who can remain silent for the whole school day. The prize…'

(There had to be some good news).

'…will be tickets to Amazing Mazes Mania.'

I could hardly believe it. Amazing Mazes Mania! Sweet!

I also could hardly believe this. Silent for a WHOLE DAY!

What was Miss Wiley thinking? She totally must have flipped her lid, gone bonkers and lost every single one of her marbles.

I mean, no talking. At all. How was I supposed to communicate? I would need to have a fool-proof plan because I absolutely had to win those Amazing Mazes Mania tickets.

Only a crazy person could waste a TOTAL weekend thinking about school. So okay, call me crazy. But getting my hands on that prize was going to be worth it.

I snuck a look at my brother's Code Book for some inspiration (Toby is a secret agent in his spare time).

There was a chapter on Ancient Egyptian hieroglyphics. You know the sort of thing: 2 birds, a triangle, some squiggles and a goat = this pyramid is private – keep out.

The pharaohs and mummies were clever at reading little pictures (which was handy for them). But there is a total shortage of clever pharaohs and mummies in my class (which is not handy for me).

Then there were the secret tapping codes. Dot – blip – dash – dot – blop. But the blips and the blops all sounded the same and could easily get mixed up.

And not only that. Tapping codes can seriously damage your free time. For example, when Toby sent dot-dash messages through the bedroom wall Mum got totally spooked and thought his room was haunted. She refused go in there for ages, even to make his bed. Toby was NOT amused because making beds takes up a lot of valuable secret agent time.

No, blips, blops and dots were not a good idea. So I scrapped that one, too.

I liked the semaphore flags. In fact I like flags, full stop. We got to wave a Union Flag on a stick last year when the Queen visited our town. She waved back. But she didn't have a flag on a stick. Maybe Her Majesty looks in a mirror and waves a Union Flag at herself in private.

Yes, semaphore flags might be a good way to communicate. But would Miss Wiley understand that I was signalling 'the answer is 27' and NOT 'I am dying to go to the toilet'.

Then it dawned on me. The absolutely perfect answer. And it was totally brilliant. I would no longer be just an almost-mega-famous-actress; I would become the greatest mime artist in the history of the universe.

Know-it-all Neville had brought the hugest writing pad ever.

He wrote: I am going to win.

I mimed: On your bike!

He wrote: The Amazing Mazes Mania tickets are mine.

I mimed: In your dreams!

He wrote: You don't stand a chance, blabbermouth.

I mimed a pig.

All day long he wrote messages. He posted them everywhere. For example, on my locker. And in my book bag. And inside my lunchbox.

Neville Nugent had totally taken a wrong turning on the road to maturity.

On the other hand, Jessica Dooley is the politest girl in our class. She was also the first one to break the silence. Sometimes being polite isn't the cleverest thing to be, especially when Miss Wiley is handing out the reading books. Saying 'Thank you' was Jessica's BIG mistake.

No, this keeping silent lark was NOT going to be easy.

There was not a lot of reading going on. But there was lots of fidgeting. And giggling. And staring out of the window at the football pitch. At least seven boys yelled 'Goal!' when one of the teams scored.

Okay, I will be honest; I had a few hairy-scary moments myself.

At times I could feel my own words bubbling up like a volcano from deep down in my throat. Sometimes sounds rolled around my tongue and tried to burst out of my mouth. I had to fight them to stop them escaping into the open and wrecking my chances of winning.

There were times when I thought I was going to EXPLODE.

And it would not have been my fault if I had exploded. It would be Miss Wiley's fault for coming up with the totally nutty idea of a Big Silence.

The clock showed 2 minutes to 3 o'clock and only know-it-all Neville and yours truly were still in the running for first prize.

Miss Wiley waved the Amazing Mazes Mania tickets in the air.

She said, 'Neville Nugent and Betsy Fudge have both made it this far without talking. It looks like they may have to share these tickets.'

'NO WAY!' shrieked know-it-all Neville.

47

The whole room went quiet. Miss Wiley looked at the clock. It showed 1 minute to 3 o'clock. Know-it-all Neville had blown it.

Well, that is what you get for being mean. But tickets to Amazing Mazes Mania are what you get when you are an almost-mega-famous-actress and the greatest mime artist in the history of the universe.

Birds of a Feather

By Lauri Kubuitsile

Bontle hated everything about the Gaborone Birding Club: the heavy shorts that swished at each step, the wide expanse of khaki vest advertising that, thus far, she hadn't earned a single birding badge and, most of all, the pith helmet with 'I'm a Gaborone Birder!' emblazoned across the front.

The club members lived in a La-La Land where the ability to tick off the various species on their bird lists and being ace at call recognition was all-important. So intense was competition that the club members worshipped their most successful birder watchers with a voracity rarely seen outside of African Evangelical churches.

Bontle, herself, featured on the bottom rung of the club's strict hierarchy but she had only herself to blame. After all, she'd only become a member through lust and a lie.

It was all Dr Kavindama's fault. She instantly fell for the tall, dashing intellectual when he gave his speech, 'Cloning – It's Always Good to Have a Spare'. Then, one day in the university cafeteria, he said, 'I love bird watching.'

Without thinking, Bontle had responded, 'Me, too.' And now, here she was.

'Don't forget your guide, Bontle, we don't want another embarrassing incident,' Lillian Molemi shouted, pushing to the front of the queue. Lillian, the Birding Queen. Bontle wondered how she moved, weighed down as she was with all of those badges; 'Best Birder' from 1989 to 2007 alone took up the entire left side of her vest. Then there were the 'Warbler Call Recognition' and 'Complete List' badges for ducks, birds of prey and owls.

The Bird Queen just needed to open her mouth and the group would congregate like moths to a cherished lamp. 'Turn to page 471 in Newman's and, voilà, we have today's bird – the long-legged buzzard. Let's be on our way, birders!'

Professor Kavindama pushed to the front of the group, his pith helmet askew. 'Lillian, let's not forget, a sighting will earn one of our members a 'Rare Vagrant' badge.' He smiled at his Queen.

Bontle looked away. Professor Kavindama of the Gaborone Birding Club was not the Professor Kavindama with a passion for clones. He likely stole hair samples from Lillian with the hope of reproducing his own Bird Queen back in his lab. Bontle felt ill.

But there was little time for such thoughts. Lillian kept a brisk pace when hunting a bird and Bontle quickly fell to the back. She'd never be the first to spot the long-legged buzzard at this rate. The members were ruthless when a badge was at stake. On a trip in the Okavango Delta, Gothata Modise, a slightly built accountant, pushed two members into a hippo-infested channel just so he could see a copper sunbird and earn his 'Complete List: Nectar Feeders' badge.

'Kraak!' Bontle strained her ears. 'Kraak!'

She knew that call. It was a white-backed night heron, a very rare bird for this area. If she found it, she'd get one of the most prestigious badges of all, the 'Rare Night Water Bird'. She looked left then right – she was alone.

Bontle set off towards the call and suddenly heard the group in the distance. They'd heard the call too and were coming her way! Bontle ran, ignoring the thorns tearing at her bare, chubby legs. She pushed through some reeds and there it was – the white eye ring and yellow legs gave it away.

In seconds, Lillian's annoyed face appeared through the reeds. 'Imagine you stumbling upon that, Bontle.'

'No stumbling involved. I just heard the call and followed it. I don't believe you have this badge, Lillian, am I right?'

Ignoring her, Lillian snapped, 'No time to waste ogling that, let's find the buzzard!' She set off, the group trailing in her wake.

Bontle sat down on the mat of reeds, happy, and watched the heron hunting in the marshy water.

'Quite a find.'

Bontle jumped. She'd thought she was alone. It was Professor Kavindama. They watched the bird for some silent moments.

'I wonder, would you like to accompany me to brunch later?' the Professor asked hesitantly.

The heron pulled its head out of the water, a wriggling frog wedged in its beak. Bontle looked at Professor Kavindama and smiled.

Blow by Blow

By Jane Thomas

The kitchen was their emotional battleground. As she beat eggs and he shook cocktails, they disputed the corners and the high ground of their marriage. He had pursued her for years, occasionally cornering her for a month or two, but she would fend him off time and again, enlisting support from friends and colleagues to set off on long jobs in Inverness or Dubai. He besieged her voicemail, her email, her snail mail. She knew theirs would be a dreadful, wounding, misalliance. But he won the battle. He engaged her in the arena of maternity, made his advances as a potential good father. So it went, year on year, until the hammer blows of biology won her over. Knowing still that theirs was a marriage of enemies not allies they marched to the registrar hand in hand. Sometimes he thought that a small unnoticed golden arrow had pierced her defences. But the mood would pass and she would return to the fray, his old and dear adversary.

And now, quibbling in the kitchen about tarragon with the chicken, he watched her strike the garlic a sharp blow and pick off the silver paper skin with her long nails; smoothly shaped nails, lacquered guardsman red; their perfect beauty at odds with her thin brown-patched hands. Although she had capitulated on the grounds of his solidly paternal character, it turned out that she was not mother material.

Call Centre

By Elizabeth Reeder

Hard like a rock face they were, his rare hands. She imagined. She watched him through her fringe: streaks of black hair surged up his arms; his knees bruised by the confines of the desk; his headpiece balanced precariously on his big bruiser skull. He walked his voice up to the mouthpiece and tried to sound gentle. But his were not gentle ways. He was a manual labourer cramming his legs into too small a space, in a hard time.

Big, like feet they were, his mammoth hands, sweeping from gorilla arms as he rushed past her desk at the end of his shift. His indiscriminate hands knocked over her coffee and her container of pens and rubberbands. She saw his back as he retreated and he came back with paper-towels bunched together like a bouquet. He made an unconscious bracelet of the rubber bands. *Charming*, she thought. With their heads close in, as he worked on the stain, she whispered, 'Take out the middle drawer; remove the arms off your chair.' He jerked up, glared, walked away.

Loud, like crashes they were. Cracks of plastic arms being torn from the body of a chair and flung to the floor. He slapped his hands on his thighs, 'It works!' he shouted.

She blushed so she did, quietly, still picking up pens. *Talking to me*, she thought. *He's talking to me.*

And then his hands rushed towards her, capable of ripping her apart. She sat back in her chair, *He's off his head*, she thought. She thought this right up to the moment he placed his large hands upon her. The onions on his breath were sweet and greedy.

His lips were pillows; his hands were unquarried like a rockface, awkward as an adolescent's, exactly like heaven they were.

Channelling Blues

By Sylvia Petter

Pierre Dufour was beat.

He crawled up the stairs to his dingy one-room flat next to the studios of Tele-7. He turned on the TV, vibes drizzled over him like the damp of a hamman bath. He sipped then gulped a stiff Pernod as images of nubile nudes traipsed across the screen. It was a rough job – or rather – jobs.

Times were tough. Pierre Dufour went door to door. Brooms, he thought, you could sell that way, but that was years ago. The gap was widening now. Everyone was into leisure. Europe was uniting. It was anything goes: tennis racquets, balls, even cricket bats in Paris. Pierre poured another Pernod and switched off the set.

It was that time of night. He needed to talk. He didn't care if no one answered. But he knew they were out there when he poured his frustrations of the day into the Minitel Rose. He knew the men and women would be keying into their little boxes supplied free-of-charge by the French deregulated telecomms companies as a face-lift for the paper phone book. He knew they'd listen, schooled ears tuned to the innuendo of English sporting terms. He'd been lucky. The language police hadn't cracked that code yet or all his clientele would be lost by now, in translation. He laughed and took another gulp and thanked Dieu he'd brought a Gallic flair to his sales pitch.

Pierre knew all about bowling maidens over and catching them out in slips. He knew all about love games and scrums. His accounts titillated his virtual consorts but it didn't sell the goods. His story of O playing cricket, tennis and rugby had started to peak in his own peep-show frustrations. He just couldn't handle both jobs anymore.

Sport was clean, he thought, healthy. He poured the Pernod neat this time. He had to cut the sex. 'Damn TV,' he said. 'It's all their fault. They'll do anything to move the body.' Pierre wondered how he'd got caught up in the bathwater drain-out of the Minitel. The box. The boxes. He had to stop. His brain fizzed as he downed the Pernod with a lump of sugar for effect.

They found him stoned, smashed out of his mind through the glass door of the studio, Tele-7, a cricket bat still in his hand.

Chatting in the Closet

By Tim Maguire

'So you want to talk about it?'

'Not really.'

'How about I talk about something else then? Something that happened to one of my friends. How about that?'

'I can't make you stop talking. I'd like to.'

'Thanks for the blessing. My friend once told me she had a set of masks, one for every person she knew. They weren't literal masks, you know, more ways of behaving around people. She'd avoid certain topics of conversation, for example, or lie about facets of her life. You ever done anything like that?'

'Yeah. So?'

'Well she said that she didn't notice she was doing it at first, you know? It was just her building a list of what not to tell her family and her friends. It was only as she reflected on it and began to notice that she had an actual structure to her lying, that she started to call them 'masks'.'

'There is a point to this, right?'

'Have you ever known me not to have a point?'

'Noodles.'

'There was a point to that. Anyway, as I was saying, before someone distracted me, she realised she was creating this series of masks, to be worn in different situations. She even started to name them.'

'I take it you think I have my own set of masks?'

'I have my own masks. You think I'm going to tell my parents all the stuff I do round here, or I'm going to tell anyone about this? Everyone wears masks.'

'I now officially have no idea what you're talking about.'

'Tell me, what do you think my friend said about her masks?'

'One of them gives her super-powers?'

'Very funny. No. She said that the big problem with them was that she began to let them control her.'

'Huh?'

'She'd 'don' the mask, and, knowing that she was doing so, it took away her courage to be a little more open with people. It locked her into these patterns and she couldn't escape. The masks compressed her, forcing her to act like a puppet. The masks dictated her entire life. Know the feeling?'

'Umm.'

'She says the masks took an entire year of her life as she fought their programming. She still has shards of it, you know? She's always forcing herself to do things, to step up and be truthful, but she's better for it, happier, in her own way.'

'So what? You're saying that I shouldn't hide who I am? That I should be truthful with everyone?'

'Oh god no. That'd be insane. Total honesty's suicide. No, her tip was something completely different.'

'Be yourself?'

'Nah, nothing that stupid. Her advice is a lot shorter: know your masks from yourself.'

'Have you been writing fortune cookies again? That's textbook inscrutability?'

'I try. What I meant is that you need to use the masks solely for protection. Wear them to protect yourself, not to hide behind.'

The Cloud Dragon

By Sarah Ann Watts

The cloud dragon trailed fiery wings across the sky. Alexander waved goodnight from his window. The cloud dragon was always splendid at bedtime. His left eye twinkled and kept the bad dreams away.

Later when the light faded you could see his shadow against the sky picked out in stars. Wherever Alexander went, even on holiday, whether he was on a boat or a plane or a train, the cloud dragon came along for the ride, following like a kite on a string or a puppy on a lead.

The cloud dragon was special. He was Alexander's friend. The first time Alexander saw him cry, he was worried until the sun came out and his rainbow smile lit up the sky.

In the morning, Grandma took Alexander out in his red Wellingtons. When he jumped in a puddle, he saw the reflection of the cloud dragon's smile burst into laughter. Rain fingers tapped him on his shoulder and, as he turned to see what the cloud dragon wanted, a car drove up to the kerb in a shimmer of spray.

Dad opened the door and Mum got out. She held someone small and very new to the world. 'This is Peter, your baby brother,' said Mum. She pulled down a corner so Alexander could see. Peter screwed up his face and wriggled. The cloud dragon gave him a raindrop kiss. Alexander took Peter's hand in his.

'You can see him too,' he said.

Clubs and Societies

By Deborah Fielding

There's a song on the radio and like all songs, it is about love. John has heard the song before, but as he sits here, in his living room, with his feet up on the coffee table, he hears what the words really mean.

For the first time, the lyrics make sense to him. There's something about beautiful eyes, something about time and dreams and being crazy. There's something about tears. John thinks he can probably leave 'tears' out of it, but otherwise, it's exactly right. He looks at his toes dancing along to the tune and he feels like he's part of the Real World now. He feels as though understanding love is a kind of society and he's been invited to join it at last. He smiles, closes his eyes and he thinks about Jane.

Jane is at work and her colleagues are complaining about their girlfriends and boyfriends, husbands and wives. 'He doesn't listen,' they say. 'She doesn't understand what it's like for me.' 'He hasn't got a clue, it's like talking to a brick wall.' 'I wish he didn't wear that dressing gown.' 'I wish she'd cut her toenails.'

Jane listens and she thinks about John. She feels as if her colleagues are in a club that she doesn't belong to.

'You'll see,' they say. 'Just you wait a bit. It'll be the same with you.' She wonders, as she sips her tea, how her colleagues felt at the beginning.

Later that day John meets Jane at the pub where they go after work.

Her face is shiny and her hair is parted in a funny way from where she's been running her fingers through it. He looks at her and wonders about those song lyrics. He looks at her with mascara smudged under her eyes and wonders about this society that he's been invited to join: the society of dreams and sunshine on rain and perfect summer days and clever lyrics. Then he notices how tired she is. And he forgets about the society.

Jane sees John ambling across the pub. He looks very peaceful, fresh from the shower. His hair's wet but she bets he hasn't actually washed it. He's wearing a jumper that she bought for him and it looks nice. She smiles. She's very tired after work and thinks what a lovely day John must've had. She can see how relaxed he is and how carefree he looks. She wishes she were carefree like that. She feels hard-done-by. Then she looks at him and she thinks about the club that she's been invited to join: the club of greyness and endless complaints and quarrelling. Then she notices how concerned he is. And she forgets about the club.

John sits opposite Jane.

Later, as she walks past him to the toilets, Jane nudges John with her hip and he puts an arm around her for a moment.

Coming, Ready or Not

By Jac Cattaneo

Dorothy fingers memories as if they were photographs, coloured snapshots of the sixties fading to tan. Hitching with Pearl along the Cote d'Azur, azure coast, turquoise sea, blazing sky. Pearl in a blue dress, chiffon scarf round jet-black curls, legs brown from the dust and the sun.

There is dust here too, at the Plumtree rest home in Dublin, but it huddles under the sofa and sulks.

'Have you finished with the Gazette, Mrs. Price?' The nurse likes to fold things.

'Just looking at my advert. See?' Dorothy clutches the newspaper with her bent hands, fearing it might be taken from her.

'Looking for Pearl. Oh, you're trying to find your friend! You'd be better off using the Internet, lovey.' The nurse points at a poster tacked to the notice board. 'There's a bus goes down the Community Centre, Wednesdays.'

A corner of the poster is curling up, like parchment. Big green letters: 'You're Never Too Old for the Web.'

*   *   *

Dorothy imagines herself a fly, caught in a maze of dew spangled threads. The Silver Surfer bus jolts into the Community Centre car park.

'Welcome!' A youngster with a pony tail helps Dorothy into the building. 'I'm Ben.' He doesn't ask her name. 'Straight down the corridor and turn left, please. I'll be with you in a minute.' He tugs at his hair.

The chairs are orange plastic. Wobbly. Dorothy sits in front of a blinking machine. A purple wave shimmers across its screen.

Ben bounds into the room.

'Right, let's begin. That's the monitor, this is the mouse and on the floor is the actual computer.'

61

Dorothy touches the stack. An oblong hole sucks at her crooked fingers.

'That's for port for the memory stick. You won't need that.'

The memory sticks. Running down the sand dune to look for Pearl, ducking behind knotted pine trees. 'Coming – ready or not!' Laughing like kids. Sleeping on the beach, under a carpet of stars.

After Pearl stayed in France, there were letters. Visits across the Channel. Photographs of grandchildren. Then, late one night, a phone call. Pearl disappeared, two years ago now, an old lady in a wheelchair, wearing a blue cotton dress.

Dorothy glances at Ben. He's looking out of the window. She places her fingers on the port again. They unfurl, become tiny, metallic. She watches her hand shrink and disappear into the computer. Someone yells. Dorothy follows her arm.

Her feet are quicksilver, gliding along fluid conduits, sparkling, electrical. Sheets of sound fall around her, colours of an unknown rainbow, ringing like a xylophone. The web smells of cookies. She taps bars of code, leaps into portals, surfs through words and images, swings around circles and circuits.

'I'm looking for Pearl.'

A flash of blue, like a kingfisher or an angelfish, deep inside the web. Dorothy glimpses a door marked 'Chat Room' and slides towards it on a torrent of light. She hears a voice, eager, girlish.

'Coming – ready or not!'

Contact

By Jason E. Thummel

'You can't be serious!' Anna said.

'Yes, I am. It was on the phone when I got it. On the contact list.' Katie shifted uncomfortably on her chair and looked around the room to make sure no one else was listening.

'God,' Anna's voice oozed sarcasm, 'is on your contact list?'

'Yes. That's what it says.' Katie put her cell phone back in her purse. You weren't allowed to have phones out during class, even study hall, and she didn't want it confiscated.

'Somebody's just messing with you,' Anna continued. 'It's probably Bob or Greg or something.'

'No.' Katie paused as if her silence would let the moment fade away. Conversations would do that sometimes, especially in wooded and low-lying areas.

'What makes you so certain?' Anna put her pencil down from where she had been sketching in her notebook and looked at her friend with doubtful but concerned eyes, most likely seeking signs of mental illness or drug use.

'Sometimes the... well... the text messages I get are about things that no one else could know. And one time I got a text not to ride home with Alan Pierce, you know, on that Wednesday when he had the accident.'

There was a moment of silence as the girls thought about Alan.

'And what else?' Anna asked.

'Usually just normal stuff. What I'm doing, movies, music, guys, you know, the usual stuff. And the mall. Messages I send about the mall seem to be a source of extreme fascination. I find our exchanges very uplifting, you know. It seems to be very interested in just... well... me.'

'Somebody's just messing with you,' Anna concluded. 'Give me the phone and let me call the number.'

63

'I've tried that. Text only. No one answers. There's not even a voicemail to leave a message.'

'That's because whoever's behind this knows it's you calling. Give me the number and I'll call from my phone.'

'I can't. It told me not to give out the number.'

Anna stuck her hand in Katie's purse and pulled out the phone. Katie made an awkward grab and there was a brief tug-of-war. Mr Ornstern cleared his throat authoritatively from his desk and Katie saw his eyebrows rise as he stared at them. She clasped her hands together and stilled their wringing by clamping them between her knees.

Anna scooted away, waited until Mr Ornstern turned back to his papers, and flipped open the phone. There was a furious bout of number punching and then Anna slipped Katie's phone back into her purse.

'Mr Ornstern,' Anna said. 'I need to go to the bathroom.'

'Period's over in 10 minutes.'

'Um, Mr Ornstern, I can't wait 10 minutes. Please please please please.' Anna had a grating whine and the teacher relented under the barrage.

'Be back in a few,' Anna whispered as she turned to leave.

The wait was agonising. Katie replayed the conversation in her mind, trying to figure out how they'd gotten on the topic in the first place, when she was distracted by Anna's return.

'The number's disconnected,' Anna said.

Katie opened her phone in a panic and scrolled down through her contact list. GOD was gone. She tried dialling the number from memory, but it was no longer in service.

'It told me not give out the number,' Katie sighed.

*　*　*

Katie flopped out of bed, pulled her new phone off the charger, and scrolled down to the contact list. It was empty. There were no new messages waiting. She sighed and gently closed the phone. *The fourth one this week*, she thought.

The people at the mall kiosk where she had bought her first phone (and all the subsequent ones as well) told her she couldn't just keep exchanging them every couple of days. This last time they'd even summoned the manager to tell her and he was not swayed by her quoting the return/exchange policy printed on the receipt.

I'm sorry I gave out the number, she thought. Sure, Anna had grabbed the phone from her, but a part of her had wanted her friend to call, had wanted to know for certain.

Katie's bored eyes scanned the yard through her window. It was autumn and falling leaves danced on the brisk air and cartwheeled along the browning grass. A board on the greying privacy fence her father had put up a few years ago had come loose and it shivered in the wind. The thin, twisted branches on the slowly balding apple tree outside her window looked like arthritic fingers and she remembered how much their shadows had scared her as a child. Silly, really.

A dove was sitting on the nearest branch, only inches beyond the glass, head cocked and looking at her. She'd never seen a dove in the tree before, never really paid much attention to doves at all, for that matter. They looked at one another, neither moving, and in the seemingly eternal moment of stillness, Katie heard a small inner voice.

Going 2 the mall 2day?

OMG! There u r, she thought. Yes, have 2 return fone. I mist u.

I mist u 2, came the reply.

Dinner for Two

By Trevor Belshaw

Has that clock stopped? No, my watch says the same time. Stop looking every 30 seconds will you?

Maisie Connolly, this is your bloody fault. If it all goes tits up, I'll never speak to you again.

Right, check the food, Sarah. It's fine. You know it's fine, you only checked it two minutes ago. Wine, where's the bloo…okay, it's on the table, should be room temperature by now. Maisie Connolly, if this wine isn't as good as you promised you'll be wearing it tomorrow. At twelve quid a bloody bottle it ought to be dynamite.

Check the mirror. Sigh, I'm sure those lines round your mouth are getting deeper; you'll need cement to fill them in if they get any worse.

Was that a car? Dare you peek through the window? You don't want him to catch you looking. Count to 30 and listen for the car door closing… 30. No, can't have been him.

I hope he likes classical music. Those free CDs from the Sunday papers were worth keeping after all and classical is a bit more sophisticated than Simply Red.

Hang on, daft girl; Simply Red is fine for that close-up chat on the sofa later in the evening. Damn, where the hell is it?

Had to be in the bloody car didn't it? Right then, that's Mozart for dinner and Mick Hucknall for afters. Lovely.

*   *   *

8.25pm. This has to be the longest night of my life. Are we stuck in a time warp or something?

Hope he likes the dress; check the mirror: not too much cleavage, not too short. Come on, Sarah, you've been through all this; it took you two hours to choose it. What if he comes in a suit though? Are you formal enough? No time to do anything about it now.

I bet he wears a suit.

Let's hope it goes better than last time, eh? Note to self: if you spill the red wine over his trousers, don't dab at his crotch with a napkin.

Why did you do that? You should have left it at a horrified 'sorry'. It was his house; he could quite easily have nipped through to change. He ended up being more embarrassed than you, and why did you keep bringing it up throughout the meal? Oh my God, then you go and lose a contact lens in the beef stroganoff.

Wonder if he'll want to stay over?

SARAH! Stop that, you slut…It has been a while though…

* * *

8.28pm. Stop looking at the bloody clock!

He's going to be late isn't he? What if he doesn't come at all? No one could blame him after our last date.

Two glasses of wine, Sarah, and that's the limit. You don't want to get the giggles like last time. For pity's sake, he only asked you how you liked it. He was talking about coffee.

It's a shame he still he has that ex-wife hanging around in the background. She shouldn't really be calling him halfway through a dinner date. He was very kind to her, though. Not many exes would offer to give her and her new bloke a lift to the airport at the weekend.

I hope Malcolm doesn't ring me half way through this meal. He'll get short shrift, the lying, cheating…Maisie Connolly; you had better not ring to see how it's going either.

* * *

8.31pm. He's late; please don't say he's going to stand me up.

How the hell did you get yourself into this anyway? You know you can't cook.

The dinner!

Phew, lucky girl. Another couple of minutes and you'd have been serving crispy chicken.

Phone! It's him isn't it? Calling it off: he's had a break-down; his ex has come back to stay; he's just found out he's gay.

Bloody cold callers. No, I don't want to change my bloody phone provider you bloody numbskulls.

You need a drink. Just a small one Sarah, remember the giggles.

Candles? You forgot the bloody candles. This is going to be a real cosy meal with a 60 watt light bulb hanging over the dinner table, isn't it?

* * *

8.33pm. Where the hell is he? If he stands me up I'll…Hang on, whose is that car in the drive? Shit! He's here. Damn that bloody doorbell, why didn't you change those batteries when you noticed it wasn't working?

Shit, shit and triple shit.

Right, breathe in, deep breaths, calm yourself. Think Feng Shui or is it Buddhist? Check mirror, you'll have to do. Don't smile too quickly… act as though this is a weekly occurrence. No, don't do that, he'll think you're easy.

He's wearing a suit. He is looking gorgeous.

Offer your cheek, you slut, not your mouth.

'Hello, Mike. Are you early?'

Dragons

By Fionnuala Murphy

'Once upon a time, many moons ago, there were dragons.' The old lady peered at her grandson, his eyes widened with fear and wonder.

She continued: 'These were immense beasts of vast intellect and more than a hint of avarice. They used to roam the world at will, stealing cattle, sheep and goats. But more terrifying than that, if they spied a fair maiden, they would steal her away and add her to their vast hoard of precious things. The people could not fight them, for their gaze was fear itself. So they would hide their fairest, to keep them safe and sound.

'There came to this land a young woman. Her beauty was unsurpassed. Her hair glowed with a silken sheen. Her skin was pale with a rosy hue, and she walked with a delicate grace. The dragons of the land looked upon her with greed. They fought great aerial battles to be the one who would claim her. She, in turn, waited for the winner to be declared. For this was no cosseted maiden, to be stolen away by beasts. She had walked the world to attract their attention, for she had a plan to trap them.

'She approached the chief of dragons and offered herself to him, but as she did so she mentioned that she worried for his safety. For if he claimed her, the young dragons would pursue him constantly. She had an idea, an offer, if he would consider it. The chief of dragons bade her continue. Inside her, she said, was a vast country, filled with livestock and precious things. If he were to sacrifice his mortal body and enter her mind, he would possess her completely.

'The dragon considered the woman. She was a small and fragile thing. Dragons were older, wiser and more powerful in every way. Except for one: greed.

'He was tempted by the offer of her mind, and so he consented. He drew his essence inwards, before exhaling it on her.

69

He surrounded her, poured into her. The woman stood her ground, welcoming him in, smiling, for she had a secret.'

The boy broke in, 'What was her secret, Grandmama?'

His grandmother smiled.

'Wait and see, pup, wait and see.'

She paused a minute before continuing: 'Once inside her, the dragon realized his mistake, for indeed there was a vast country filled with jewels, but there was no way out. Her mind snapped closed, trapping him within.

'The woman picked her way carefully out of the dragons' lair. She walked throughout the country, removing the dragons one by one until none remained. Once she had collected them all she disappeared. No one could remember where she came from or who her people were. Some speculated that she had been a witch, but other wiser heads knew the truth.

'Sometimes when a brood leaves the nest and misbehaves it is necessary for a mother to come and bring them home. She had been no girl, but a ruse. An older, wiser and more fearsome beast, and she had come to chastise her children.'

The little boy sighed. 'But where did she go, Grandmama?'

The old woman smiled: 'Who knows? Some people say that out there in the world is a woman with dragons in her head; some say it's just a tale, a legend, like the dragons.'

She ruffled his hair and stood up. 'Sleep well, pup, and dream of flying.'

Emergency Response

By MCM

The first thing Tim noticed about the supplies tent was the water. The second thing he noticed were the boots floating in puddles. It was oddly serene, next to the world outside, and yet completely and utterly wrong.

'Dammit! Clear!' said Morris, pounding at the side of the replicator. A second later, another pair of boots fell out.

'Uh, Morris?' asked Tim, carefully navigating through the muddy terrain. 'Whatcha doing, guy?'

Morris turned, face ashen, expression switching between false calm and utter panic every half-second. He laughed, then cut it off, and shrugged. His face was twitching.

'Technical difficulty,' he said. 'I've got it covered.'

'Where's the food? The trucks are ready to load.'

Morris said nothing for a moment then turned back to the replicator, pushing a series of buttons in a pattern so deliberate, they seemed informed.

Another pair of boots fell out.

'Morris,' repeated Tim. 'Where's the food?'

'I don't have it yet,' said Morris, voice cracking. 'I just need a few more minutes, and then I'll—'

'Why is the replicator spitting out boots?'

'It's not clearing the—'

'Morris, please tell me you didn't replicate your boots. Please. Please tell me you're not that stupid.'

Morris had nothing to say, apparently.

'Oh god,' sighed Tim, sitting down on an empty crate. 'Oh god, I'm so tired.'

'It's not clearing the memory!' whined Morris. 'I'm doing it, see? Memory bank three, clear, OK.' Another pair of boots. 'It's broken or something!'

'It's supposed to do that, you idiot!' yelled Tim. 'They went over that on the plane! Weren't you listening?'

'To most of it, yeah!'

'Not enough!'

'Obviously!'

Morris pounded buttons, and this time a large tub of water materialized. He threw it across the room in a fit of anger. It added to the mud.

'We've had people collecting rubble for converting all day, and now there's nothing to convert to,' said Tim. 'Unless the people here eat rubber. And leather.'

'Kevlar,' corrected Morris, and very nearly caught a boot in the face.

'Guys,' said Marissa, peeking inside, 'the trucks are— holy crap, what happened?'

'Morris replicated his boots.'

'You what?'

'I missed the tutorial on the plane.'

'What tutorial?' Marissa asked, looking between them. 'It was in the manual!'

'There's a manual?' asked Tim.

'Yeah, and a chapter that says 'do not replicate your stupid boots, you dumbass!''

Morris sulked some more. 'Just get the manual and tell me how to clear the memory, and I can get the food copied out,' he muttered.

'You can't clear the memory!' snapped Marissa, splashing over and pushing Morris away from the replicator, as if he could do any more damage. 'It's a safeguard. It's the safeguard.'

'What kind of safeguard is that?' he said.

'To keep warlords from using it to make guns,' she said. 'Penicillin and vitamin water are built-in, and the third one is left blank for the local food staple.'

'Fun fact: not boots!' cracked Tim.

'You get one shot to set the food slot, and that's it,' said Marissa, running her hand down her face. 'And you did footwear. This is just … oh my god, Morris. How dumb are you?'

She trudged back to the door. 'I'm going to see if I can get someone stateside to send us an unlock code or something. Anything.'

She left Tim and Morris alone. Neither spoke for a few minutes. Tim was nudging a boot through a puddle like a toy boat in a pond.

'They're nice boots, though,' he said.

'Yeah,' said Morris. 'Got 'em right before we left. Didn't realize it would be so … rough, y'know?'

'Disaster zones are like that.'

'Never been before.'

'Won't be going again, let me tell you.'

Morris scratched his cheek, tapped a button on the replicator. Another pair of boots fell out.

'I just thought: it's not a big deal, right? If I back up my boots, I won't be shy about ruining these ones. Made perfect sense! It wasn't hurting anybody. I mean, all things considered, it might have even saved lives!'

Tim laughed, went back to nudging his boat.

'I'm really sorry, man,' said Morris. 'I thought I was being smart. I even made sure I wasn't wasting the rubble, so I converted my own stuff instead.'

'Like what? Your passport?'

Morris rolled his eyes. 'I'm not that dumb. I used the stupid press kit for the replicator. I was careful, Tim. My heart was in the right place. You've gotta believe me.'

Marissa came back in with the satellite phone, nodding broadly. She pushed a button on the side and set it next to the replicator.

'Okay, you're on speaker with our co-ordinator, Tim Rosco, and Morris MacIntyre. The boot guy.'

'Hey, guys,' came a voice from the phone. 'Brett here. I hear you're havin' some trouble?'

'Morris copied his boots,' said Tim bitterly.

'Third slot?' asked Brett.

'Yeah,' said Tim.

'Happens a lot,' said Brett. 'Between you and me, the plane ride over is the worst time to run a tutorial. Nobody's listening. Big waste of time.

'The good news is that it's so common, we have a protocol for dealing with it. There's an override code. Unique for every machine, very secure, and it clears the third slot.'

'Oh thank god,' gasped Tim, a smile breaking onto his face. Marissa was saying a silent prayer in thanks. Morris was having trouble breathing.

'So what you're going to do is open the keypad on the front of the replicator, and hold down the reset button for three seconds, and when the light flashes red five times, you enter the code and hit reset one more time.'

'Got it,' said Tim, making his way to the machine. 'What's the code?'

'Oh, I don't have it here,' said Brett. 'It's written on the inside cover of the press kit we sent out with the box.'

Emily's Stone

By Julia Bohanna

I was the one who spotted the strange cracked stone embedded in the riverbank – then took Richard there to help me capture it. He flipped his bike down onto the river path, not caring if the creaky thing got another bump or anything fell off it. 'You should have a rest too, before we head back,' he said. But I had seen him puffing as if he was a hundred, not twelve. The sun had buttered our backs all the way.

There it was, sticking out from the bank. Big as a peach and cracked enough to let us see something glittering inside. Something red. I sent Richard clambering down the slippery bank, his feet only just holding on.

'Be careful!' I yelled.

I was half anxious about him but the other half was worried about the stone. Pebbles and bits of dirt were already plinking down into the dimpled water.

'Emily – it's stuck!' he yelled.

Already he had his penknife to lever it out. His tongue was hanging out as he worked, just to the side of his mouth. It was his concentrating face.

I would have been gentle about the operation, taking my time. But he would never have let me use his knife. He rushed at the job and the stone split in half. Then he climbed back up to me with one hand clutching the bank, more ape than boy.

We sat on the grass, him holding the pieces out on his filthy palm. Inside the dull rock were delicate red crystals exactly the same colour as the boiled sweets I liked. The ones that always stained my mouth afterwards. Some were as pointy as pencils and when I touched them they were cold and sharp on the end of my finger.

It should have been easy: two bits and two of us. But he put them in the dirt and began chipping away at those crystals with his knife. I was too afraid to snatch up my half, but I let him know the score.

'I want mine with the crystals still in,' I said, trying to let my voice stay calm.

The earth was reddening with crystal dust.

'Typical girl!' he sneered and kept at it like a hen at a snail.

The light was failing. I was cold and thirsty. Richard was uncaringly dressed in clothes a boy grabs from a chair, or his bedroom floor. I had known him since he was a toddler and he had always dressed as if he was in a hurry. Labels on the outside, same ketchup stain three days running, that sort of thing. But both of us were in short-sleeved t-shirts and I was shivering.

It was as if he couldn't see, intent as he was in getting all the booty separated from the mother stone. I thought of the pictures of men I had seen in history books, the old prospectors from the West, panning for gold. How greedy their eyes had been; as if the telltale glint of those bits in the water held all the answers. This was more like treasure than the pretty birds' eggs we found, or even the pebbles we buffed with our sleeves to try and make them look shiny and special. He always shared those. There was something different; something darker in his eyes that I didn't like.

He was shuffling all the chippings into his pocket, where it would probably lie with all the lint and rubbish that was already there.

'I should have the bigger lot because I'm older,' he said finally, holding my pathetic share of dust up to me. He was grinning, as if that was fair. Final justice.

There was no point crying but it didn't stop my eyes reacting just a little. Life was what it was and I had the crumbs at everyone's table because I was small and quiet. Funny, I had never noticed that his nose was a bit crooked and he had a big brown mark like my grandfather's mole, on one of his bottom teeth. Funny too how it was always the flaws in boys that made people interested in them, but it was the flaws in girls that just made them less pretty.

I wanted to go home.

'OK,' I said.

76

I held out my hand. He bit his lip as he gave it to me, as if even that share was too much. We cycled home without speaking and it was my turn to throw down my bike, against the dry stone wall of my garden. I ran up the path. Like Grandma Ethel, who even looked at Grandpa as if he was not fit for purpose. I saw something in his face, just for a moment – as I was giving him my best we certainly aren't going to be friends now stare. But I gave another tilt of the chin. Then I was inside the house.

It was then that I hammered up the staircase, sat on my bed and let myself cry. I took out the sparkly red dust from my pocket and tipped it without reverence onto my dressing table. It didn't really distinguish itself with all the stones and the funny-shaped sticks that we had found together.

I was having dinner when the doorbell rang. My mother tutted and made me go. There was nobody there; on the step was a clean, white, bundled handkerchief. I put it on the table and finished my dinner. Then when my mother took my plate away, I undid the knot. To find two parts of our stone, what looked like most of the crystals, and a slightly crushed pink flower.

'Looks like a lovely present,' said my mother, looking over my shoulder.

I laid out all of it on my dressing table, the fast-wilting flower at the centre of it all.

But I wasn't thinking about how I had got my way, or admiring the find.

Not one bit.

The Encounter

By Francesca Burgess

Roy looks at his watch for the fifth time, then checks it against the clock tower outside the café. She's late. He'd suspected she might get cold feet and decide not to come after all.

The bell above the door clinks as it is pushed open, and there she is. The resemblance to the photo she had emailed him is exact. He thought – expected, in fact – that she might look older.

The woman looks timidly around the café, so he stands and waves at her. She smiles faintly, then click-clacks over to him in stiletto heels. Her cream, cotton dress with its wide, petticoat skirt, gives her a look of the Fifties. In her hand, she carries a red clutch bag. Her dark, wavy hair curls around the olive skin of her face. Such a pretty face.

She puts out her hand in greeting and he stands to properly receive it.

'I'm Marita,' she says, taking in every inch of him with her eyes.

'Roy,' he replies, bobbing his head respectfully, but not moving his gaze from her.

They stare at each other for some seconds, embarrassed, yet fascinated, before he breaks the spell with, 'What would you like to drink?'

'An Americano please. No milk.'

'Anything to eat?'

She surveys the counter at the end of the café.

'No, thank you.'

He knows that she is watching him the whole time he's at the counter. It pleases yet unnerves him. Does he come up to scratch?

When he returns with the drink, it is evident she's been thinking the same thing.

'Am I what you expected?' she asks.

'I'm not sure what I expected. You're as young as your photo – that was a surprise.'

'On the basis that women always lie about their age?' she asks, clutching the cup with both hands and glancing at him with her head tilted to one side.

He laughs briefly, looking down at his coffee, abashed.

'No, not lie. Who of us would willingly give someone a photograph that didn't flatter us? I guess it's human vanity.'

He closes his eyes against the probable faux pas he's just made.

'I'm sorry, I didn't mean …'

'I know you didn't,' she smiles. 'I'm only 15 years older than you. I've worn well, I think. Charles seems to think so.'

At the mention of her husband, their eyes lock. Hers are sad, his enquiring.

'What have you told him?' he asks.

'That I'm meeting an old friend. I don't believe it to be entirely untrue. And what have you told Anna?'

'That I'm visiting a client. She's taken the children to visit my mother for the day. They get on tremendously well.'

'What do you think your mother would have to say about this?'

'She'd be upset.'

There's silence as he finishes the last of his sandwich. She just sits, staring at the table.

'Tell me about yourself,' he says.

'I've been married for 25 years. My husband is an accountant. I own a bookshop.' She shrugs her shoulders. 'There isn't much to tell.'

'And your children?'

'Two boys, well, men now.'

'How old?'

'Carlos is 23 and Emilio is 21.'

He considers this for a while.

'What do you think they'd say?'

'They would be shocked. But it's Charles I'm worried about.'

'I don't suppose Anna will be thrilled,' he replies.

'Does she not even suspect?'

'I don't think so.'

He watches her fiddle with her hands. He longs to take hold of them in his. When he looks at her face, her expression displays the same emotion. But they sit stiffly and very much apart.

'And your children?' she intones softly, her eyes wide.

'A girl and a boy, six and four. Joanna and Edward.'

'Joanna. That's very pretty. And Edward, such a strong name.'

'Yes.' His answer seems to comfort her and a small smile plays on her lips.

Roy checks his watch.

'Must you go?' she asks.

'I don't want to, believe me, but I should. I told Anna I'd arrive mid-afternoon.'

Marita's face is passive, like a statue carved purely for beauty's sake. This meeting was a mistake thinks Roy. She's disappointed with me.

He is about to rise when her hands shoot out to grab his.

'Please. Can we meet again?'

He sits back down, sighing with relief. Tears well up in her eyes and he clutches her hands as tightly as she did his.

'Yes, I'd like that. I thought maybe you regretted coming.'

'No, no. Never. It will be hard though, for our families.'

He nods. 'My mother will take it particularly to heart, but it can't be helped. I'll tell her and Anna tonight.'

'And I will tell Charles. They'll all come round to the idea – eventually. I look forward to meeting my daughter-in-law and grandchildren. Grandchildren! Fancy that!' says Marita, wiping her eyes with a hankie.

'And I'll look forward to meeting my brothers,' says Roy.

They exchange phone numbers and finally hold each other in farewell.

'Bye for now ... Mum,' says Roy.

'Bye for now, my son.'

Enohn Jarrow, a Warning

By Emily George

When I was a boy growing up in Cornwall there were stories that used to scare the living daylights out of me. We would be sitting around the wood burning fire at my nan's house, safe and secure in armchairs, with blankets and the smell of Granddad's pipe tobacco and damp. Mum would finally give up the dishes and shift me off a chair, and I would lie flat on the floor next to Kath and stare into the dying embers.

Time didn't pass in the usual way on these evenings.

We used to sit, unmoving, me, Kath, Mum, Nan and Grand-dad. Like we were all under a spell.

Not that Nan ever moved very far anyway. She hadn't left the cottage for 21 years.

'No point in going out.' She would not be moved. 'Nothing good ever came of the outside. I'm happy as I can be here with your granddad.'

But she told such stories of Cornwall; I began to understand why she was happy to stay inside. If it wasn't giants hurling rocks, it was ancient lands, sunk under the sea. Mermaids sang to fishermen and bewitched young lads; maidens danced under still moonlight. It was more exciting in Nan's head than ever it was in the outside world.

I believed every word she said to me.

'Nothing but the truth passes these lips, my boy. It's history, I tell you now, and you'd do well to listen carefully.' And she would stare at me and Kath, and we would stare back, until one of us couldn't hold it in and a great splutter would erupt from our mouths.

We took notice of her all right, though. Especially when she told us the tale of Enohn Jarrow.

The night she first told us about Enohn, there were storms coming in. On the news we'd seen pictures of a tornado hanging above Land's End. The damp was worse than usual and the mould had begun creeping up the walls of the tiny fisherman's cottage, making Granddad cough.

'This one's worth listening to, you know,' she said. 'Every Cornishman from Sennen to Saltash knows to keep an eye out on stormy nights for spirits that may gain access to land again, clinging on the winds from the sea.'

'Like ghosts, Nan?' I asked. The heat from the fire was making my eyes water.

'Worse than ghosts, my boy. Worse even than the spriggans down the mines. Those'll avoid you if you keep yourself to yourself and a polite tongue in your mouth. No, the spirit of Enohn Jarrow will track you down. He's out at sea most of the time, riding the flurries and swirls of the Atlantic, but when there's enough storm heading our way, he'll find passage back to Cornwall. Always does, and then by God you'd better watch your back.'

Kath and I were upright now, eyes wide.

She told us it all that night.

How in life, Enohn Jarrow had travelled the length and breadth of Cornwall looking for true perfection. Some had said he was a madman, tormented. He received letters from those who had heard of his quest, telling him that the perfect sculpture had been created, that the perfect picture had been painted, or that the perfect child had been born. With each new letter his hope was renewed, and he would set off, desperate to set eyes on perfection, and rest his troubled soul.

But wherever he went, he was left disappointed.

As the years drew on, Enohn became more and more dejected. He would walk the cliffs of Land's End, ranting and raving and throwing insults to the wind.

'Can you not quieten down there, wind and storm? What is this whistling and howling, and can you not see how you lash my ears and sting my eyes? Wind should be sure about where to go, not this endless turning, this way and that and this way and that. Make your mind up, damn wind! And the noise! Oh, how I wish I were the wind, and I could show how it should be done!' And so he would go on, night after night, teaching lessons to the wind that blew in from the sea.

Finally, he disappeared, never to be seen again.

Most of Cornwall forgot about Enohn Jarrow and his quest. Until there came to be strange reports from the people who lived in the countryside up by Land's End.

There had been noises heard along the cliffs on stormy nights. Strange moans, which did not come from the wind. Anyone who dared walk the coast paths in a storm would come back enveloped by a despair and disappointment in their lives that could not be shaken.

Eventually people stopped walking out on those cliffs. But then the shadow spread. Mostly it was artists and writers, exhilarated by their latest creations, who were struck down with melancholy and disappointment, unable to put brush to canvas or pen to paper again in their lives.

These reports became legend over time.

'But I know folk who'll tell you they've felt it come over them like mist settling over land, my boy,' Nan sighed. 'They say it's the spirit of old Enohn. He couldn't find perfection in life, and he makes everyone pay the price for it in death. But once touched by Enohn Jarrow, you never feel happiness in quite the same way again.

'Just you be warned, you two, look over your shoulder on stormy nights.'

Kath and I stared at my nan in silence.

'Nan, have you ever ...' came Kath's voice, daring to ask. We knew better than to ask questions, but we did wonder about Nan and Enohn Jarrow.

Escape from Crete

By Ozzie Nogg

Amanda wanted wings so badly she could spit.

'Stop bugging me about them wings,' her Momma said. 'You gotta be patient.'

Amanda pitched a regular conniption. Tore ribbons from her braids, stomped on her baby-doll and held her breath, but Momma paid no mind. Just kept stirring the gumbo.

In the yard, on the branches of an old hickory tree, abandoned birds nests hung like magic beads. Amanda climbed, searched, found a few tufts. 'Phooey. These here sure is piddly old things, but they can help me some.' She licked the wispy feathers, stuck them on her shoulders and floated to the ground.

Her cat laid a dead sparrow at Amanda's feet. Shouting, 'Hallelujah, praise the Lord,' Amanda plucked the feathers, licked them, stuck them on her shoulders and soared to the kitchen.

'Are them feathers you got stuck on you?' Momma asked.

'No. They wings.'

'Uh-huh. Wings. Just like that. Well then, eat some gumbo. You gotta stay strong, girl, if you gonna fly.'

Eve

By Billy O'Callaghan

Stefania watches Michael as he sleeps. Three years old now, he looks more and more like her father with every passing day. Already, he has the same strong chin and the same way of wrinkling his nose to laugh.

There are times when she struggles to bring her mother's face to mind, but one glance at Michael and her father, Jozef, might just as well be standing there before her, large as life.

Tonight is Christmas Eve. Back in Tarnów this is the most precious night of the year, a night for family and all that family means, all the laughter, tears, tales, and longings. But Ireland is not Poland and tonight, sitting here in a bed-sit apartment and watching her son as he sleeps, home has never seemed further away.

She sighs, a long tired breath that spins gossamer curls from her thin mouth. The cold has crept in this week, turning everything ideally seasonal. For the past few days there has been rawness to the air that makes smiling easier than usual. At the beginning she gave herself willingly to the spirit of things, braving the hectic streets, spending money she didn't really have, on things that neither she nor Michael really need. But that's Christmas.

Once the night-time has fully settled, she gives in and switches on a single bar of the electric fire. An hour of that heat will make all the difference. If she still feels the cold after that then at least it will be late enough to go to bed. The apartment feels more bearable in the darkness. She draws her chair in close to the fire and sits forward all the way to the edge so that she is perched to savour the fullest throw of heat.

She has lived in this city for almost six years now and Cork is not so bad. Like many of her friends, she had listened to the stories of money to be made, of life to be lived, and great adventure to be had. What she has isn't squalor, though it's a long

85

way from the lavish world she'd been led to believe. But that's the way of the world.

As it turned out, hers was the old story, tumbling headlong into love with a man who knew exactly the right way to flatter and coerce. For the better part of two years, his word was gospel and she feasted on the very sight of him, adoring everything from the premature salt-and-pepper sprinkle of his crew-cut all the way down to the caked mud of his steel-toed work boots. And when that bubble burst, her life was changed forever. Well, she wasn't the first ...

At home, they'd have the table laid for the Wigilia, the Christmas Eve dinner. Days would have been spent decorating the house and preparing the many traditional meatless courses. Her father would lead the family in prayer, a place would be set in memory of their wayward daughter and, after the meal had been eaten, carols would be sung.

Tears form at a surge of childhood memories and her throat tightens with a dehydrated ache. But instead of giving in, Stefania rubs her hands together, drawing in the yellow nourishment of the fire's heat, then stands and drifts around the dark bed-sit apartment, tending to small details by touch.

Christmas in Ireland is different than in Tarnów. If there is one lesson she has learned through all her mistakes, it is that regret is a useless emotion.

Her son, Michael, is Irish. This, really, is the first year that he understands anything of the season. Tomorrow he will wake to a Christmas morning of presents carefully wrapped and placed underneath the small decorated tree. His eyes will light up as she tells him that, because he had been such a good boy for his mommy this year, Santa Claus visited during the night and delivered very special gifts. They will drink cocoa for breakfast as a special treat and walk hand in hand to First Mass, smiling widely and wildly through the cold. Afterwards, he will play with his new toys while she cooks a dinner of roast chicken, sprouts and potatoes. This can be the start of a new tradition for them; their Christmas will be special because they have one another. Two is more than enough to make a family.

Stefania pulls her cardigan closed across her narrow chest, strikes a match and lights the candle that she has placed in the window. This is one of the traditions that Ireland and Poland share, and maybe the best one. A small, flickering glow, giving hope to wanderers everywhere.

Fleeting Thoughts

By Nadene Carter

Tessa moved steadily along the dimly lit street. She'd walked this neighbourhood before, but somehow, tonight was different ... she was different. She stopped and studied her hands, her arms, her legs, and measured the sensations she felt as she rotated her arms full circle.

I feel. I'm aware. But why now and not ever before? Thoughts crowded her mind, one after another, assailing her with questions that had no answers. Puzzled, she walked on, now keenly aware of motion, first moving very fast, then more slowly, enjoying the contrast.

Ahead, she saw a break in the darkened shop fronts. In a flash, she decided, 'When I get to that corner, I'll turn right. I always turn left, but today I need to do something different.' But when Tessa came to the corner, she turned left, against her will.

'No, no, no! The other way!' she cried aloud. 'Why can't I turn right?' But her voice had no resonance, as if the sound died just a few inches from her lips. She passed more shop fronts, all indistinct and shadowed. At the next corner, she paused as a taxi went by. Just a yellow taxi, nothing worth remembering. Like the neighbourhood, really.

Tessa approached the next corner. 'I always turn left here, too. This time I'll turn right. I will!'

But she turned left and continued walking, wondering why she had no will of her own. On this street, store windows were lit up, but the objects inside appeared as if they were painted on the glass. The next block had only one lit shop front. A striped pole rotated by the door, with the words Barber Shop emblazoned in green on the glass.

Tessa stopped at the window and looked inside. Couples waltzed across a gleaming wooden floor. Muffled music coming from within startled her with the sudden realization that her journey to this place had been silent. No heel-taps from her shoes on the concrete. The taxi, silent, as it had passed by. And something else was strange ... no rectangle of light from beyond the glass splashed onto the sidewalk where she was standing.

Tessa glanced down and nervously smoothed the heavy satin of her lovely blue gown. *I've just been preoccupied*, she thought. *That must be it.*

Blue? The thought captured her.

She quickly looked from her dress to the green lettering on the window. Everything else along the streets had been grey ... except for the taxi. That had been yellow. Three spots of colour in a charcoal world. She wondered about that, for a moment, until the music coming from inside caught her interest again and enticed her to enter.

Tessa put her hand on the door and hesitated, letting the music wash over her. Then, standing tall, she squared her shoulders and went inside. A man dressed in a black tuxedo rose from his seat, as if he'd been waiting for her and, without a word, they began to dance. She studied him, trying hard not to be obvious. Tall, dark and handsome, of course. But then, he always looked that way. In a moment or two, the older, distinguished gentleman would cut in. She knew this without question.

And that was exactly what happened. The older man didn't speak, even when Tessa asked, 'We've met before, haven't we?'

He merely smiled and led her through the waltz without hesitation or error. A perfect dance partner.

As they moved across the dance floor, she glanced at the window. The words Barber Shop, so distinct when she stood outside, were no longer visible. The glass was opaque.

Confused, Tessa chose to sit out the next dance. She noticed that while the music was perfectly audible, the people around her made no sound. There was no murmur of conversation from the tables, no shuffle of dancers' feet from the floor.

Then another man approached, interrupting her thoughts and, obediently, she rose and danced.

'We've met before, haven't we?' she again asked.

He didn't reply, but held her correctly, turning her in time to the music, without showing the least flicker of emotion.

Tessa gathered her thoughts in one supreme effort. I must break this pattern! The effort caused her to miss a step. Her partner appeared not to notice.

Overcome with confusion, she wondered, 'Why must I break the pattern? Why is a pattern important and what is the point of breaking it?'

Unbidden words formed in her mind. 'So I can see. This is a new reality for me. I must learn to function in it.'

Tessa shook free of the mental chatter and tried to focus on her partner. 'Do you like this place?' she asked, not really expecting an answer.

With precision, he twirled her across the floor, smiling all the while. But then, he always smiled and never missed a step.

For a second, something stirred within her. If she had to give it a name, she might call it anger. He cannot change, but I must! I must make a difference. But different how? What will happen if I do change the pattern?

Tessa gently removed her hand from his.

'There, that's a start.' For the first time she heard joy in her voice. She almost felt it.

She allowed him to lead her through another turn, then she took her other hand away. Still they danced, apart from each other. Her partner showed no reaction, whatsoever, to her withdrawal.

'I've had all of this I can stand,' Tessa said, her voice indignant.

She stopped dancing. It was almost beyond her strength to do so, but she stopped. For a tiny slice of time, her partner danced on without her. She watched his back move away from her as he swung through the next turn.

And then things started to change. The music became garbled. She stared at her partner's back. Change accelerated upon change, until he appeared only as a collection of squares within a ragged outline. He seemed to be made of tiny blocks that quickly grew more and more disorganised.

Completely bewildered, Tessa saw her surroundings fragment. The people, the room, the walls, everything turned into squares that became disconnected from each other. The change progressed, faster and faster. She only had time to say, 'Oh, no!' before her own body formed into blocks, too. She watched it all go, until even her mind – her newly-made mind – disintegrated.

And then, nothing.

* * *

'It was so close,' Dr. Whitaker sighed. 'So very close. We actually saw her begin to react.'

'It was fantastic!' his assistant replied excitedly, as she shut down the device and put it back on the shelf. 'She was self-aware for 27 milliseconds! Artificial intelligence is possible. We just need a larger memory matrix, that's all.'

The assistant turned off the lights and pulled the door shut as they left the laboratory. All was dark. All was silent. And then the device whirred to life and an image appeared.

* * *

Tessa moved steadily along the dimly lit street. She'd walked this neighbourhood before...

Folding Paper

By Debz Hobbs-Wyatt

'Why the urgent text?'

Kai looked at the large square of paper and carefully folded the edges together.

'They're wondering where you are.'

He looked down at his hands, carefully drawing the edges together, left point to right point, crease and unfold.

'Is this to do with the dreams?'

Only then did Kai turn his head. Maybe it was the light, the milky glow from the lamp, maybe it was something in the air, but she looked different.

'Well? Why did you summon me?'

He lifted the top corner and folded it to the bottom.

'Kai?'

Outside it was dark. He imagined them all at the pub: bright lights, music spilling out into the street. They'd be waiting. But there was something he had to do. Something he had to finish. Something really important.

His fingers moved faster, turning the paper over in his hands, left to right, top to bottom.

She smelled of flowers. He felt her behind him, her hand at her sides, brushing lightly against him. 'Kai?' she said. 'You're missing it all.'

'No,' he said. 'There'll be other birthdays.'

'You're only eighteen once.'

'Maybe.'

He felt her stare, felt something shift, coldness against skin, déjà vu. It was the feeling he got when the dreams came, when he was looking into the old man's face – familiar – a shadow standing in the corner of a room.

'Kai?'

He scooped the paper in his hands and felt the shape emerge, like a diamond, as he pushed the edges inwards.

'What are those?'

Kai turned his head, looked into Naomi's face, studied the shine of her eyes. 'Wow,' he said.

'What?'

'Nothing.'

He felt the paper give as he folded, edge pressed to edge. She was watching him. Press and fold. Press and fold. Press and fold.

As his hands moved, his eyes shifted to hers. Until she'd walked into the college a month ago he'd never been friends with a girl, never been able to talk to a girl.

'What is it, Kai? Did you have the dream again?'

His hands moved, as if not his own. The smell of her perfume grew stronger.

Kai closed his eyes. He saw the face of the Japanese man, the face that had grown younger with each dream, younger when he talked about her. 'It's about love,' he'd said. 'It's about fulfilling the prophecy.'

'What prophecy?' Kai had said

Later Kai had laughed it off – a combination of that awful Japanese beer, Happoshu, and over-sentimental sub-titled films.

'But it felt real,' he'd said. He'd said it out loud to his empty room.

'Perhaps it is real,' he'd heard in his head.

Way too much Happoshu.

But the dreams came again. Each time showing him a place, a place he felt he already knew. A woman. Great happiness. Great sadness. A promise. 'When you find her again, make her remember. You have to.'

'Who are you?' Kai had asked. 'Who is she? What is this?'

'Look in the reflection,' is all the man said.

'Kai? What's happening?'

The memory faded. He was back in the room, hands moving. Folding. Creasing. Folding. Faster and faster.

She looked at the table, at the paper. 'What are they?'

'For Obon.'

'Obon? Why do I know that word?'

'The festival.'

'Now you're freaking me out,' she said. 'We should go.'

Naomi stepped away, watching him. 'What is it?' she said. 'Just say it.'

'I think I understand. But you need to come with me.'

'What about the others?'

He handed her one of his paper creations.

'It's beautiful,' she said, 'How did you learn–?'

'Just come.'

They followed the path, each holding on to the paper lanterns.

'Where we going?' she said. 'What we doing? What about the party?'

'Five hundred years,' he said. 'That's what the man told me. It has been five hundred years.'

She slowed, looked back along the path. 'You're scaring me. The others are waiting—'

He remembered the last dream, the urgency in the man's face. 'When the time comes you have to make her remember. There's not much time.'

'Her?' he'd said.

But the man had already gone.

They moved away from the path, grass wet beneath summer shoes, her moving faster, trying to keep up, she'd know where they were going now. She'd see the lake, star reflected in the faded light.

'Kai, we should get back—'

'You have to trust me.'

'But what about—'

'Trust me.'

When they reached the water, they stopped, Kai looking into her face. 'Try to remember,' he said.

'Remember what?'

As they stood he pressed his hand into the pockets of his jacket, found the candles. 'We're supposed be here, like this – together, at my coming of age.'

94

'What do you mean? Is this to do with the prophecy?'

She copied him, lowering her lantern to the wet grass at the edge of the lake.

Kai turned, trailed his finger against her cheek. 'Close your eyes and remember, Hanako.'

'What did you call me? I know that name. How do I–?'

'Watch,' he said kneeling, lighting the candle, placing the lantern on the water. 'Do the same.'

'What is this? Why do I know this?' When she turned to look at him she fell silent.

'Here,' Kai said as he placed his hand over hers. Their faces changed in the reflection. Their faces became Japanese faces, young faces in the stillness turning old in the ripples, and then the faces they knew. That's when he looked back at her. Her lips gaped open. She was crying.

'Madoka,' she said. 'You're Madoka. I do know you.'

'Yes, Hanako.'

'I was supposed to find you, Madoka. I know you. I've known you before.'

'Set them free,' Kai said, shifting his gaze to the lanterns. 'Like this.'

Together they nudged them gently into the lake.

'We did it,' Kai said. 'We found each other.'

And they watched the trails of orange glowing against the blackness of the lake.

The Forgetting

By Layla O'Mara

I received a note from a man in the post today. It said it was the longest time since we had met, so many years. He wrote with such familiarity, albeit coupled with hesitance, almost like an unsure teenager.

'Hello, this is Ella,' I said down the phone to the man who had written the note. He said hello back and remarked how good it was to hear me after all these years. And I said yes, yes, yes it was and little sparks flew off his voice as it jump-started something in me.

He asked if I would like to meet for a coffee or a drink. I said, 'Yes, Jay, that would be nice', and suggested meeting at the Patrick Kavanagh bench. I have no clue why the bench came to mind. But it did. I said it and his voice smiled and he answered that that would be fine.

*   *   *

It felt like a first date. Which was stupid, really. Getting dressed with that same butterfly attention. Seeing myself in the mirror as he might. Which was stupid, really.

I stepped out into the grey day. I had left a little late deliberately, wanting to arrive with him already sitting there on the Patrick Kavanagh bench.

I had it mapped in my head. Over Harold's Cross Bridge. My old jogging path. I used to jog along with music driving me, pumping on one of those CD players and then later with an iPod, so tiny in my hand.

The morning-time rush was calmer by the water – the swans, the ducks and the drunks not so harried by traffic or appointments. Past Portobello. Middle-aged men sat alone on benches by the water, reading the paper and swigging on their first cider of the day. I used to shoot music videos in my head as I ran, the beats in my ears narrating everything around me, all those daytime thoughts and worries sucked into a three-minute video. Jesus, it seemed like such an epic time ago. How fresh and excited and completely lost I had been.

Suddenly the city and the canal became a blueprint, a memory-print. The whole stretch seemed so scratched and scarred and glowing – virtually leaking back-bits of me into the glinting autumnal water. My mind and memory, or whatever it was that I was losing, for at least those short minutes, was at my command again.

The fact that these moments had come up for air created something very close to an out-of-body experience for me. I questioned why there was still space on my blueprint for this man and me to lie out that night on the now-gone pontoon, he after cycling me on the crossbar by all the red-brick houses, showing me where his father had grown up and telling me how his mother was so strong. That there was still room for summer pints with him outside The Barge and chats that changed what you thought about things and made you want to do new things and do things better.

Jesus. I tried to snap back, to be present, but my brain, having lost these things for so long wanted to linger a while ... someone once told me a wonderful word for it all. Palimpsest. Layer upon layer of manuscript and paper lie one on top of the other, each page borrowing the indentations of the page before and lending snippets of its own markings. It was strange, the marks that were left and the indents that were smoothed away to nothing – no logic there at all, it seemed. And no logic to where and when my mind will slip and when it will soar ...

Leeson Street. His old basement flat, where we had danced and giggled and held each other. He played music I had never heard before, music that I fell in love with and could never quite listen to again. The flat's peeling yellow door and a flash of myself in a bus window, peering at the door, eyes stuck on it as the double-decker pulled away over the bridge.

And now for my favourite stretch – the leafy patch from the Bridge down to Baggot Street – the locks silent, stubbornly holding the water in, the fiery leaves, the proud swans, the padded silence. I was always aware that the city was living, pulsing, working all around me on this stretch, yet something about it seemed defiantly unhurried, quiet.

Suddenly, I desperately wanted to turn right back or walk on by. I didn't know who I was going to sit with. I could not quite fully jigsaw this man into my past. I did not know what to say to him or what I should be remembering. How rude not to be able to properly share the past with him. How sad, this forgetting.

I was about to leave. About to turn around, escape, But he saw me and called my name.

'Ella.'

Those sparks again.

Sitting straight and tall in the chilly light, he waved and then stood to greet me. He hugged me and my body remembered his hold and we sat, like two old fools, talking and laughing and somehow remembering for the whole afternoon, him crossing the road to pick up two coffees and some cake and me feeling like I was 20 all over again. And when it grew dusk, we stood, two inky silhouettes, and he looked at me and into me and through me and he kissed my cheek and pressed my hand as he left.

The Garden

By Gwen Grant

They had been there a long time, Sharon and Mrs Garvin. Sharon, three months, Mrs Garvin, six, and now they were almost well.

'They're only keeping me because they like me,' Mrs Garvin said.

Sharon wished she could say something like that but she never did because she knew it wasn't true.

'When I go home,' she would tell anyone who would listen, 'I shall be out of the house all day.'

The problem was, Sharon couldn't sleep. She would lie awake all night, tossing and turning. She thought she would have gone on not sleeping forever if Marilee hadn't come.

'Marilee!' Mrs Garvin said. 'Very fancy. But you all have fancy names.'

'Who do?' Marilee asked.

'All you lot who come to work here,' Mrs Garvin grumbled. 'You artists-in-residence, writers-in-residence, sculptors...'

'I get your point,' Marilee said hurriedly.

'Best of it is,' Mrs Garvin went on, 'is that you're not in residence, are you? You don't live here. You go home at night.'

'I don't like the night,' Sharon put in, 'I can't sleep.'

'Why not?' Marilee asked.

'Because of the thinking,' Sharon said.

'You need a quiet mind for sleep,' Marilee told her, 'and the way to get a quiet mind is to think of something nice.'

Sharon spent hours trying to think of something nice but she just couldn't.

'Nothing, Sharon? Not one single thing?'

Sharon shook her head. Then, she smiled. A long, slow smile.

'There was my Dad's garden, Marilee. It was really beautiful. Everybody said so. People came from miles around to look at his garden.'

99

Mrs Garvin shrugged.

'It wasn't that good, Sharon.'

But it was good enough for Marilee.

'What I think you should do, Sharon,' she began, 'is make a collage.'

Sharon liked, no, loved, the idea of a collage. It sounded exotic, glamorous. Better than knitting a scarf or sewing a toilet roll cover.

'What shall I make a collage of?' she asked, and Marilee looked at her.

'Your Dad's garden, of course.'

The collage took up all Sharon's time. Marilee had to talk her down from making it life-size, with all the little paths and the black iron pump, to something a bit smaller.

'I never saw a pump in your Dad's garden,' Mrs Garvin protested. 'You've made that up.'

'My Dad put that pump in,' Sharon said sharply, and a ripple of excitement ran round the room because Sharon never answered back. 'It was for the parrot tulips.'

Sharon started cutting out pictures of flowers and grass and trees for her collage garden. No magazine was safe. A story that began on page 10 and continued on page 45 was never finished, for page 45 had become a big flower-shaped hole.

The collage grew more and more beautiful, a riot of colour and texture, as Sharon had cut out the fabric flowers from the bottom of the curtains. The sunflower was especially lovely.

Marilee went in even on her days off, just to admire the collage garden and follow its progress. It wasn't until it was almost finished that she began to see the big black hole in the centre.

'What are you going to put in there, Sharon?' she asked.

'Parrot tulips, Marilee. No one could grow them like my dad. It felt like you were standing in the middle of a rainbow when you stood in the middle of his parrot tulips. Red and white striped. My favourite. He gave me a bunch for my birthday one year. I tried pressing them but they didn't keep their colour.'

'Your dad never had parrot tulips,' Mrs Garvin said flatly. 'Never.'

'He did,' Sharon said. 'You just didn't see them.'

Mrs Garvin was also making a collage garden but her garden, she said, was going to be realistic.

'Social realism,' she added smartly.

'Well, it's certainly that,' Marilee agreed, as the collage sulked at her.

Where Sharon had flowers and grass, a water pump with a bird bowl, birds and trees, Mrs Garvin had dirty plastic bags, broken glass, shards of wood and dots of old brick, with vicious green wool for weeds and grubby yellow lace for mould and rot.

'That's what the gardens in our street looked like,' she said.

Sharon could not find a picture of a red-and-white parrot tulip to cut out anywhere but when Marilee offered to paint her some, she smiled, 'You paint very nice, Marilee, but this is my collage. I'll find tulips somewhere.'

But the empty dark hole was still there when both collages were hung on the wall.

Sharon's collage was a sunburst of light and colour beaming into the room. People would stop and stare at it, sometimes even pull up a chair, although the big black hole could be disquieting.

Then Mrs Garvin came across a picture of two red-and-white parrot tulips. She cut them out and stuck them under the green weed wool in her own garden, where they glowed and shone among the crumpled plastic bags and bits of broken glass.

Sharon didn't care.

'My collage,' she told Marilee, 'is the best thing that ever happened to me. It's the realest thing, too. I can practically see my dad in that black hole, looking for his parrot tulips.'

On the day she went home, Sharon took her collage with her and the longer she lived with it, the more she liked the empty black bit the best for it was that bit she could fill with her hopes and memories.

Mrs Garvin never got to like her collage. Never got to like the red-and-white striped parrot tulips either, but she left them because, in some queer way, they summed up her past. One thing she did do was ask Marilee to tear off the green wool weeds and winkle out the mouldy yellow lace.

And when she'd done that, Marilee cried, 'Now that is powerful.'

And it was, Mrs Garvin thought, but not quite in the way the artist-in-residence meant.

Going, Going … Still Going

By Danny Gillan

The day before you're planning to do something monumentally stupid is always a bit odd. The plan is made, the time is set – in twenty hours his life would be irrevocably changed, in the most final of ways. Should he just go for a pint, in the meantime? Maybe catch a film?

Carson Campbell decided to visit his aunty.

'Come on away in out the cold, son. Your arse cheeks must be freezing.'

'Cheers, Aunty Jean. It is a bit nippy.'

Carson shuffled through Jean's tiny hall into the living room. He took off his jacket and sat in one of the two ancient armchairs that faced the electric bar fire.

'Tea?' Jean asked, going into the scullery and filling the kettle.

'Ta.' Carson didn't want tea but he loved Jean's kettle. She was the only person he knew who still had one that whistled.

'So,' Jean said, handing Carson a mug with a picture of Mao Tse-Tung on the side. 'What's wrong this time?'

Carson smiled. 'Do I really only come here when I'm in trouble?'

Jean's lips pursed. 'Yes you do, son. Don't worry, I know all I'm good for is digging you out of the holes you keep jumping into. It's fine, makes me feel needed. Besides, I told your dad I would. What's happened?'

Carson drank some tea, burning his tongue on the super-heated brew.

'I've made a decision.'

Jean nodded. 'Thought as much. You've thought it through?'

'I think so …'

'Seriously, Carson,' Jean said. 'I know things have been … difficult, recently, but this is drastic, even for you.'

'I know that. Christ. Of course I know that.'

'Yes, you do know that. But has it occurred to you that do-ing … this thing … might make it … easier for you, but it's going to hurt a lot of other people. People who care about you.'

Carson bowed his head, unable to meet his aunt's eye. 'What the hell else can I do? I've got nothing left, Jean. Nothing.'

'Sorry, son, but that's a pile of bollocks and you know it. There's always something can be done; there's always hope. Even in the darkest darkness, there's the chance that someone will come looking, that someone will find you and lift you out of the pit. Do you really want to give up on that?'

Carson laughed. 'I've been waiting for a fair while, Jean. No one's come to rescue me yet.'

'Aye, cheers for that, son. I'm just your daft aunty with the funny kettle, then?'

'You know what I mean.'

Jean stood up as quickly as her hips would allow and snatched the mug from Carson. She looked directly at him, daring him to meet her gaze, not speaking till he did.

'No, son. I don't, anymore. I used to think I could help you, but if you do this, you'll really be alone. Far more alone than you seem to think you are now. Do you even understand how final this is going to be?'

'I might be mental but I'm not stupid, Jean. Of course I know.'

'Aye, well. I wonder about that, sometimes.'

The kettle whistled. Carson sat in the threadbare chair. Jean made more tea. Carson wished the wee telly on top of the sideboard was on. David Dickinson would have been a friendly presence, just at the minute.

'Here.' Jean thrust Chairman Mao back into Carson's wilt-ing hand.

'So,' Carson said, without much hope.

'Is this life actually so bad, son?' Jean's mug sported the famous Che Guevara photo.

'You tell me,' Carson said. 'How much fun have you had recently?'

'Maybe not as much as I used to,' Jean admitted. 'But a shit of a lot more than you, apparently. I'm not for giving up, just yet.'

'Aye, fair enough. But you know what I'm facing, Aunty Jean. No offence, but you've already had your future, and you enjoyed yours.'

'You know how to endear yourself to people, don't you?'

'Sorry, but you know what I mean. What's the point of me going on, the way things are? You can talk all you want about hope, but sometimes you have to accept there isn't any left. I've tried; I've tried everything I can thing of.'

Jean placed her tea on the mahogany-effect laminate mantelpiece and leaned towards her nephew. 'You told me. You told me they said you could last a couple of years at least. How do you know what's going to come up? How can you say there's no hope? Things could change, Carson. They could change.'

'Hah! Nothing changes, Jean, nothing. You know that better than anyone.' Carson looked round the damp-ridden room. 'What's changed for you, eh? You've been in this shithole for twelve years, what's changed for you?'

Jean took a breath, smiled, and slapped Carson sharply across the cheek.

Carson sat back in his chair, shocked.

'You're my nephew and I love you dearly, son. Do us both a favour and don't bring me into this particular argument, eh? I'm an old, feeble woman and I know exactly what my future holds, as you so kindly pointed out. I'd imagine, though, that you getting your arse kicked by an OAP would be an added humiliation you're not really after, given your plans. Wouldn't be the image you're hoping to leave behind for posterity, so behave yourself.'

Carson nodded. 'Sorry.'

'Fair enough.' Jean lifted her tea from the mantelpiece and sat back, taking a swallow. 'Don't mistake caring for weakness, son. That's dangerous.'

Carson took a breath and sent his eyes to his thighs. He'd hoped not to cry today, but he knew how unreliable hope was.

'I can't think what else to do, Aunty Jean,' he said.

'I know, son. I know.'

'I've been living with the news, living alone with this news for six weeks.'

'I know, son.'

'Two years, tops? That's it, that's all I've got. Two fucking years? Getting progressively more miserable; the pain getting progressively worse. Can you imagine me at the end of those two years? Cos I can, I can, and it's horrible.'

'I know.'

'I can't do that, Jean. I'm sorry, but I can't.'

'I know.'

'It ends tomorrow.'

'I understand.'

'It has to end, Jean. I can't keep going like this, with this uncertain fucking certainty.'

Jean's eyes clouded. Carson knew she had finally accepted his decision.

'I'm not the only one who'll miss you, son.'

'I know,' Carson said, crying openly. 'Tell her, tell her ... Christ, I don't know. Just tell her I'm sorry, will you? I know she'll hate me, and that's okay. But, just say sorry for me, will you do that?'

Jean finished her tea, put the cup back on the mantelpiece and reached over to Carson, hugging him.

'If this is what you think you need to do, I'll tell her, son. I can't promise she'll forgive you, but I'll tell her.'

Nineteen hours later, Carson Campbell stood up on the platform. He walked towards the edge and tried to smile. It was a decision. He'd finally made a decision. Even though he knew it would mean his damnation, he was glad.

Carson looked down, took a deep breath, and made that leap...

Carson Campbell, newly redundant factory worker with two years' redundancy money in his back pocket, and the surprise

Conservative Party candidate for Govan South, received fewer than four hundred votes and lost his deposit.

'Daft twat,' Jean said, switching off the television and heading for the scullery. 'He'll be needing a whistle.'

Home

By Gillian Best

Home, it's such a small word that can mean so many things: a country, a town, a house, people, food, familiarity; family.

Home means may things to me. A backyard in San Francisco, my first apartment in Toronto, several apartments in Chinatown, a sea view in Cornwall, a reasonable walk to work in London, an old tenement flat in Glasgow, and a blue house in the suburbs. Home is fresh peach pie in the summer, BBQ salmon, curry goat and roti, the ten dollar Ethiopian special, the number two at the taco place, traditional steak pasties, bun at the BYOB Vietnamese in East London, Marks and Spencer, and chicken soup.

But home is people too, people who will cope with you, put up with your moods even when you're being unreasonable. Home is comfortable, secure, knowing where everything is. It's the smell of eucalyptus in salty sea air, the business end of a deep fryer, shrimp frozen in the winter snow, foxes, and breweries.

I'd always been of the opinion that it was possible to have only just the one home, but I think I'm able to feel at home in many places. However, there will always be only one Number One Home.

I left Canada a few years ago to move to England to study. When I came home during the summer break to sort out another visa so I could move up to London and work, I foolishly referred to England as home. As in, 'I'm going home in a week.' Word to the wise, don't do this in front of The Mom. Ever. Under any circumstances. Regardless if you've been away for twenty years, wherever it is that you're currently living, if it's not The Mom's house, it's not home.

And there's a certain logic to that. The Mom's home, the home you grew up in, those four walls that felt like they might suffocate you during your awkward teenage years, the house that you fled as soon as you could, that's always going to be your

Number One Home. Because you can always go back. It won't be quite the same, but your Mom will be there, ready to cook, clean, do laundry, put up with your unpleasant moods, do whatever it is she thinks will make you happy. The door to your Mom's house will always be open, even when every other door on earth is shut.

When my visa expired for good, I had to go back to Canada. I'd come to call England home and leaving was the last thing I wanted to do. I felt a thrill when the plane began its descent into Heathrow. I was excited because I knew how to take the train from the airport. I knew it was too expensive to take a black taxi; I was armed with the number of a reputable minicab firm. I understood the local lingo. In my head, I was the coolest person ever.

With a heart heavier than my luggage, I boarded my flight. I treated it like the last time I would ever live in the UK. Several nostalgic hours were spent wandering around Heathrow.

When the plane landed in Toronto, my stomach flip-flopped. The airport is overly familiar to me. The Parents dragged us all around the world from a young age; I could negotiate customs before I'd worked out how to take the city bus. But the familiarity of this place was off-putting. I didn't want to be back, I was working on becoming – in the most pretentious way – English. Or at least British. I was living my life. I was living an exciting life, worthy of real jealousy. And now, I was back home, a place I was certain would be absolutely no fun.

The Mom was only too happy to see me when I arrived on her doorstep. I'd packed everything into my case that I could; everything that reminded me of the mates I left behind. If I could've packed all of East London into the case, I would've done. Hugs, kisses, laughter and a nice meal awaited me, but sullen as ever because I didn't get my way, I didn't appreciate it.

It took me a while to come to terms with living with The Mom again. I'd left home at nineteen and I'd never been back. The Brother and Sister had both kept ties, and friends, in our hometown. Not me, I went to The Big City and never looked back. Came to visit often, but never to live.

But now, here I was, at the ripe old age of thirty-three, and living with The Mom.

I'm sure she had her anxieties about our new living arrangements as well. Once the children had all left home, she'd had the house to herself. For the first time in her life, she was living alone. It took her a while to get used to, but she really came into her own. She thrived on it. She had her routine with The Dog, with the birds, with her walking, her friends. And it was completely disrupted when I arrived.

One of the things The Mom has always had going for her is that she's cool. She is the coolest mom you will ever meet. She doesn't judge, doesn't forbid, and very rarely scolds. We were raised to use our own good judgement. So you can come into the kitchen at 11am with a raging hangover and The Mom won't tell you not to drink so much next time, she'll just laugh at you, loudly.

I arrived home in early April. And thus began the summer of The Mom. At the time, all I could think about was getting back to the UK, getting back to my life. But when I look back on it, we had a pretty good summer. Most people don't get to experience their parents in the same way.

There were things that drove me crazy that summer, and the following one as well, but what I remember most is laughing. The Mom, for reasons known only to her, thinks I happen to be the funniest person to have ever walked the earth. What she fails to realize is that I need a foil, and that she's it. The funniest times we have are the times spent together, and those times seem to happen at her house. At Home Number One.

Hope in a Strange Corner

By Tony Cook

It's not often you find hope in a strange corner. It normally creeps up on you in moments of despair or sits upon your mantelpiece, beaming, in times of plenty. But to find it in a strange corner is rare.

This piece of hope was not self generated. I wasn't looking for hope at the time and I wasn't aware that I needed it – but when it's found, it's found, and it shouldn't be ignored.

I've always possessed fortitude and I'm very good at managing persistence but sometimes, it is true, I do lose hope. I look around and I see what's what and I just lose it. That, of course, weakens the defences and allows despair, misery and sloth into life.

Today, though, I wasn't aware that I was losing hope. I was, as the Americans might say, chipper. I prefer top hole or lashed up tight myself, but then I've always had a thing for 1930s upper-class English, and not many people understand that these days.

So, there I was, all chipper and lashed up tight and strutting about town like a puffed-up trumpleton. I was handing out cheery greetings and dispensing bonhomie like a pharmacist on happy pills. I made a witty quip to a downhearted acquaintance, who told me I'd brought a smile to his lips for the first time in an age. I told a fella I know about another fella I know who would definitely do him a turn and both would be pleased by the link. I suppose you could say that I swaggered. I certainly preened. I was a man on top form and the world was my oyster, the pearl my undoubted reward.

That's when the fall happened. It comes soon after the apex of the puffed-up trumpleton stuff and it's well deserved. It was a woman, it's often a woman, but she told me in plain and simple terms that I didn't have what it takes. She didn't just say it. She spelled it out. She made it very clear that her grounds for these statements had real body – and I found it difficult, nay impossible, to counter her claims. And she did this in the open. Some of the fellas heard and a fair number of the women heard. Disdain was generated and I couldn't gainsay it, nor did I wish to do so. I was flattened and I deserved my flattening. Like the cartoon wolf under the heavy anvil, I was spread thin upon the ground and was available for walking upon by all and sundry. I know when I'm licked, all over.

That was when I looked in the corner. There, seated upon the ground, were two children, snot smeared and knock kneed. Now I am not, by nature, a children person. I am a character, a charmer, a wit and an aesthete. I will wink at a child, I will produce a penny from behind its ear, I will smile and fawn, but I will not spend time with the creature. If the child is the route to the mother, or, on occasion, the father, then so be it. But God forbid that the purpose of the game is the child itself. That would be too, too vile.

But I am metaphorically flattened. I am down on my uppers. I am cast out and put aside. Time, I am telling myself, is what I need, for I cannot utter a cliché about healing.

Then one child starts to blubber. Shaking and sobbing, it is. The tears are rolling down its blotched and puffy cheeks. And the other child is head down upon its knees, arms folded round the caps. Then one arm sneaks out and holds the hand of the other child. And the other arm reaches into a pocket, in which are probably kept old conkers, an inky handkerchief, an apple core from last week, hardened and spongy as it approaches fossilisation, a penknife that is jammed, a foreign coin and a plastic dog keyring with no keys attached from a long-gone Christmas cracker. The hand finds a toffee, dog eared and sticky. The boy hands it to the other, who peels back golden paper as strands of sugary brown gloop reach out and stick to inner wrap. He places the paper close to his mouth and scrapes the toffee from its shell with his front teeth. He stops crying. He smiles as he presses the sweetness into his gums with his tongue. His snotty laugh bubbles through and he turns and thanks his pal with smiling, brown-tinged dribble. The boys stand and run away, jinking through the crowds.

There went hope revealed in a selfless act, a hand that reaches out, an unequal division of spoils. Nothing is offered in return. Nothing is expected.

Impact

By Dan Powell

The moment the sound becomes audible enough to notice, Sam is dragging his feet to school, swinging his rucksack back and forth over the rough path through the field behind his house. A light in the sky burns towards him and the noise blossoms into a sustained boom that threatens to crack the sky. The meteorite, for that is what Sam later discovers it is, strikes him, slicing a scar into the back of his hand before knocking him down. He lands, dazed and utterly alive, staring at the pea-sized rock that sits in a foot-wide crater punched into the ground.

Years from now, Sam will hold his dying wife's hand and weep. He will cling to the weak pulse that resonates from palm to palm, squeezing tighter as if doing so will keep the old woman from leaving. It is then Sam's eyes will alight on his childhood scar and he will marvel that the impact of this moment hurts in so many more ways than his collision, so long ago, with a nugget of rock that fell upon him from space.

Indian Dance

By Martin Tyrrell

'Here it is,' said Aidan's Dad, after he'd rummaged through every cupboard, getting angry. 'I thought someone had thrown it out.'

He handed Aidan a music case. It smelt of old, mildewed leather.

'Was this yours, Dad?'

'Margaret's. Mum's, I mean.'

'Could Mum play piano?'

'Once upon a time.'

Aidan opened the case and breathed in its must. He'd not known his mother could play. Even when she was well, she'd never touched the old upright in the front parlour.

Dad unlocked the piano the day before Aidan's first lesson.

'Play it, mind,' he said. 'Any thumping and I'll close it for good.'

The keys were yellow with age, many of them chipped and cracked. When Aidan tried to play a run of notes it sounded less like a piano and more like plucked strings twanging, flat. Deterred, he glanced through the beginner's tutor Dad had bought him in Tughan Crane. A child's book, a little too young for him, he reckoned, all those cartoon elves skipping between the staves, pointing out clefs and dotted notes and time signatures. The first dozen pages looked simple enough. After that, though, the elves were gone, the pieces trickier, whole bunches of notes dripping from a single stem, chords he could not imagine his fingers ever finding. He closed the book and slipped it into his mother's case.

'You have to creep before you walk,' Miss Cullen told him that first lesson. 'Just a few years ago, you were a baby, you couldn't walk. Now you walk to school. You walked all the way here.'

Miss Cullen walked with a stick.

'She's a cripple,' Dad had advised. 'Polio.'

Thanks to Dad Aidan had known not to stare when she opened the door and ushered him as best she could to the piano. He'd felt a little shaky himself. This was a part of town he'd never seen, a place of grey, breeze-block terraces, where broken glass crunched under his shoes. A gang of older kids had hurled a clod of tarmac onto the pavement in front of him and he'd hurried, almost running, afraid they'd come after him, throwing more. It had been a relief to round the corner and see a blue, three-wheeled invalid carriage parked at the kerb.

'Middle C,' said Miss Cullen, after she'd instructed him to keep his wrists high, his fingers bent. 'Easy to find. The white note, here beside the lock. And easy to find on the stave as well.'

She had him open his piano tutor to the first page where it showed the note as bass and treble, crotchet, minim and semibreve. Then a piece he could play – Indian Dance, four middle Cs to the bar, one bar with the right thumb, one with the left. Miss Cullen played it first, each note ringing pure and yet also, strangely, percussive as, inside the piano, mallets nodded against strings. And somehow, Aidan thought, Miss Cullen managed to make that single note sound like Indians dancing, like moccasined feet on parched soil, like the throb of a buffalo hide drum. It sounded nothing like that when Aidan played, just the same four notes being struck again and again. He shrugged.

'Try again,' she said. 'Creep before you walk.'

He made to play but the front doorbell rang and Miss Cullen hobbled to answer it, keeping close to the wall. He heard her open and close the door. Then she made her way back. No sooner had she eased herself into the seat beside him than the doorbell rang again.

'I'll get it,' he offered, but already she was on her feet, shuffling the length of the hallway. He heard the door open, a chorus of jeers, the door being quickly closed.

The third, fourth and fifth rings she ignored.

On the hour, the lesson finished and he handed her the twenty-pound note his father had given him.

'How's Ray managing?' she asked.

'Fine,' he lied. For a moment he thought of telling her how his father had stopped going into work, that he hardly spoke except to scold, that they lived on toast and chips.

'I'd imagine he still misses her a lot,' she said. 'Margaret was the one, you know. A lovely girl. My best. Then she gave it up. And now she's gone. She'd be pleased at you, though.'

How could she be pleased, Aidan wondered, when he couldn't manage Indian Dance, a string of middle Cs?

Back home, their piano made it all the worse, just one flat, discordant twang after another. No hint of wood-smoke fires or drums or tee-pees.

'I think your Indians have danced enough, son.' Dad was looking over Aidan's shoulder. 'They can do it all again tomorrow.'

Aidan closed the piano lid. Tomorrow, he'd play again, listen for those drums. It was far too soon to stop listening.

An Island's Story

By MG Farrelly

Long after the storm, Vara still dreamt about the rain that cleaned the whole world.

She had been just barely six when the storm had come and gone, changing the face of their island forever and always. Grandmama talked of the time way before. She told stories of big white men in big black suits smoking itty-bitty cigars.

'They would toss candy in the air, toss it right up and make us run for it,' Grandmama said. She would shake her head and twist her lips; a look that Vara knew meant trouble. 'I would not run. No, no.'

Vara listened to Grandmama's stories in the mid-afternoon. This was the middle of her day, when the island people rested beneath trees, took in the air, and did not work too hard because it was too hot for such a thing. The middle of Vara's day was the end of Grandmama's. She would tuck off to sleep as the light drew down.

'I miss the stars,' Grandmama said.

Vara nodded and listened.

'I miss the fine young men, all smart in their skinny suits. Did you see Dennis Lonogo? Riding on that scooter. A fine man, strong and smart. I kissed a young man like that. Under a hundred, hundred, hundred stars.'

The first half of Vara's day was down at the waters. Since the storm, the fish came biting, jumping even, to the basketmen. Vara would sell them foldaway bread, a name she'd made up for her simple little food.

Take some cornmeal, sugar and milk, and a bit of flour. Get a big egg from the farmer next door. His son will eye you, but just smile because he is so young. Mix in some mango fruit, bits of shrimp and cinnamon. She was always folding new things into the bread. Taste for sweet, taste for sour. Cook to taste and sell near the waterside from a big tray. Hungry basketmen and their sons, some of whom are not so young, will smile and tell you what you want to hear.

'Vara, this has too much meat. Too heavy! I liked it sweet. I have the sugars, the sweet teeth.'

'Vara, penny-beautiful, this is all fruit and nuts. A man needs meat on his bones. Come to my house, my son will fry conch. That's him, in the water. Straight and tall.'

Vara took their compliments and enjoyed their money. In town, she bought her ingredients, those she could not get anywhere else, the spices, the good flour. The only shop left after the storm was Pennel's. The old man who ran the shop was blind, but no one bothered him. When the storm came he lost his sight saving a mother and baby. A nice story, probably not true. What mother was saved? What baby? People like nice stories. The old man's story was likely not a nice one.

Vara would go to the tailor's stall and look at the dress she was buying for Grandmama. Two more weeks it would be paid for in full. The fabric was off-island, very rare. It was a rich, dark red satin. Vara loved to hear it sluice under her fingers, slick. The satin was cool even in the high morning sun.

Then home to Grandmama and her stories. Her skin was getting more slack and floppy every day, as if she was a great deflating balloon and every breath reduced her.

Come dark, Vara would meet the sharp-faced boy from up the road. Grandmama would not approve, as he was Blanco. Since the storm came and went she had become only a bit more prejudiced, but just enough that Vara did not want to fight her.

Not about the sharp-faced boy.

She did not love him, no. He was too quick on her for love. He wanted her like sweets and he would run and run to get them, she was sure of that. Some nights they would walk to the edge of the water. It was not always safe there, so it was said. When the storm came and washed away the old world it left many bad things in the water. The men talked about night things, ghosts and sad voices weeping over the radio waves for the long-gone

Blanco world. The sharp-faced boy liked to scare her with these stories, and when she was in the mood to, she let him.

At the far tip of the island, on a still and cloudless night, you could see fires, or ships, or lights burning far off. The island was not alone, but after the storm people kept to themselves. The storm changed the world, left its mark. Vara remembered the rain, and how her Grandmama was there, the whole night through and come morning round.

'Someday I will take you on one of those boats. We will sail to Old New York,' the sharp-faced boy lied. He would hunt for a kiss then, reward for his cleverness.

No boat would come and the sharp-faced boy would break her heart it was true. But someday a fine boy would be worth her heart and she'd give it freely. And many summers from now she'd tell her granddaughter stories about lights on the water and candies from the long-ago time that made her Grandmama twist up her lip. And Vara would be asleep before sundown.

Jacob's Ladder

By RJ Newlyn

At the site of Bethel in Palestine there used to be a visitor centre, situated near the spot where (according to Genesis) Jacob had his vision of a staircase to heaven. The building lies in ruins now but the staircase remains. Tired of a broken and sad world, I climbed up a little way. I did not mean to go far – just to leave life behind for a while.

In Jacob's time, apparently, the stairs were thronged with angels ascending and descending (I remember the picture in my Children's Bible). However, those days are long gone. I met one who was kind enough to stop and talk for a while as we took in the view of the Earth's curve, spread out below us. He said that most of his colleagues work under cover and are rarely recognised.

I've left the world far behind now. Our heaven no longer has Dante's seven planetary circles or the wheeling lights of the empyrean. Instead there is this infinite expanse of dark empty space between vast masses of rock and gas. But I'm not worried. The silence is comforting and ahead of me, up the stairs, is the tiniest twinkling star.

I'll keep climbing.

Jeremy's New Pet

By *Justin Stanchfield*

Of course Jeremy knew he couldn't have a Brontosaurus for a pet. For one thing, as his mother patiently explained, Brontosaurs were enormous and, from all accounts, impossible to house train. And for another, they weren't even Brontosaurs anymore. They were Apatosaurs, having been demoted from 'Thunder Lizard' to whatever an Apata was a few years ago because of some clerical error.

'Besides, honey,' she had continued, a bit more kindly, 'Brontosauruses were tropical animals that liked big fern jungles and swamps and such. I don't think one would be too happy living twenty miles from the Canadian border. A Montana winter is no place for a dinosaur.'

'We could keep him in the barn,' Jeremy had insisted. 'It's big enough to keep one in, at least most of one, and only his tail would stick out and I could cover that with a tarp when it got really cold. And they're plant eaters, so it's not like he'd eat the milk cows or anything.'

But his mother had only smiled, given him a cookie, and sent him outside to play. Grampa had been even more adamant when Jeremy broached the subject with him.

'A Brontosaurus? Now what in the name of hell gave you that damn fool notion?' The old man had actually looked affronted by the idea. 'Hasn't been one of those lumbering buggers around these parts for a million years or better.'

'But—' Jeremy started to say more, but Grampa had already closed the subject as far as he was concerned. He hitched up his pants, spat out a soggy wad of sunflower seed husks and shuffled off towards the beat-up tractor he was repairing. Jeremy could see this was going to be a lot harder than he had expected.

For a minute or two he toyed with the thought of asking his dad, but decided against it. It was the middle of haying season and the weather was threatening rain, and Dad was never in a good

122

mood when that happened. Besides, he would just do whatever Mom told him to do anyhow, especially whenever the subject of pets happened to come up. No, he decided, if he was ever to have himself a Brontosaurus he was just going to have to do it himself – which is why, promptly after supper when everyone was still watching Wheel of Fortune, he headed out back to the henhouse.

'It's like they say,' he told himself as he fluffed straw around the big, leathery egg and moved the incubator lamp in a little closer. 'Sometimes, it's just better to beg forgiveness than to ask permission.'

Journey of Hope

By Pam Howes

Phil Pearson stood twentieth in line as the restless queue snaked around the main concourse of Grand Central Station. It seemed to him that half of New York City was travelling home for Thanksgiving. The throng shuffled forward a few paces and he checked his watch. Fifteen minutes. What if he missed his train? Beads of perspiration broke on his brow at the thought. Then two family groups moved away and he was at the head.

'Round trip to Irvington, please.'

'Twelve dollars, sir. Happy Thanksgiving.' The clerk smiled and looked to the next customer.

Phil dashed across the concourse to Zaro's. He popped his head inside, savouring the heady aroma of pumpkin, cinnamon and hot pastry. Great! No queue. The large pie he chose was placed in a box. 'Thank you, keep the change,' he called as he hurried on his way. He rushed downstairs to platform 103 where the gleaming silver train to Irvington was standing. Passengers crowded on board and Phil found a window seat on the left. He sank into the comfortable leather and stretched out his long legs, the box on his knee. Ebony loved pumpkin pie, especially Zaro's.

He closed his eyes then opened them as a large black lady squashed in beside him. She wore a yellow hat, decorated with nodding sunflowers, and balanced a bulky shopping bag on her lap. She smiled and Phil's heart sank. He hoped she wouldn't try and strike up conversation. He was tired. The last day had been hectic. A delayed flight from Heathrow, late meetings and no sleep.

As the train pulled out of the station, his travelling companion spoke.

'You going to your family for the holiday?'

'No, I'm visiting a friend. My family live in England.'

'Oh, you're a long way from home.'

He nodded, struggling to keep his eyes open.

'You tired, son?'

'I am.' He returned her friendly smile.

'I'm going to my sister's home,' she announced. 'We're a big family. My niece is meeting me off the train. She's real excited. Thanksgiving's her favourite holiday.'

Phil smiled as they rattled through Harlem, past 125th street, home of the Apollo Theatre. He glanced across the carriage and to his right he could just make out the bulk of the Yankee Stadium. Thanksgiving was Ebony's favourite time of year, too. As the train skirted The Bronx, he lost his battle and closed his eyes, only to be awakened two minutes later by the conductor who punched his ticket.

'No peace for the wicked!' Phil muttered as the lady beside him chuckled.

It was a clear day and Phil could see New Jersey across the mighty Hudson River. The flanking trees were shedding their colourful fall foliage, the red, gold and orange leaves now fading fast as winter approached. He gave an involuntary shiver in the warm carriage.

'You cold?' the lady asked.

'No, I was thinking of your cold winters.'

'So, it's not cold in England?'

'More damp than cold.'

'My niece goes to England on business. She says your weather is very different.'

'It has its moments,' Phil replied as the train pulled into Yonkers.

There was much gathering of belongings and assorted off-spring as several families alighted. Phil shifted in his seat, wondering if the lady might move somewhere with a bit more room. But his hopes were dashed when further passengers piled on and the spare seats were quickly filled.

'That bridge always looks as though it's floating on the water.' Phil's companion pointed to the Tappan Zee Bridge straddling the width of the river.

That's exactly what Ebony always said. He closed his eyes again and let his thoughts wander. This journey was one of hope.

125

But supposing she didn't want to know? They'd parted on bad terms when she'd left England in August. His hand crept into his pocket and closed around a small box. She'd given the ring back. Relationships like theirs had enough problems and could never work long distance, she'd said.

Well now he was here to tell her that he'd got a transfer to New York. But what if he was too late and she'd found someone else? His heart raced and his stomach rolled at the thought. She'd no idea he was on his way. She didn't even know he was in the country. He hoped the surprise would be a welcome one.

'My niece fell for an English boy!' His companion's voice disturbed his daydream.

'Did she?' He smiled politely as the train pulled into a station and more passengers departed.

'She sure did. But it wasn't meant to be.' The lady gathered up her large bag and transferred her bulk to the seat opposite.

Phil stretched out and placed the pumpkin pie in the vacant space. 'And why was that?'

'What, honey?'

'Why wasn't it meant to be? Your niece's relationship.'

'Problems with his job and family, she told us. We never got to hear the full tale.'

'She found someone else?'

'No. I think she still loves her English boy.'

Phil smiled. Hopefully Ebony felt the same and was still in love with him.

'Your accent makes me go weak at the knees,' she teased and heaved herself to her feet, swaying as the train slowed to a halt. 'Here we are, next stop Irvington.'

'My stop, too.' Phil jumped up and took her bag. He helped her down to the platform.

'Aunt Grace! Aunt Grace! Oh, my lord – Phil!' A tall girl, black curls bouncing on her shoulders, stopped in her tracks. 'What on earth are you doing here?'

He spun round as Ebony, big grin splitting her face, ran towards them.

126

A twinkle in her eyes, Aunt Grace whispered, 'I recognised you right away from the photograph she carries in her purse.' She patted his arm. 'Everything will be just fine.'

Juno Out of Yellow

By Nuala Ní Chonchúir

Is it vain to love a portrait of yourself? My mother didn't think so. Juno Out of Yellow hung – still hangs – in the City Gallery. We used to visit it. Mother would squeeze Father's arm and say what a great artist he was, and how lovely she herself looked in the painting. Father had wanted to paint her like Botticelli's Venus – powerful and demure – but she argued for a Flemish-type Bathsheba and he obeyed. He portrayed Mother being helped out of a yellow cloak, her alabaster breasts pouched, her face turned away.

I am in the painting. Well, my twelve-year-old self is: I'm the girl behind Bathsheba, who pulls the cloak – in real-life it was a towel – from her arms. We look alike: long noses, dark hair, prim mouths. Like most people, I own a postcard of Juno Out of Yellow, but sometimes I love to go to the gallery to see it. I enjoy looking at Mother and me as Biblical mistress and maid, and at Father's brushstrokes. He was lavish with oil; it took months for his paintings to dry. Linseed and turpentine were the scents of my childhood.

*　　*　　*

Mother sits, shawled in the yellow towel, on the edge of a chair; I'm on the floor. The seat's cane-work has made a criss-cross pattern on her behind; I see it when she rocks her body, but I don't tell her, in case she gets angry. My eyes linger on the bush of hair between her thighs, comparing it mentally to my own spare sproutings. She holds up a hand-mirror and slicks one finger over each eyebrow. Tilting her chin, she re-does her lipstick.

'I'm fed up prinking; if I fiddle any more with myself, I'll look like a fucking corner-girl. Can we get on with it?'

'No cursing in front of Isabelle, Juno.'

'Oh, piss off, Desmond.'

Father crosses his eyes at me and I smile. Then I glance at Mother; she doesn't like being left out.

'Fix Izzy's hair,' he says.

Mother pulls me between her legs and pincers me with her knees. Her smell is sweet-sharp like buttermilk. She flicks the ends of my hair with a brush, then pulls it from the crown in even strokes; the sound fills my ears with a comforting thrum-thrum-thrum.

'Your turn now,' I say, hopping up. I start on her hair; the tines snag and she jerks.

'Go easy!'

I run the hair-brush gently over the smoothening strands. Mother purrs and wiggles her neck. I look at her nipples pointing from under the towel like two plum-coloured hazelnuts.

'Thomas is visiting us today,' she says.

'Thomas?' says Father, distractedly. He continues to mix paints, his face creased.

'Yes, Desmond. Thomas.' Mother snaps the brush from my hand.

'Is he visiting us, or visiting you?' Father asks.

'Where do you want Isabelle to stand?'

'Does he have to come today? I wanted to really start on the painting.'

'Will here do?' Mother pushes me behind her and faces him.

'Yes, Juno. There will do.'

*　*　*

Father tells Thomas to wait in the parlour.

'I'd like to stay and watch, if it's all the same to you,' Thomas says, smiling, 'see the master at work.'

He perches on Father's paint-mixing table and tips cigarette ash into a jam-jar. I can't see Mother's face, but the air has shifted around us. I lift my eyes. Thomas has sideburns; he is jauntily handsome, like a film star. I want him to look at me and I wish that I was naked too. He pouts a small kiss across to Mother, catches me watching, and winks.

'Can we have wine, Desmond?' Mother asks.

'Isabelle. Eyes down, please,' Father says.

'Red or white, Thomas?' Mother says.

'Mmm, red for me.'

'I want to do another hour.' Father stands with his palette tucked in front of him, like a shield.

'We have tomorrow,' Mother says. 'And the day after that. And the day after that.' She giggles. 'How often do we have guests?'

'Isabelle, get your mother her robe,' Father says.

*   *   *

Mother is tucked on the couch in her silk robe, with Thomas at her feet; they drink wine until their teeth are grey.

'Don't you have something to do, Isabelle? Dollies maybe?' Thomas says.

'Oh, shut up, Tommy; she's excited by visitors, stuck out here in the back-arse of nowhere. Aren't you, Izzy?'

'It depends on the visitor,' I say.

Mother hoots. 'Isn't she a scream? So serious. Just like Desmond.'

Thomas stares at me. 'Be a good girl and get more wine for Juno and me.'

I look at Mother and she nods.

The kitchen is dark, though light spills across from the studio. I make two cheddar sandwiches; Father and I eat them in silence, looking at the painting.

'It's going to be special,' I say.

'Yes, my love. It is.'

*   *   *

I stand in the doorway. Mother's robe is peeled back and Thomas is leaning onto her, cradling her breasts with his long hands and sucking at her neck. She grunts and I can hear the sloppy noise of his mouth on her skin. He must be squashing her, I think.

'Here's your wine.'

Mother slides below the couch and Thomas plunks into a sitting position.

'You shouldn't sneak up on people,' he says.

'I thought you were gone to bed, Izzy.' Mother's lipstick is fuzzed around her mouth.

'Father is still in the studio,' I say, and leave.

*   *   *

Look closely at Juno Out of Yellow. Lift your eyes past the nude figure and the clothed one; past the folds of the cloak and the blue walls. Most people haven't realized that there's a third person in the painting. In the mirror, behind Mother and me, you will see a face – a Le Brocquyian ghost of whites, with two slashes of black. Nicotine-brown smoke rises above this figure, whose mouth is a stretched leer.

Justice for Cody

By April L. Hamilton

She drifted back into awareness as the voice intoned, '… but we're afraid your son's …' the doctor glanced at the chart, 'Cody's vision impairment is permanent.'

'Vision im … you mean, the blindness?' she whispered.

'Yes, Mrs Cortez.'

She didn't react, just sat there, pale and blank, in shock. After a full minute of uncomfortable silence, Dr Whaley cleared his throat and motioned for a nurse to take Linda by the elbow. 'Mrs Cortez, Carrie will take you to a private lounge where you can lie down and rest for a while. Is there anyone you'd like us to call?'

'My husband,' she mumbled.

Two long, blurry days later, Linda and her husband sat at the breakfast table in their small apartment. Linda slapped the Formica surface hard with an open palm and raged, 'No, Rafael! Paying the medical expenses is the least of this. Our son is blind! He will be blind forever!' She stood up and paced the room as she became desperately businesslike. 'He'll have to quit Little League, and you know how he loves it. Then there's karate, I don't see how he can keep going to karate. The fun run in May, he'll have to withdraw.'

Rafael grabbed her by the shoulders, forcing her to stop her frantic movements and thinking. 'Linda, please. Forget about all of that for now, none of it matters. What Cody needs most right now is both of us and his best friend.'

Linda's eyes narrowed and her jaw clenched. 'A proper best friend wouldn't have made him do anything so dangerous. I never liked that Steven, I never trusted him!'

Rafael pulled her firmly to his chest. 'Shhh! You know that's not true. We both love Steven as much as Cody does; he's a good boy. It was an accident.'

'No!' she shrieked, and Rafael hugged her tighter. She buried her tears in his chest. 'Don't you care? Don't you want … justice for Cody?' she whimpered.

'Baby, there is no justice for Cody. This is nobody's fault.'

Linda yanked herself back from him and fixed him with a hateful stare. 'You can give up on our son, but I never will.' She grabbed her purse and stalked out, leaving Rafael to gaze out the window.

It took weeks to find the right attorney, but at last Linda was satisfied the Lynch boy's family would pay and pay dearly for what their son had done to hers. She knew Steven's mother would be bringing him to visit Cody at 4 pm today, as she did every day after school at Steven's insistence. All of this Linda had learned from Rafael, having successfully avoided running into those awful Lynches herself during visiting hours.

Linda clutched the papers in her hand as her heels clicked curtly on the tiled hospital floor; she was looking forward to seeing the reaction on Debbie Lynch's face. Rafael's ultimatum sprang to mind one last time like a warning bell, but she shoved it aside. If Rafael didn't want to do right by his only son, then she didn't want to stay married to him, either.

She took a deep breath and threw the door open. 'Debra,' she said, flatly.

Steven rushed up to her, shoving brochures and papers up toward her face. 'Mrs Cortez? I been learning about all the things to help Cody – well, my mom helped me look on the Internet ...' At this, Linda shot a glance at Debbie, who averted her reddened eyes and lifted a Kleenex to her nose.

'– an' I found out there's this special school for the blind right here in Austin, an' I got this application for a seeing eye dog an' my mom and dad said it's even okay if I wanna raise a puppy to be Cody's seeing eye dog, an' I can help Cody learn his way around the neighbourhood till then, an' I'll walk him anywhere he wants to go, an' ... an' I'll ...' He burst into tears and threw his arms around her hips.

'Mom?' Cody's small voice called from the bed, his bandaged head swimming to try and locate the sound. 'Is Steve okay?'

Linda's hand curled into a fist, crumpling the papers. She weighed them for a moment before tossing them in the wastebasket. She put a hand down to stroke Steven's head. 'Yes, honey,' she said. 'Steven's just fine.'

The Kids Are All Right

By Jennifer Domingo

The train was late. The train was always late. And yet Michael still had to run up the escalators, taking two steps at a time, thinking that maybe tonight would be different. What an idiot. When would he learn?

He could feel his shoulders sag under the weight of the perky woman's voice announcing the train company's apologies for the late running and inconvenience this was causing to his journey. Of course they were sorry, he thought, feeling more hunched over than ever, his heart pounding. Not only had he just finished another overtime session at work, but the temperature was three below zero and he'd made a complete fool of himself charging up the stairs as if he were being chased by a swarm of bees. And to make matters worse, just look at who was heading towards him.

He tried not to stare but to his left, ambling along the near deserted platform were two lanky boys wearing their jeans sagging down their hips, the bands of their underpants showing brazenly. They had their hoods pulled up over their baseball caps and what was that he could hear? Oh yes, one was holding his iPod without the headphones so that he could hear the tinny juddering music and, yes, the boy was singing along too. Not exactly singing, he thought eyes rolling up to the heavens in dismay, more like shouting along – voice broken and resounding.

Michael took a deep breath. Hopefully there were CCTV cameras around and maybe he ought to make his way to the ticket area? Then again, why should he? So far, the boys were only walking along the platform. Admittedly, walking directly and with seeming purpose towards him, but that's just how kids walk these days. Like marauding hungry cats.

Stop it. He hated sounding so old and he wasn't old, not really. He only turned 38 two months ago and that doesn't make him old, does it?

Who was he kidding? Only yesterday, Sandra had noticed a few wisps of grey at his temples.

Sandra. Michael tried to focus on his beloved, all warm and soft and waiting for him (he hoped), but the thundering bass juddering out of the boy's iPod was nearly upon him. Actually, they were already so close to him, he could reach out and touch. Not that he dared. The boys, on closer inspection, were lean, mean and really well built. They looked like they worked out in some gym. He could tell because he used to go to his company's gym and be able to get those same taut contours himself.

Poor Sandra. Now that she had lost her accountancy job, she was more and more obsessed about the marriage thing, the starting a family thing – especially the family thing. Did he want a family? Maybe, he didn't know. Maybe in the future, but not now, not yet. When? Well, he didn't know exactly when. He just knew he wasn't ready in the way Sandra was.

Besides, he wanted to ask her, 'Who in their right minds would want kids in this day and age?' Kids who'd grow up to be young guys like these guys. In his day, he wouldn't even have been out at this time on a school night and he certainly would not have had all the gadgets and gear that these boys had. Which made him wonder how come they could afford such brand names being so young – 15, maybe 16 years old?

He tried not to think of the rows they've had over such things. For now, he just wanted the train to turn up and whisk him away from this depressing station, this depressing weather, this night, this cold and these guys.

'Hey.'

Great. Now they were talking to him.

'Yo, geezer.'

Maybe he could pretend he was deaf.

'Geezer!'

Just turn around slowly, be casual just pretend you're not some lone white man in a suit holding a briefcase looking harassed and fed up –

'You want your wallet or what?'

'Sorry?'

'Your wallet. You dropped it running up them escalators.'

Michael stared at his wallet being held to him by fingers encased in chunky manly gold jewellery.

'Do you want it or what?' the boy asked looking thoroughly bored.

Michael took his wallet. It felt heavy and warm.

'Let's go now man,' iPod boy said not waiting for any reply, his back already turned.

'Told you it was his,' the bored boy said.

'Yeah, yeah, whatever.'

'Er,' Michael cleared his throat, 'thank you.'

'Later,' was all bored boy said as he and his friend ambled off.

He didn't know how long he stared at their receding backs or at the length of the semi-lit platform nor at the tracks disappearing into the night.

The perky announcer repeated how the train company was sorry for the late running of the train and the inconvenience it was causing to his journey.

His wallet weighed fat and heavy in his hand.

Larger Than Life

By Sherri Turner

After years of expensive face creams and serums, Claire finally had to admit that Newton was right. Gravity was winning and south seemed to be the only direction everything was going. It wasn't too bad in certain lights, but here at the dressing table with three times magnification and harsh daylight it was like looking at the surface of the moon. As she had applied her luxury Swiss night cream the previous evening, her teenage daughter Becky had commented: 'I don't know why you bother. It's like throwing a bucketful of water into the Grand Canyon.' Claire had to agree. Maybe it was time for something more drastic.

The young woman at the beauty salon welcomed Claire eagerly.

'So this is your first time for a facial? You've left it a bit late, haven't you?'

She examined Claire's skin minutely, tutting and sighing as she went.

'You need our special emergency rescue package today and then weekly top-ups. Let's get you started.'

Claire was led into a white room and given a paper bib to protect her clothes. She wondered what they would put on her face that could actually damage her clothing, but didn't like to ask. So she lay back and thought of smooth, young skin as the beautician massaged and rubbed, pummelled and scraped and applied creams, lotions and potions. As she left, she caught sight of herself in one of the salon mirrors and was horrified to find that her face was red, blotched and puffy.

'Excuse me. Am I supposed to look like that?'

'Oh yes, it will die down in an hour or two. You can't expect a miracle though – don't forget the follow-ups.'

Claire paid the extremely large bill and decided to wait before booking any further torture. If she could see a result, it would be worth it, but she didn't hold out much hope.

The next day she sat in front of her magnifying mirror, counting the lines and wrinkles. It was a tricky operation. Did that large line with the slight break in the middle count as one or two? Should she count the wrinkles that only appeared when she smiled, or just ones that were there all the time? However, after a number of minutes, she had to conclude that the treatment had had no effect whatsoever. Claire had hoped she could avoid anything surgical, but was beginning to think that it would be the only way.

She spent the next few hours in front of the Internet. Typing 'facelift' yielded nearly two million results. It was astonishing, the range of treatments on offer: high frequency electro-therapy; a 'thread' treatment, that yanked up the saggy bits with stitches; the 'cut-it-all-off-and-reposition-it' thing. None of them filled Claire with much enthusiasm. And she really didn't want her face removed, even if they would put it back on. The cost was also way out of her range.

After dinner that evening she went over and over the options. Even her husband Steve could see she was concerned.

'Hey, don't frown like that, you'll give yourself wrinkles!' he joked.

'Too late!' she wailed, 'I'm just one big wrinkle already!'

Steve took her face in his hands.

'Well, yes, there are a few,' he said. 'That big one on your forehead – you got that when you studied for your French exams. We were so proud of you when you got that A grade. And these around your eyes – they're from that holiday in Greece when you didn't want to wear your sunglasses so you could see all the colours properly.'

He gently touched the edges of her mouth.

'These are my favourites,' he said softly, 'from when Becky was born and you didn't stop grinning for days.'

The Last Boy on Earth

By Maire Cooney

I noticed him straight away, head bent and feet just clearing the ground with each step. He crossed before he got to me – most of the older ones do – and seemed to be trying to figure out how slowly he could move towards the school gates without actually stopping. I really felt for him. The next thing the sky darkened, like a dimmer switch had been turned down. Drops started falling, then hail, pelting the cars and pavement like machine-gun fire. Everything looked different.

People started running, hands and bags over their heads, tearing about, left, right, left, feet slapping the pavement. But I wasn't watching them. I was watching the boy. He stood, a full minute, head up and arms out, soaking it up, basking in it. His hair shining, flattened against his face. Then he turned a full circle, slowly, arms wide and smiled at the sky. The hail was falling harder now, pounding the scorched grass until it split into muddy circles. Most of the kids had gone inside. A few watched the boy, same as me.

He'd put his bag down. Shirt and trousers clinging, water pouring off him. Next he took a few steps back and ran, full out, folding one leg under him as he went. His mouth opened into a wide grin as he slid, 20, 30 feet, cutting a muddy chute into the bank as he went. He could have been the last person left on earth.

The noise stopped like a tap turned off. People slowed and stopped, glanced about, shook their heads. The boy just stood, arms dropped to his sides. Then he smiled a beautiful, broad, smile, picked up his rucksack and walked through the gates.

The Last Bus to Montreal

By Jenna Wallace

I don't know why I let you stay. A friend of a friend who needed a place to sleep. You wanted to see America, jumped on a bus, and now are seeing one small, small square of America called Apartment D. And my bedroom. A gentleman, you offered to take the floor. I let you, showing you the side of me that is the mismatched shoes, wrinkled clothes and last year's magazines under the bed.

I am in my bed, watching the city lights reflected on the ceiling and listening to you breathe. It worries me that I am not scared at all, lying here in the company of a stranger.

Morning finds me alive, despite everything my mother would have said. You are awake, sitting on your makeshift pallet, spit shining your shoes. You are dressed, an advantage you have over me. I almost dare you to look at me as I get out of bed. You deliberately look at your shiny shoes.

We eat eggs for breakfast and you tell me what you have seen so far. To you, it sounds like so much, but it is nothing but a postcard America at 60 miles an hour. I give up work for the day to be your tour guide. There is more to America, I say, than a Greyhound bus and Apartment D.

We sit at a dirty table in a pizza parlour, drinking beer from plastic cups and smoking Marlboro Lights. There is more to America than the Statue of Liberty, I say. This is what the huddled masses yearn to do once they break free.

You tell me about Her Majesty's Royal Navy and the family you haven't seen in a year. I ask about Montreal and where you belong. You tell me about the city and say you belong nowhere. I can see the adventure and anger in your eyes and the something else that aches.

Volleyball on the lakeshore. It doesn't matter that there is snow along the boundary lines. We take off our shoes and spike and dive barefoot in the sand. You are in better shape than I am, and you talk effortlessly while I can answer only in gasps. This game will be the death of me. You laugh at me and call me Sunshine.

Tonight, I take you to the only movie theatre in town – maybe in America – that still uses real butter on their popcorn. The movie is French and you whisper the translation in my ear. You could be making it up as you go, teasing me more. Your voice is butter smooth and your fingers on mine are oil-slick. I gain a new appreciation for foreign films, especially those that come with their own translators.

We return to Apartment D and check the timetable for the bus. There are two to Montreal. You say you will take the earlier one; you can't be late returning from leave. I'll take you to the station, I say, and pour us each a glass of wine. It is American, grown at a vineyard six miles away. You try to teach me French, but I murder your language and you tease me in words I cannot understand. Canadian French and French French are different, I am told, though it matters little to me right now.

The wine is gone. We sit on the postage stamp floor looking at everything but each other. I still can't speak French but the way you speak it makes me want to. I guess we should sleep, I say, unconvinced. You take my hand and kiss it. I am sure you know what that does to me. You hold onto my hand as I get in my bed. You are still holding it as you lie down on the blankets on the floor. You caress my fingers, which are still polished and fragrant with butter. We are distant, intimate and silent. I do not know who falls asleep first. Maybe our fingers made love into the night.

Morning finds me again, though I try to hide by keeping my eyes closed. The clock shows its nine o'clock face and I know the early bus left you behind without even a backward glance. You are still sleeping. I stare at you because I can. You must feel it because you open your eyes. And smile.

It is the last bus to Montreal. I stand in the parking lot and try to understand the self that is mirrored in the chrome of the bus. I should not feel sad. You are a stranger to me. This was not a one-night stand – no stand was involved at all, other than the one our fingers had while we slept apart. But there it is. That pull, that sting, that undoing inside.

Goodbye, I say. You kiss both cheeks and then my hand. Je t'aime, you say, but you really mean goodbye. You squeeze my hand and board the bus. I watch it drive off and feel like part of me has gone with it.

One Morning

By Greg McQueen

I sit up on the edge of the bed. Floor cold under my feet. I yawn and rub the sleep from my eyes, head heavy.

Tiny hands hook onto my shoulders, and my daughter's bright little face pops into view. 'Mummy making breakfast?'

'It's Daddy's turn today, sweetheart.' I slide my arms so she can climb on my back. 'What would you like?'

She frowns, as though deciding what to have for breakfast is the most important decision in the world.

'You need the bathroom, darling?' I ask.

She shakes her head.

'You sure?'

She nods.

I'm desperate for a pee. But I get up and glance to my wife still dozing under the duvet before piggy-backing our daughter downstairs and depositing her on the sofa.

'I'd like yoghurt and toast and blueberries,' she announces. 'And can I watch television?'

I smile and pick up the TV remote. The news comes on. BBC World. A reporter standing in front of a collapsed building, something about the rescue efforts in Haiti continuing, despite the fading hope of survivors. I flick away. Cartoons. Then I glance at my daughter – she's giggling, good, the news didn't register – before wandering into the kitchen.

Our house is small. Three bedrooms, a bathroom, an open plan lounge and kitchen, fake wooden floors throughout, and a garden the size of a postage stamp. We love it.

As I stick the kettle on and pop a slice of bread in the toaster, I hear the shower upstairs. Routine. My wife gets ready, while I make breakfast, so our daughter gets to day care by 9AM.

'So, do you want butter or honey on your toast?' I ask my daughter.

Again, she frowns, the weight of the world on her eyebrows. 'Butter,' she says. 'No wait ... Honey,' she nods quite vigorously, 'honey, Daddy, honey.'

I finish making my daughter's breakfast and pour myself a cup of tea before joining her on the couch. Honey covers her mouth and chin, as we watch cartoons, together.

I sip my tea. Head filled with an image of a reporter and a building reduced to rubble. I get an idea. Forget all about needing to pee.

Ten minutes later my wife comes downstairs. 'Hey, why aren't you dressed?' She's talking to our daughter while looking at me.

'Oh, yes, time to get dressed, darling.' I switch off the television, and my daughter cries and kicks, as I carry her upstairs.

I raid my daughter's wardrobe. None of the clothes I put on her match. They never do. I don't know the 'What not to wear' rules, as long as she's warm and comfortable and dry, that's what matters.

My daughter is still snivelling as we make our way downstairs. She wants to watch more cartoons, but we're running late.

Routine. Wipe her nose. Ask whether she needs to pee. Coat on. Shoes on. Gloves on. Hat. Kisses.

'Have a lovely day, sweetheart,' I say, waving from the front door, as my wife and daughter climb into our ice-covered car.

I close the front door, and a shiver hijacks my body. It's been snowing on and off in Denmark for two months. It's bloody freezing. Yet, most mornings, I stand in the doorway of our house wearing nothing but a t-shirt and pyjama bottoms.

I go upstairs. Wash. Throw on some clothes. Then I wander into the spare room and switch on my computer, intending to start writing the last bit of the novel I've been working on for nearly a year.

Idea. Reporter. Rubble.

'Right,' I say aloud. 'Must do something ...'

I type some notes. A few strung-together facts from the news reports I've seen about the earthquake in Haiti. I print them.

145

Switch on my webcam, and … Like a shiver, the idea hijacks my body. I glance at the notes, but I am not really reading them. The words come out because they are already there.

'Dear Twitterverse,' I hear myself say. 'On January 12th, 2010, a 7.0 magnitude earthquake struck near Haiti's capital …'

When I am finished, I post the video to YouTube, and embed it on my website. I post it on Facebook and Twitter for good measure, and then wander downstairs and stick the kettle on.

As I am making tea, my mobile phone chimes. An e-mail, someone commented on my YouTube video. Blimey, I only just posted it. I read the comment. Then I read it again. Thought. What the heck have I done?

I hear the front door open, and my wife comes in. She smiles, peels off her coat, and dumps it on a chair before joining me in the kitchen.

She slips her arm across my shoulders and kisses my cheek. 'The drop-off was fine,' she says. Then she frowns, because she's seen the look on my face. 'You okay?'

'I don't know … Think I might have just made a total arse of myself.'

Her frown deepens.

'I just posted a video online, asking writers to send me their stories. I am going to publish a book and donate all the money to … I don't know, Haiti. Maybe, the Red Cross.'

She's still frowning.

'Some guy on YouTube posted a comment,' I glance at my phone, not because I need to, because I am nervous. 'He says I'm taking the piss out of the aid workers over there.'

'What about your novel?' she asks. 'I thought you needed to finish it?'

'I do. But …' I shrug. Don't know what else to say.

'You haven't thought this through, have you?' she says.

I shake my head, as though I am a ten year-old confessing to breaking a window.

My wife smiles. Now let me tell you something about that smile, because it deserves at least a paragraph. It's a fantastic smile. Stunning, actually. My wife never half-smiles. It's always teeth, and always gums, and there's something in it, as though she somehow has hidden knowledge of the workings of the universe. When my wife smiles at you, you'd best be prepared … It's as if she knows that some mystical force is going to bless you.

'I think it's a wonderful idea,' she says. Smiling.

'Really?'

'Yeah. I'll help you make the cover if you like.'

'Cover?'

'Books need a cover, don't they?'

'Yeah,' I say, 'A book needs a cover …' Shit, she's right … I haven't thought this through at all. 'And it needs quite a lot of other stuff, too.'

The Law of Attraction

By Teresa Ashby

Something about the old man made me slow down as I came up behind him. He looked so dignified in the bustle of the shopping centre as he walked slowly with the aid of a stick.

'You dropped something,' he said as I hurried past him.

He bent to pick up my scarf.

'Thank you,' I said.

'You're very welcome.'

It was now touch and go whether I caught my bus. 'Thanks again.'

I had a job interview and my car had chosen, today of all days, to break down.

I looked back and saw the old man fall, his stick flying from his hand.

I hurried back to help him.

'I'm sorry,' he said as he brushed dust and dirt from his clothes. 'Clumsy old fool.'

'You're not,' I said.

He held onto my arm. He was shaking.

'Let me get you a cup of tea,' I said.

'Really, there's no need,' he said, but he was breathless and still shaking.

'Well I need a cup of tea,' I said.

'But you were in such a hurry. You must have been going somewhere important.'

Funny, but it didn't seem so important now. I'd missed my bus, anyway.

I found us a table in a quiet corner and went to get a pot of tea.

'Get proper tea,' he called after me. 'I can't stand that new agey herbal stuff. I like mine good and strong with milk and sugar.'

I couldn't even call to cancel the appointment. I had no credit on my phone and the public phones were out of order.

'You look very smart,' he said when I returned.

My suit had seen better days. It was distinctly out of fashion and I'd noticed, too late, that a button was missing from the jacket.

'Job interview?' he asked.

'How did you guess?'

'The clothes, the nerves,' he smiled. 'Will you be late?'

'I've changed my mind about going.'

'Why? Because of a silly old man who can't stay on his feet?'

'Because I wouldn't get it, anyway,' I explained. 'It was stupid even applying. It's very different to my previous job.'

'Which was?'

'Bank call centre,' I said.

'You should be more positive. You've heard of the Law of Attraction haven't you? What was the job?'

'Receptionist at the complementary health centre.'

'Ah, the crystal palace,' he chuckled.

'I know people think it's a joke,' I said. 'But a lot of people are helped by alternative therapies.'

He grinned as he heaped three sugars into his tea.

'Phone them,' he said. 'Tell them you'll be late. They'll understand. Remember the Law of Attraction. To draw good things to you, you have to ask for them.'

'Can't,' I said. 'No phone credit.'

'Use mine.'

He pushed a mobile phone across the table.

'I don't know what half the buttons do,' he said. 'But it's pretty obvious how to make a phone call.'

I'd been for countless job interviews and never got anywhere.

'There's really no point,' I said.

'Defeatist,' he said, smiling. 'Make the call. And be positive. Do it for me.'

I made the call.

'No problem,' my interviewer said. 'Can you be here in an hour?'

Easy! If I had to walk I could be there in an hour. And that was the first positive thought I'd had in a long time.

'There, that wasn't so hard was it?' he slipped the phone back in his pocket. 'You'll get that job.'

'I wish I could be so sure.'

'But you are sure,' he said. 'You know that you are good enough.'

He was right. I was sure of it. There was no reason why I shouldn't get the job.

I was presentable – no one ever got turned down for a job because they had a button missing.

'And you're a sympathetic human being,' he said as if he'd been reading my thoughts. Or maybe I had spoken aloud. Who knows?

'I'm going to have another cup of tea, but you should get on your way,' he said.

He assured me he'd be fine and I looked back as I was leaving to see if he'd vanished, but he was still there, smiling and waving.

I have to say it was the easiest interview I'd ever done. I sailed through.

And at the end, Grace smiled warmly at me and folded her hands on the desk in front of her.

'I'll send you a formal letter,' she said. 'But as far as I'm concerned, the job is yours. How soon can you start?'

Three days after deciding my life was a mess, I started my wonderful new job.

In the first 10 minutes, I met John the reflexologist, Doris the acupuncturist and Suzanne who does crystal therapy. The centre offered a wide range of treatments from reiki to hypnosis.

And who should come in the door but my friend from the shopping centre.

He was walking in that slow, careful but proud way and he beamed at me.

'You got the job,' he said. 'Congratulations. I knew you would.'

'Thank you. I owe it to you and your insistence on positive thinking. Are you here to see someone?'

'Only my clients,' he said.

He lifted his walking stick and pointed it at one of the doors.

Joseph Atkins, Hypnotherapist.

'That's you, isn't it?' I said.

He closed his eyes and nodded.

'At your service,' he said.

'Would you like a drink before your first client?'

He leaned across my desk and grinned.

'Tea please,' he said.

'Proper tea with milk and sugar?' I laughed.

He laughed too. I knew he couldn't stand that new agey stuff and he called this place the crystal palace, but I also knew he was good at what he did and, as he walked off towards his consulting room, I knew from now on things would go on getting better and better.

The Layman's Solution to the Causal vs. Final Conundrum Or How Two Men Became Insomniac and One Man Slept

By Jane Roberts

I am asleep. I dream that I enter a vacuous room and there is a closed door in front of me with a key in the lock. Freud propounded theories on causality: what happened to get me here? Jung preferred finality: what is there on the other side of the door? Freud would have leapt upon that key and proudly declared it to be a phallic symbol. Jung would have wanted to unlock the door with the key and discover the mystery behind the door. Freud and Jung then appear in the room and begin expostulating – vociferously – with each other. With whom should I agree? What should I do? I'm no philosopher – in the real world I work a twelve-hour day. My solution to the conundrum? I curl up in a ball on the floor of my fantasy room and sleep.

A Lesson in Magic

By Robert Freese

'Dad-eeee!'

Marc Dunn was in his computer room working when he heard his seven-year-old daughter slam the front door. 'In here, pumpkin. Try to be quiet. I just put the baby down.'

The baby. That's all her parents talked about since bringing the little toad home from the hospital. Prudence could already see a big problem with her baby brother.

Bouncing into the computer room, where she found her father working, she approached him and held out an object in her small hands.

'Look,' she beamed.

'It's a stick,' Marc said, looking away from the screen momentarily. He loved the way his daughter smiled with her entire face. She lit up the room. She took after her mother.

'No. It's a magic wand.'

'A magic wand?'

'Yeah. It does tricks.'

'What kind of tricks? Do you twirl it around, throw it in the air, and catch it like a baton?'

'No.'

Marc tried not to laugh at the look of bewilderment on her face, like she could not believe that he did not understand what kind of tricks she meant. One brow was cocked, her hands on her hips. She was so much like her mother.

'What kind of tricks then?'

She perked up immediately and said, 'All kinds. I can change stuff, make stuff disappear, make stuff appear.'

'That is magic. Where did you procure this magic wand?'

'Huh?'

'Where did you get it?'

'Mister Boone at the end of the street made it for me.'

Leonard Boone was a retired elementary schoolteacher. A bit eccentric, he loved telling the neighbourhood kids fantastic stories of faraway lands, dragons, and brave knights. He was wonderful with the children and they were in awe of him.

'How did Mr Boone put the magic in the wand?'

'He said everything's magic if you believe enough in it.'

'I see. Well, Daddy's got a lot of work to do. Unless you can wave that thing and fill in these reports, I'm stuck here for the next hour or so. Do you think you can play quietly in your room?'

'Sure.'

'I'll make grilled cheese sandwiches for lunch. Sound good?'

Marc watched his little girl leave. She waved the wand around like a conductor leading an orchestra. He envied her that she still believed in magic wands and felt an ache in his heart. If only he could, he would keep her seven forever.

In her room, Prudence lined up all her dolls and waved the wand over their heads.

'Abracadabra, Alacazam, make me a plate of green eggs and ham.' Giggling, she took a doll and said, 'You can dance like a ballerina.' She touched the doll's head with the tip of the wand.

There was a sudden flash of light, like Mum's camera, and all of a sudden the doll was alive, leaping and pirouetting elegantly from one end of her room to the other.

'Uh-oh!' Prudence didn't know what to do. She looked at the magic wand and dropped it as if it were white hot. She ran downstairs to her father.

'It works,' she blurted.

'What works?' Marc asked without looking away from the computer.

'The wand. It's magic!'

'That's great, pumpkin, but Daddy has a lot of work, okay. Please don't wake your brother up.'

Daddy didn't seem upset. He must have had a magic wand when he was a kid. She ran back upstairs.

Peeking around the corner of her bedroom door, she saw the living doll spinning.

Next was Pennington Bear, the bear that told stories.

'You're a handsome prince.'

There was a burst of light and then Pennington Bear was no more. Instead, a man in tights and a crown sat in the rocking chair.

'Fair maiden, I've searched the entire kingdom for someone as radiant as you.'

'Uh-oh!' She ran back downstairs, the wand in her hand.

'Pennington is a prince!'

'Yes he is.' Marc was getting a headache from staring at the computer screen. 'Play nice and I'll make some lunch soon. And don't play Pennington on the highest volume or you'll wake your brother.'

On her way upstairs, Prudence heard Adam crying in his crib.

'Pru, check on your little brother,' Marc called out. 'Try to rub his tummy and put him back to sleep.'

Little brother! Marching into Adam's room, she peeked over the crib rail. Adam was fussy, crying, and waving his little fists about.

'Be quiet,' she said, but the baby only cried louder. 'Adam, shush!'

'Fair maiden...'

Prudence spun around and said, 'Be quiet Pennington and go back into my room.' Shrugging his shoulders, the bear prince retreated. Prudence turned back to her brother.

'You're a little toad.' Without thinking, she tapped Adam's head with the wand. There was a bright flash of light.

'Uh-oh!' How would she ever explain this to her parents? There was no way she could dress that warty little thing and make it look like baby Adam. Worried sick, she ran downstairs.

'Adam is a toad,' Prudence announced, entering the computer room.

'I really wish you'd be nicer to your baby brother. He loves you so much.'

155

'No, really. I changed him into a toad with the wand.' She held up the incriminating object.

'Well, change him back.' Marc was studying the screen. 'Do it before your mother comes home. I think I'll order us a pizza for lunch instead of cheese sandwiches.'

Change him back! Yes! She bolted upstairs.

'Change back!' A flash of light and the baby reappeared. Prudence repeated the words twice over and the doll stopped dancing and Pennington transformed back into a toy bear.

Over lunch, Marc asked, 'Did you figure out how to do tricks with the magic wand?'

'No,' shrugged Prudence, 'maybe I'll just learn how to twirl it around and stuff.'

Life Behind a Motorway Billboard Hoarding

By Kate Tough

We are gathered at the top of the slope. Jostling, animated, we are stepping this way and that way with no purpose. Talking over each other, we do not even know what we are saying.

Sofia is saying, 'Move back – keep back – watch me!' Paulo says, 'Give it here, it's my turn.' She says, 'I'm not finished yet. Watch me. Watch!' Sofia is pretending it is better fun than it is. It was a good idea, but if your idea doesn't work you should say.

The sledge and Sofia are moving down the steep slope of our back yard, but with a lot of help from Sofia's feet.

What grass there was has been worn away by our games, leaving dry bare ground. We don't get snow here. The people who lived here before must have realized that, leaving a blue plastic sledge among the junk in the old hut.

For the second time, she is positioned at the top of the slope, sitting in the blue sledge, feet either side on the ground.

She pushes against the earth to launch. But doesn't quite. She goes a short way, slowly, and then out come her feet for another push. This happens many times before she stops at the bottom; beyond the front of the house, beyond the terrace, beyond the dog wire.

Paulo and Juan both ask, 'When is it my turn?' We are bored with watching her. We are not saying so though, not to her, instead expressing impatience in our little frowns and shrugs. And none of us is leaving; we don't dare.

I do not want a turn on the sledge. It doesn't even go properly. The earth is not slippery enough. The earth is not snow. It was a good idea, though, to use the slope of the garden for speed. I have given up on the sledge but I have not given up on the idea. Perhaps something else would move better on the uneven ground.

I go, unnoticed. I am running down to the front terrace. The dog is there, doing what he does all day. We ignore each other. I have my little green push-car in my hand. I am trying to run up the slope but it is pulling heavily behind me. I get there. No one has noticed me. No one has guessed my idea. Sofia is at the bottom, again, standing up from the sledge. I place my car at the top and sit inside, carefully, because the car wants to move already. I keep a foot on the ground either side, as a brake.

I don't ask Sofia if I can go. She would only say no, and something about the youngest goes last, and she is not finished yet.

When I get back to the top the others will want to have a go in my green car and I will let them. I lift my feet. I am going fast! Too fast for the steering to work. I head left into a rock and stop. I reverse by pushing on my feet. Pulling the wheel round as hard as I can I straighten up and I am off! Soon after, the front of the car tips towards the ground and the back end flies up, almost sending me over the front. Maybe I hit a dip.

I right myself. I go on. Suddenly it happens again. I get my feet down just in time not to tumble over head first. Why is this happening? Why isn't my car speeding freely down the slope? I get out, embarrassed to look around and face the others, but they have gone: wherever Sofia wanted to go.

I start back up the slope, hauling my little car. At the top, I get into position. I look down at the clear run ahead. I make sure the steering wheel is straight and I lift my feet. I go fast! I nearly go over! The car is tipping dangerously. I recover. I lift my feet. I go fast! I tip forward!

I am over half-way down. I get out and sit on the ground, holding the back of the car. I think about my plan. I am the problem in my plan – too heavy for the lightness of the car, or maybe the steepness of the slope. I am disappointed my idea didn't work. A high-speed journey to the bottom did not happen.

I stand up and look at the remaining run ahead. The only way the car can make it to the bottom is without me. I stand behind it, straighten it up and let go. It trundles and bumps its way down without stopping. Past the terrace, past the dog wire, it settles to a stop. Ha! A new game for my car! I am happy.

I run back to the house. I run to find the others.

Lily's Room

By Alison Dunne

Lily's room smells of talcum powder. Lily drifts it in clouds, which thicken the air, then settle on the surface of her dressing table.

Lily, I think, is too pale and fine for this life.

'Don't draw in it,' she says, sharply. I have made a heart in the powder on her bedside table. I am just piercing it with an arrow.

'I am pierced, Lily,' I tell her. 'You have done that to me.'

And she has. Lily laughs and, as always, it is the sound of blossom falling.

The first time I saw Lily was in the library. I work there, see. Lily came in and I thought she was a ghost; she had on the palest shades. A lilac coat, the lightest pink of chiffon at her neck, I thought her shoes were satin ballet slippers. I had the greatest lump in my throat.

'I need something,' Lily said to Margaret at the desk.

I almost fell over myself, jumped up from the table and hit my thighs against it. Both the women turned to see what the commotion was and I saw Lily's eyes were such a pale shade of blue and her skin was etched glass, her lips were chapped.

'I can't wear strong colours. They make me feel tired.' She is standing by the wardrobe, looking at herself in the long mirror. 'This isn't my era,' Lily says.

I am lying on my side on Lily's bed. Looking at Lily. Sometimes she reminds me of an exhaled breath in winter air. Or someone's half-thought idea. Sometimes I think about kissing her. I don't think she would want me to kiss her.

'I am not what you would call pretty,' Lily says. She is peering closely at her face. She draws back her lips and shows her teeth. She has a gap between her front teeth that she can fit a matchstick in. She proved it to me once. 'I should only be viewed by candlelight.'

I'd followed Lily. For weeks. I wanted to touch the things that she touched, to look at them and see if dust had come off her hands, like from a butterfly wing and transferred itself. I wanted to see if the racks of clothes in charity shops were silvered somehow where she had run her fingers along them.

One day I trailed her into the antiques market, followed her from stall to stall. Watched how she handled things. I saw her touch a piece of glass, pick it up, hold it to the light and look through it. Then put it down and drift on. I picked the glass up, too, carefully by the edges. And I saw her fingerprints, I was sure of it.

'From a chandelier, that is,' the gruff woman behind the stall said. 'One of them country houses.' She was bundled in her coat and scarf, she had her hands linked over her belly, I saw thick fingers, yellow nails. '£3.50,' the woman said. And I got the money from my pocket. 'Shall I wrap it for you, love?' I shook my head.

At the end of the aisle, Lily was waiting. I had the glass in my pocket, a sharp secret wrapped in my own handkerchief. Lily was looking at me. I felt hooked on her two eyes, panicked.

'I saw you buy that,' Lily said. I couldn't speak. Her voice was like rain that is light, but wetting. Insistent. Soaking. 'Why do you follow me?'

I thought she might be angry. I couldn't make my throat work. It felt plugged, like I had swallowed that glass and it had stuck there, wouldn't go down. I shrugged.

'Come on,' Lily said. She stuck her arm through mine, a surprising human limb. She steered me through the streets of the town. We didn't say a word. She took me to her house, a house she shared. Made tea, carried the two cups to her room and sat me there in the chair by her talc frosted dressing table. Made me drink it.

'Did you think I wouldn't see you?' Lily asked.

And Lily is right; she is not what you would call pretty. But to me she is like an opaque thing, lit from within. I can see all the things inside Lily playing on the outside of her like shadow puppets. I can see her.

'I can see you,' I say to Lily.

And Lily turns to me. Pins me on those eyes. Lily comes towards me; there is no sound as she comes. I think I hear my heart stopping inside me, train brakes squealing. Smoke behind my eyes. I can't hear her feet on the boards of the floor of her room. I can't hear anything as Lily bends.

'You funny thing,' Lily says. She places her small cool hands either side of my face. 'Funny, you are.'

I want to make this moment stretch for ever. I want it preserved in amber like a tiny prehistoric insect.

I want it wrapped in a handkerchief and kept in my pocket. I close my eyes to hold it, Lily filling my vision, a fog. The smell of talcum powder, her skin on my skin. Lily.

And then Lily kisses me.

Lola Loves Loving

By Martin Reed

So many messages. I don't know why hers caught my attention. Maybe it was the moment. Colleen off for an early night. Just me and the computer and an inbox packed with strangers' voices. Win Millions in a Single Spin. Learn how MR BIG satisfied YOUR girlfriend. Canadian Pharmacy: V14gra, Ci4l!s—

But hers. I couldn't explain. I was sure it flickered as it appeared, looking unsure whether or not to arrive, its date blank as though really it hadn't. The sender: Lola. Email: lola@lola.love. Subject: Lola loves loving.

Straining to hear if Colleen was still awake, I clicked to open the message. It was blank, but as it opened I caught a waft of cinnamon. Nothing more, and before it faded I clicked reply. Oh Lola, I wrote, I'm so glad, I love loving too.

I don't write to her every day. That would be too much. But most days I do. Whenever I catch her scent. Not that she writes back. She doesn't need to. It's enough to know that she loves.

Marco's Ice Cream

By Clare Reddaway

Marco was notorious for his sour nature.

'Morning Senore Marco! Still single?' Renata said and grinned at him as she crossed her long legs.

'Can't trust women,' said Marco.

'How's business?' Senore Caspari asked.

'Terrible. I'm about to go under,' Marco grumbled. 'These taxes don't help.'

Senore Caspari nodded sympathetically, but he didn't believe a word of it because Marco owned the most popular ice-cream venue in a town that loved its ice-cream. And Senore Caspari doubted he paid his taxes.

No one knows why Marco decided to add the new ingredient to his famous chocolate ice-cream that day. Perhaps it was absentmindedness. Or perhaps it was sheer ill will. Marco was at the café at 6 am as usual, sorting through the deliveries, when he found a small brown paper package in the bottom of a shipment of blood oranges. The label stated that it was a new mystery ingredient, designed to enhance appreciation of any food. Marco opened the package. Inside was some powder that looked like cinnamon. It didn't smell of anything. Cautiously, he wet his finger, stuck it in and licked. It didn't taste of anything either. He put it down and forgot about it, until later when he was beating the ingredients for his chocolate ice-cream.

What the hell, he thought, and he sprinkled the ice-cream with a shake of the powder and gave it a stir.

That day he was very busy so he didn't notice anything strange until local tough Silva Da Remo came in with a big grin on his face. Marco fingered the baseball bat he kept beneath the counter as he greeted Silva nervously.

'Marco, the ice-cream, it's delicious, delicious,' said Silva. He grabbed Marco and gave him a great big kiss on the lips. Marco was surprised – but not half as surprised as Silva's mother when she opened the door later to find Silva holding out a large bunch of flowers.

'Mama, I missed you!' he said. She didn't point out that he lived in the next street but she made him dinner and nearly had a heart attack when he washed the dishes. He's turned over a new leaf, she prayed.

Marco decided Silva must have had a win on the horses. Then he noticed some of his other customers were behaving oddly. Professore Lagio, a tall, lugubrious aesthete, ordered the chocolate ice-cream and left the café with a definite spring in his step. Although Marco didn't know it, the Professore went into his office, locked the door and swept his secretary of ten years into his arms. Kissing her passionately, he told her that he loved her and that she was the most beautiful woman in the world. Entranced, she'd kissed him back. The Professore missed three important meetings that afternoon.

Outside, under the awning, Marco saw little Letitia De Palma leap to her feet shrieking as she flung her arms around Antonio.

'Yes yes, yes yes, yes!' she cried.

'We've been dating for ten years. I thought he'd never ask!' said Letitia and Marco rolled his eyes because he knew how many girls had sat on Antonio's knee under that same awning.

Then Marco put two and two together and looked at the chocolate ice-cream. The carton was nearly empty. Maybe ... no ... maybe the powder? Marco surreptitiously spooned a scoop into his mouth. He was still swallowing when Sergeant Cassale came into the café.

Sergeant Cassale took his job as the senior policeman of the district very seriously. He had a uniform which was ironed crisp every morning. He could always see his face in his knee-length boots. The Sergeant knew immediately that something was wrong as Marco was smiling broadly. The Sergeant proceeded cautiously. He said there had been a number of incidents in the town this afternoon, and there was one link between them all – Marco's ice-cream.

'What incidents?' asked Marco.

The Sergeant told him that Lucia Pietro, a jeweller legendary for her meanness, had opened her shop and started to hand out gold chains. The ensuing scramble had left one boy with a broken leg. Then three middle-aged spinsters had to be pulled out of the fountain and begged to put on their clothes. Finally, the police had been called to an orgy at Paulo's café and had sustained a number of injuries trying to separate the couples.

Marco remembered serving Lucia Pietro. She'd counted the change three times as usual. Paulo always had a carton for his lunchtime sitting. The three old ladies, he remembered, had come back for seconds. Marco gulped. He could still taste the chocolate on his tongue.

'There is only one conclusion – you have laced your chocolate ice-cream with drugs!' ended Sherlock.

'But Sergeant, why would I do that? And what drug has this effect? Look, here, try some,' said Marco. The Sergeant stared at the remains of the ice-cream. It looked innocent enough. It didn't smell odd, or taste odd – in fact it tasted surprisingly good, better than any ice-cream he'd ever had before....

Passers-by were astonished later that night by the sight of Marco and Sergeant Cassale tangoing up and down the length of the marble-topped bar in their underwear, roses clenched between their teeth.

The town woke up with an almighty hangover. There was a lot of explaining to do. Antonio was besieged by fourteen girls who had planned to be Mrs Antonio. Letitia fought them off. The Professore's wife demanded he sack his secretary and buy a dictaphone, but instead he left her, set up home with his mistress, and took to having long, languorous siestas. Silva spent months trying to stop his mother popping over with a hot lunch and a clean hanky, which is not the image a hard man needs, but eventually he gave up and became a car mechanic. The three spinsters founded a nudist colony. Only Lucia Pietro remained unaffected, and demanded her money back, with interest. Some people never change.

Of them all, perhaps Marco was the most different. He sang as he worked, he smiled at his customers, he enjoyed the sunshine. He wondered, however, whether he was at his most blissfully happy when he polished Sergeant Cassale's boots and ironed his uniform, ready to wave him off to work.

Marco doesn't serve chocolate ice-cream anymore and even the most persistent of the townspeople have given up asking for it. But he does keep what remains of the brown paper parcel stashed away in a secret place, just in case. Well, you never know, do you?

Messenger

By Peter Morin

He sits with his mother on the patio of her Florida home, relaxing in a wicker chair and swirling his wine as she speaks. Although it is well past her bedtime, she keeps right on talking from her wheelchair. Even addled by stroke, there is plenty going on behind her glaucoma-dulled blue eyes.

'Have you seen the two new wings on the house?'

'I can't find them.'

She describes the secret door inside the walk-in closet.

'How do you get there?'

'There's a trick door in the closet, and up a hallway, there's a door to a big outdoor room, where thousands of people lie in their beds. We watch the sky for shooting stars. Sometimes we see the northern lights. I figure the others are like me, sharing the rest of their lives with hired help.'

He asks if she recognizes any of them, but no. He wants the conversation to continue, to distract him from his anguish.

He has learned that there is a time to dispel her delusion and a time to indulge it. Tonight, this is her world, and he wants to go with her. It is just the stream of consciousness of an old and sick woman whose mind is chocked full of thoughts and images, and she flips through a random catalogue of them. As she speaks, he imagines that they become more vivid in her mind, and she adds colour and clarity to them, and he wonders if she hasn't actually seen these things. He wants to inspect the back of the closet for himself.

She begins to talk about his father. 'He was perfect, your father,' she says.

'Everyone says that.' He inspects the legs of the wine in his glass.

She asks if he remembers the songs his father sang.

'Sweet Betsy From Pike!' he says, and she laughs with a rasp. He sings it. 'Do you remember sweet Betsy from Pike,

167

who crossed o'er the prairie with her lover Ike, with two yoke of Oxen, a big yellow dog, a tall Shanghai rooster and one spotted hog.'

She laughs so hard she coughs deeply and Sandra rushes to her. She hacks through it and waves Sandra away.

'Your father loved music. Before we were married, we went to the jazz clubs. We saw all the Big Bands.'

'What a time you must have had.'

'You have no idea,' she says. Her eyes sparkle, and then they narrow and she lowers her voice almost to a whisper. 'But your father wasn't really that perfect.'

'No?'

'Other women,' she whispers, with not a hint of anger or hurt, but a big knowing smile.

'No!' He tries to act surprised. His father was discreet and inscrutable, and never gave him the slightest reason to think it. But he always had.

'Even the strongest men have a weakness,' he says.

'If it's only one, it's women,' she says, and she laughs. She begins to say something, and stops. He is sure she would to ask if he has always been faithful to his wife, and he is relieved that he doesn't have to lie to her.

'Do you think…' he begins to say, and stops. But he can see her mind working.

'That he felt he was paying his debt after I had my stroke?'

'Something like that.'

'Your father had a sense of duty that was unshakable. So no, he wasn't paying his debt. He was doing what a man does for his wife.'

He thinks that is certainly true.

'I wonder if he's mad that I'm telling you this,' she says.

'You'll have to ask him, when you see him again.'

'Oh, I'll see him again, don't you worry,' she says, and looks at her son. 'I'm not afraid to die. What the hell's so good about hanging around here all by myself? I got things to do up there, old friends to look up. Your father's waiting.'

It is after midnight, and she announces that she is tired. The nurses wheel the Hoyer lift in and deftly winch her up in her sling.

'I'll be out on the sky room for a while,' she says, and he kisses her.

He goes to his bed, tired, drained. It is a tough business, reconciling that kind of loss, and it is something you do without practice. With a parent, you think you have your whole life to anticipate such a certainty, but it's never enough. You can accept the fact in your mind, but you can never train your heart to accept the void. He wonders if it is easier for a son who does not love his father, if the void left is a source of relief and not pain. But he decides not. The pain of loss cannot be lessened by hate or estrangement; this would require an order of existence that rendered love worthless, and that could not be. He falls asleep and doesn't dream.

He awakes in the morning, and goes to her bedroom. She is in her hospital bed. The oxygen machine hums, churns air; the clear hose at her nostrils hisses. He puts his hand on her shoulder and her eyes open.

'Did you sleep well?'

'Not a wink.'

'Why not?'

'I was concerned that I had told you too much. I don't want you to think less of your father.'

'I could never think less of him.' He bends over and hugs her. 'There isn't anything weak about overlooking a man's faults. It doesn't hurt me to know that he wasn't perfect. I was afraid I wasn't good enough.'

'He was very proud of you.'

'And I of him.'

Her teary face beams, her eyes bright and soft. 'I'll make sure to pass that along.'

He bends over again, squeezes her shoulder, kisses her and leaves the room.

A Miracle Cure

By Jim Harrington

Angel Franklin entered the waiting area and Marlene covered her face with a six-month-old copy of Golf Digest, like a rumpled detective in a B-movie. The last time they were in the same room, Angel had threatened to kick the receptionist's skinny butt to Buffalo if she had to wait much longer to see Dr. Schmidt. Today, Angel smiled as she limped across the room toward the anxious receptionist, with two sprigs of Lily of the Valley in her hand.

'I brought you this from my garden, Claire. I hope you ain't allergic.' Angel held out a single stem filled with a dozen tiny, white, bell-shaped flowers. 'The other one's for Janet. I'll give it to her when she takes me back to the exam room.'

Marlene could see Claire was as perplexed as she was by Angel's offering.

'Thank you, Angel. It's beautiful.' Claire said, taking the stem.

Marlene pinched her arm to see if she was dreaming. This couldn't be the Angel Franklin she'd known since high school. Overweight and boisterous, Angel wasn't popular in school. By ninth grade, she'd become mean and angry and remained that way for the past thirty years. The only person who got along with her was Freddie Merkle. The old saying, opposites attract, fit them perfectly. No one was surprised when they married.

Marlene peeked over the magazine and watched Angel take a seat across the room. Curious to find out more, she spoke without lowering her hands.

'Hello, Angel.'

'Hey there, Mar. How're they hangin'?'

Marlene's face heated up at the question. 'Except for this migraine, I'm well.' She closed the magazine and put it on the table. 'That was nice of you to give Claire a flower.'

'It's the new me.' Angel moved over two chairs to sit opposite her.

'I'm glad to see you're happy. I was concerned about you after Freddie passed.' Wary of Angel's response, Marlene looked away.

'It was a rough time, Freddie getting hit by a car right after I got the leg replacement.' A hollow sound resonated through the room when Angel reached down and tapped her right leg like someone knocking on a door. 'Then three months later I learn I'm dying.'

'What?'

'Yep, ain't that the luck. Diabetes. Took my leg, and now my kidneys are failing.'

'I'm so sorry. How long...?' Marlene looked at her hands. 'Can't something be done?'

'Turns out I ain't a good candidate for a transplant, and even if I was, I got no insurance.' Angel swallowed and looked as if she might cry. Instead she smiled and handed the remaining lily to Marlene.

'Oh, I can't. That's for Janet.'

'I got more in my garden. I can bring her one next time.'

'Thank you.'

'I was real sad about everything for a while,' Angel paused, 'then I heard on the TV about this study that showed people who receive gifts and people who give them both feel happier. Funny thing was people who watched gifts being given also felt better. It was then I decided I wanted to make up for being such a bitch all them years by doing nice things.'

'You weren't —'

'Yes, I was.' Angel took a breath and adjusted the hem of her flowered dress before continuing. 'I don't have much money, but I can give folks flowers and say nice things to them.'

'I think that's wonderful, Angel. I'm just sorry about...you know.'

Angel shrugged and toyed with the handle of her purse.

Marlene walked over to Angel and held her hand. It was cold. 'Well, I'm glad we chatted. In fact, you cured my headache. Maybe there is something to that study.'

171

Marlene patted Angel's hand before letting go. She gathered her purse and sweater and headed toward the reception desk to let Claire know she didn't need to see the doctor today. On her way to the door, she heard a soft voice say, 'Maybe we could get together for lunch sometime.'

'I'd like that, Angel,' Marlene replied. 'How about tomorrow?'

Mother's Theorem

By Katherine Spink

My Mum's invented a theorem, but she won't tell me what it is.

She says she can work out how much rice a paddy field will yield, or how long it will be until we are out of the recession, or when I am going to get married.

She says she can predict the results of the Grand National, or the X Factor, or what my GCSE results are going to be.

She says she knows how many cows are in the field opposite our house, or how many tadpoles are in the pond, or how many children I will have.

But she won't tell me the equation. She says only mothers are allowed to know it because it's Mothers' Theorem.

I think that's one of those things your Mum says when she wants you to shut up and stop asking questions.

I've invented my own theorem. It's called I Will Not Go to Bed When I Am Told, And I Will Not Tidy My Room or Do My Homework Theorem. The equation for it is x equals the number of teenage years I have lived divided by y, and then times by the number of things I have broken that day. It equals troublemaker, except when it is in the negative, and that's because that day is one of the exceptions when I want something from Mum, like more pocket money.

So far I think my theorem is winning and Mum's isn't, because she only won a fiver on the horses, and we're still in the recession, and I'm not married with children yet.

I did get an A in my mocks though.

Mr Trick Speaks

By Joel Willans

Mr. Trick stands, thumb out, next to a road that hums like a pipe. A Merc's brakes snarl. He knows it's a Merc without even looking because Mr. Trick knows cars. He knows cars better than he knows people and that's just how he likes it. Cars do what you tell them, they're predictable. More or less. Not that he drives anymore. He had no need and, until today, he had no reason.

How they'd found him, he didn't know. But he supposed that anyone with the money, the time and the inclination could if they wanted to. He'd been in the park, the one with his favourite statue, sitting beside the pond counting his ducks.

'Excuse me, sir. Are you Mr. Trick?' said a bald bulldog of a man wrapped in a long black Mac.

Mr. Trick ignored him, and carried on with his survey. Ten mallards, six drakes and fifteen little 'uns. There were two new pairs he'd not seen before. Mr. Trick quacked at them, welcoming them to his park.

They looked at him, surprised. Mr. Trick smiled. It always surprised the new 'uns that he could speak bird.

'Sir, I understand you're Mr. Edgar Trick.'

Mr. Trick coughed and spat.

The bulldog man handed him a letter. 'This is for you, sir. It's from your daughter.'

Mr. Trick rubbed his hands over his face. It had been a long, long time since he'd heard that word used in connection with his name.

'What she want?' he said, the words feeling like strangers.

When the bulldog man spoke, his jowls wobbled. 'I don't know, sir, I've just been employed to find you and give you this.'

Mr. Trick took the letter. His fingers leaving grimy smudges on the swan white paper. The bulldog man said goodbye and, with a lumbering gait, walked away. Mr. Trick watched him until he left the park, then he sniffed the envelope. It smelt of stale trees' innards and glue. He stuffed it in his pocket and carried on speaking to the birds.

It was only later that evening, as he settled in one of his skips, that the envelope started teasing him. Scared to open me are you, Edgar Trick? No surprise there, hey? Some things don't change do they?

'You don't know a damn thing.' He pulled it out of his jacket and ripped it open, enjoying the way the tearing silenced it. 'I haven't been scared for a long time.'

When he read his girl's words, under the soft fizz of a street lamp, he instantly regretted his bravado. He never expected to have to see her again. Not after she'd gone and shacked up with the monkey she called husband. And now this. Now, she had a baby girl to share and shouldn't he care? He had a last chance to see her before they went far away. Crunching the letter into a tight, tight ball, he tossed it high into the air. An owl called out hello and he answered back, wishing he could fly, just once.

Days passed as they do. And Mr. Trick, finishing his bird survey, found himself staring more and more at those ducklings, skimming across the water, speeding yellow fluff balls, scared and hungry and excited all at once. He wondered if she was like that too. He wondered it more and more. He wondered it so much that this morning, when the sun ignored his beard and kissed his cheek, he said to the sparrows.

'I've got to know, don't you think?'

They twitted in agreement.

Mr. Trick, dragging himself from his skip, pulled a fistful of crumbs out his pocket and tossed them into the wind. 'You lot will say anything for a bit of grub.'

Yet that day, he scrubbed his face and he trimmed his beard and he dusted down his jacket. Later, he sneaked into a department store, squirted himself with scent and bought a plastic orange comb. He couldn't look the cashier in the eye, or bring himself to say hello or goodbye or even thank you. But that would come, he hoped, once he learnt to speak a few words of baby.

175

Mugs

By Tania Hershman

They meet in pottery class. Her coffee mugs are misshapen, clumsy; his espresso cups are identical, boring. He envies her creativity; she craves his perfection.

After class, they walk to the bus stop. Shy. Hands in pockets.

'Do you...?'

'Yes?'

'I mean... are you...?'

'Am I...?

'Hungry?' They laugh, relieved.

The air is warm with tomato sauce. They order gnocchi, spinach ravioli.

'My mother wanted a boy, made me wear trousers when everyone else was in frilly dresses,' she says, after two glasses of house red.

'My brother shut me in the wardrobe for hours,' he says, looking down at the plastic flowered tablecloth. She shifts her hand so her fingertips touch his, just for a second.

At the end of the final class, they show off their work, then carry heavy bags towards the bus stop.

'Hang on,' he says. He steers her past and along, to a dark alley beside the bank. Nervous, she follows. Putting down the bag, he gets out a parcel and unwraps the newspaper. Then, sudden as lightning, he throws it at the wall.

Bang! A thousand tiny white splinters.

She stares, amazed, then laughs. Laughs and laughs until she cries. He grins, watches as she scrambles to unwrap one of hers and then, like a bowler, swings her arm and flings.

Thud! A shower of clay handles and coloured chunks.

He throws another, and then she, and they take turns until there is only one left of each.

'Please,' she says. She takes his smooth espresso cup, cradling it. He holds her clumsy mug to his heart. They stand in a pool of pottery pieces in a dark alley, looking at one another, in a city of a thousand sighs and lonely souls.

Named After

By Teresa Stenson

I am ten when my no-good-father (I've only seen his photograph) arrives on my scene (front garden) where I'm playing Kings And Queens (it's my game) with Kirsty and Becky from next door and I'm just giving my latest Royal Instruction (bath of milk – ASAP!) when his car pulls up and honks its horn and my mother's face comes to the window, all skin pulled back and tight lips, and my no-good-father gets half out the car with half his mouth smiling at my mother who is now fully out of the house, cardigan flapping up the garden path and Kirsty and Becky (mouths open) have definitely forgotten where they are and that I'll probably be needing a towel and my no-good-father looks at me, nods at his car and says, 'Cleo – that's where we made you,' and my mum goes, 'Cleo, it's not true,' but then it is because she won't swear on my life.

Thirty seconds later and I'm looking at the back of his car and he is saying, 'See?' a finger (fat) running along these letters that aren't quite my name, so I walk away and give the nod to my ladies, who really should be fetching more milk.

Naming Finbar

By Vanessa Gebbie

This is a story about Finbar Dermot O'Flaherty.

Not Finbar Donald O'Flaherty, mind, whose brother Colm, the one with the port wine stain on his left cheek, who ran away with a fisherman's wife from Bantry and had to emigrate to Texas...Finbar Donald O'Flaherty who was good at woodwork at school, married a girl from Holland he met in Texas, and went into the clog making business, remember? Not that one.

Finbar Dermot O'Flaherty was born under a damp and dripping gunnera plant by a wet roadside in Kerry on a late Thursday afternoon, only the second child, until that moment, of the sweet but rambling and rather too willing daughter of a mostly drunken travelling family by the name of O'Connor.

Not, you understand, the mostly drunken O'Connors of Castletownbere, who were the prime cause of the burning down of the bookshop. No, not those O'Connors. Those O'Connor's don't live in caravans, so how would you think it might be them in any event? These are the O'Connors who live in caravans...not the Vincent O'Connors, mind, who have well groomed horses...these are the O'Connors with the smaller caravans and the donkeys.

And that was the main cause of the misfortune that surrounded the birth of Finbar Dermot O'Flaherty, for his mother, the sweet and rather too willing Nathalie O'Connor, after she had wrapped Finbar up in a red and lilac knitted shawl, and after she had taken several swigs from the nearest bottle to dull the pain, announced that Finbar Dermot was not to be an O'Connor, as she thought the name was unlucky.

'I christen this child,' she said, wiping her legs with leaves, and taking another swallow of the whiskey (for that is what it was, a bottle of good single malt purloined by accident from a passing shop), 'I christen this child Finbar Dermot O'Flaherty.'

Tom Seamus O'Connor, her father, not the Tom Seamus O'Connor from Dingle who built a turf house on the island and lives as a hermit only coming back to the mainland every five years...and not the Tom Seamus O'Connor who fell into a bog on his way home from his own wedding to Phalaenopsis Flynn and was never seen again (but they are hoping his body will be recovered in centuries to come complete with the brand new wedding ring he borrowed from his best friend Michael)... Tom Seamus O'Connor, her father, the biggest, roundest Tom Seamus O'Connor this side of Cork, the strongest most drunken Tom Seamus O'Connor to have been in jail for a month and no one knows why exactly in this part of Ireland... was not amused.

He was an educated man, but on occasions such as this his education fled like education does when the drink takes over.

'Call the child Finbar Dermot O'Flaherty? The devil you will,' he said, and he retired into the lead caravan to investigate the second bottle of single malt to have been purloined by accident from the passing shop. He left young Nathalie with her red and lilac bundle to reflect on this momentous thing, all on her own. Nathalie reflected in the only way she knew. She took another swallow of the whiskey and sat on the caravan steps, watching dusk fall.

Now had she been less rambling and less sweet, Nathalie might have muttered, 'Niggardly old father,' under her breath. Or indeed, 'Decrepit case for euthanasia if there ever was one.'

Instead, she whispered loudly, 'Father, you are an old fool.'

Alas and alack. Tom Seamus O'Connor was not as hard of hearing as she had hoped. Unlike the really deaf Tom Seamus O'Connor from Killarney, who did not hear the new mechanical peat cutter coming until it was too late, and the slightly less deaf but still deaf enough Tom Seamus O'Connor who was banned from Mass by Father Patrick for singing 'Happy Birthday' because he was confused by all those candles...no, her father Tom Seamus O'Connor heard her every word.

'Right, that's that,' he said, coming out of the gloom of the caravan, and descending like a veritable holocaust on the steps where poor Nathalie was sitting. 'You know what's coming now, young lady.'

180

'Ah shit,' said Nathalie.

'It's the gusset factory for you, my lass. O'Mahoney's Gussets in Tralee. We'll drop you off on our way through and pick you up in December.'

'But Father,' said Nathalie, her eyes filling with tears, 'Father, please, not the gusset factory...terrible terrible things happen to girls at the gusset factory, Father. Why, remember Sinead Flannery? Oh Father, only two weeks and she ran away to become a nun. Please, not the gusset factory, give me one last chance?'

'OK,' said Tom Seamus O'Connor, sitting down on the step next to his daughter, and taking his latest grandchild on his knee.

''Tis a fine evening to be sure,' he said, rocking the sleeping Finbar Dermot O'Flaherty and raising his eyes to where the very first star had appeared in a flawless Irish sky. Nathalie sensed a moment of epiphany was approaching.

For a moment, she was quiet. Then, 'Father?'

'Aye?'

'Father, why may I not call the child Finbar Dermot O'Flaherty? For, to be sure, it is a fine name?'

Tom Seamus O'Connor sighed and began adjusting the shawl round young Finbar. 'To be sure,' he agreed, 'it is a very fine name, and to be sure, names are important. They define who we are. However...' the shawl fell apart and the baby kicked its chubby legs in the breeze, 'this, Nathalie, is a baby girl.'

'Ah,' said Nathalie. 'So Finbar's not a good name then?'

Tom Seamus O'Connor thought for a moment. Then he shrugged. 'Ach, to be sure,' he grinned. 'Whoever heard of a wee girl called Finbar? Maybe she'll have more luck than we did?' He raised his bottle.

'A toast,' he said, holding the wee girl over his shoulder.

A wee girl they, of course, called Finbar Dermot O'Flaherty.

Necklace

By Nina Adel

We were 14 years old, Asil and I, two girls on the shore of the Black Sea, summer girls in the mountain dorm of an international camp above the sea, above the camp centre. We didn't ask about each other's lives, but walked up and down the camp's long stairs and small paths for hours. Though Arabic was her language, she spoke a little bit of English, and though I can't recall barely a single word we exchanged that summer, I remember linking arms, holding hands, her perfectly white teeth, short, wavy hair and the necklace she always wore.

By then I was already alone, cut loose in life by the premature death of my mother, by the departure of my sisters for lives never again based in the house where we'd grown up. I felt like an odd, marked creature, as if M, for Motherless, were tattooed on my forehead. I felt certain the other American kids in the group I'd come with perceived me as utterly unwanted and strange. And I accommodated that perception.

Asil and I were joined by our moment in that beautiful place, but separated by our lack of common earth in all the moments preceding. Because she and I had no shared cultural imprint, she couldn't feel my awkward motherlessness, or perhaps she could. I never learned her life story. We were just two girls from opposite ends of the world, walking together arm in arm, learning Russian songs, eating Russian food there on the Black Sea.

There were beach days, our turn to walk the downward trail to the crescent of shore, of black and brown pebbles. Our companions were from Iraq, the U.S., and Bangladesh, all balancing themselves on the pebbles. It wasn't cold, but we shivered in an unfamiliar wind which hovered in layers alternating with the warm air. At first we hesitated, but Asil and I finally ventured into the indigo water holding onto each other, and the other children followed. The next time it was our beach day, we could not go in at all, as the sea was filled with small, sinister-looking parachutes, jellyfish of relation to the Portuguese man-o-war which kept us from ever having another beach day there again.

On some days we roamed late in the afternoon, when activities planned for us were over. We would meet on the linked trails between the common areas. From ours, the highest camp, we could see all the way down to the seashore, the hill and forest camps in between, the lines of trail connecting each to the others. We followed these trails to where we were not supposed to go, listened unseen to languages spoken by other children, touched the green plants and flowers that varied noticeably from one camp to the other, returning quietly to the authorized spaces of our own designated area.

We tried on each other's clothes, showed each other our artefacts and trinkets from home. We had both brought stones, shells, beads, not the kinds of things that I had been told to bring to share. We'd brought candies, bandannas, scarves, colourful pens, tiny notebooks.

On our final day together, she gave me the necklace I had admired, a chain with an attached name charm – her name, Asil – in curly, silver, Roman letters that I could read, not the Arabic alphabet, a detail that I didn't notice at the time. I gave her my address at my father's house in the lakeshore city where I lived; she handed me hers on a bit of lined paper with her name neatly printed: Asil Mohammad Reda, the address on some street whose name I can't bring to mind, though we corresponded long after that day.

Her address: Iraq, Baghdad.

For years it echoed in my head, not Baghdad the city Iraq the country, like Paris the city France the country. Not like that.

Iraq, Baghdad.

Where Asil lived and grew up, a place I'm sure I imagined like the cheesy movies and ill-informed references in I Dream of Jeannie, a TV show I loved for its magic. It's true: despite the unusual and broad cultural horizons of my family of origin, despite the fact that at that very moment I was a member of a US teen delegation to the Soviet-era international youth camp and therefore assumed to be a global-minded and well-informed young person, Baghdad was, in my mind at 14, like that: a glittery bazaar sprouting through clusters of old, dull, connected, beige and brown buildings with courtyards full of children like Asil and mothers dressed like Jeannie, but with olive skin, black hair and more coverage.

Iraq, Baghdad.

Perhaps I am being harsh in my memory towards my younger self, but, at the time, I was a budding teenage Latin Americanist, and the Middle East did not yet register much on my radar. How different the images are now for my own children when they hear those words – Iraq, Baghdad: American tanks, camouflage, bombed-out villages; traumatized toddlers staring into a camera; streets permeated with acid dust and laid-out corpses wrapped in white gauze.

Iraq, Baghdad. Asil, where could you be? I wonder now, grown. I have a daughter who smiles and waves as she walks into her school, I comfort my little son in the doorway of his class-room, where he is safe but does not want to be. Do you, too, have children, Asil? Are they safe? Can you comfort them? Do you live there, on that street where you returned with my trinkets at the end of summer? At my present home, when I turn from my children each morning to start my day, I whisper a silent wish for their wellbeing, and then, after a pause, for yours, not knowing if you are even alive.

Iraq, Baghdad.

There was a day, years after our Black Sea summer, when I took the necklace from my jewellery box to put it on, and it broke in two, the metal jagged between the 's' and the 'i' of the name, Asil. I kept it for a long time anyway, in a box with other things – a tiny, broken, wooden doll from my grandmother, a piece of my mother's dress lining, an unsigned note to me left in my college apartment by a man I didn't want to let go. The box eventually disappeared as I moved from one place to another, one life to another, yet at times, I feel the necklace here, in my hands, just now broken, and I ponder whether it could be fixed, welded back into one whole name, a longer name that could roll from my tongue in one soft, complete murmur:

Asil Mohammad Reda.

Iraq, Baghdad.

The Painting

By John Booth

In a shoebox full of yellowed postcards that smelled like cinnamon and pencil shavings, I found one with a picture of the Eiffel Tower.

The air inside the antique shop hung thick with the rain cooling the summer pavement outside. I held the postcard and looked from the watercolour greys and greens to the rippled panes of the storefront windows, watching the building across the narrow street glaze and drip.

I dug for change in my pocket, laying 75 cents on the glass counter by the cash register. The thick-nosed man there may have looked through my eyes, I don't know. May have seen me, spaced out and lost and elsewhere. Maybe didn't care at all. I hardly remember walking to my car.

I used to have a painting of the Eiffel Tower. Impressionist-style, I guess. More of a feeling than a scene. Nina gave it to me in our senior year of high school, before she went back home to Germany. I remember the day she started it, copying from a postcard a friend gave her. (Odd, that circle, I guess: postcard, painting, postcard.) The tower was a blur of sidewise strokes on a blank canvas, sitting in the white space looking unnatural.

Nina was becoming frustrated trying to get the symmetry of the tower to work, overcompensating here, adjusting a curve there. It wasn't working.

She grabbed one of those little paint spatula things and set to work with a dizzying and hypnotic motion, patching blobs and bits and dabs of colour as the foreground, the sky, the cityscape, the faces, the air of Paris. It was the sort of thing that will always amaze me, looking at that kind of art, fingers touching and placing paint just so, the effortless-seeming whims that are in fact every intention of the creator. Or maybe not. Maybe that's too much, and the art really is spontaneous and springing, I don't know.

It stunned me. It drew me in and spat me out a dazzled, dripping spirit just back from the realm of the impossible. There in the converted-auto-shop art room of Lake High school, the oil-stained concrete floor vanished, the high, bare ceiling opened to possibility, the walls fell to the wind, and I stood shock-still and smiled.

When she framed and matted it for me that June, as a graduation present, I held it in my lap and stared.

The day she left for home, I sat in my room on the edge of my bed and held it again, turning it over now and then to read the back:

Matthew,

Germany and America: Too far away.

But never forget that above both there will always shine the same moon and the same stars.

Someday I will see you again, and maybe someday we can visit Paris together.

Love,

Nina.

It was written in both German and English.

My freshman year of college, the painting hung on the end of my loft. I had to climb over it to get into my bed and I often smacked my knee on the sharp corner of the frame. When I sat at my desk, I'd often stop whatever I was doing just for a second or two, and look at the whirling jewelled kaleidoscope of city and river and sky clinging to the soft but resolute grey tower in the middle.

My roommate often worried about me: I got lost in that painting too easily.

The painting followed me; it hung by my desks in many rooms, in many apartments, as I moved around during the school years and the summers in between.

When I met Susan in May after my sophomore year, the painting was still there. But after Susan and I began dating and eventually moved in together, the painting was left in a corner, unseen. Susan hated it.

I let the painting gather dust. Susan and I decided to move to Florida, and she finally forced me to give it away. I left it in the parking lot at the local Salvation Army store, dumped in a rusted red bin behind a drab yellow-brick building full of abandoned junk.

It was raining, of course, at the time. I stood there, holding it for the last time, watching water gather in droplets on the canvas, puddling in the deep acrylic swirls. I hoisted it up and let it fall into the bin.

That was four years ago.

Susan and I eventually broke up. I never saw Nina again.

Hanging above my desk is the postcard from the antique store, tacked to a corkboard. I still miss the painting. Not just because of Nina, but because it was something I lost and looked for during dark times, and while I have renewed friendships I thought long gone, the painting of Paris will always remind me that not everything lost can be found again.

But the postcard says that losing and forgetting are not the same thing.

The Path of the Faerie King

By Robert J. McCarter

The Faerie King was in a foul mood as he headed down his path from the forest to the meadow. Below, he could see the odd rectangular dwellings that were beginning to spill into his last, beautiful meadow.

His path now passed behind a series of houses that had been built recently. Although he was loath to be near humans, it was his path and he would not yield it–after all, he had already yielded so many paths and so many meadows to them.

It was there that the small human girl-child saw him and called out. 'Squirrel?' She was young, young enough to still see his kind, perhaps 3 years of age. She had bright blue eyes and cascading locks of yellow hair. She sat right on the Faerie King's path, encircled by wild irises.

He was taken aback; it had been such a long time since a human had seen him. He stopped, tugged at his bark tunic and puffed out his chest (vainly hoping it would extend further than his belly). 'Squirrel? I should say not. I am a king, the Faerie King,' he said, looking up at the girl towering over him. Beside her was an open gate and, beyond that, one of those rectangular human dwellings. 'You best get home now, shoo.'

'Tea?' she asked. He hadn't noticed it before, but set up in the ring of irises was a tea pot and several tea cups. Next to one cup was a rumpled doll. She pointed him to an empty spot next to another tea cup.

'I... Well... Hrmph.'

'And nuts?'

Right then his large and rebellious stomach growled. 'Well, I could use a bite,' he said.

The girl, whose name was Dawn, clapped and squealed. 'Squirrels like nuts!'

*   *   *

The Faerie King was whistling as he headed down his path in a very pleasant mood, and Dawn was the reason. Despite her insistence that he was a squirrel, he had enjoyed the last two summers they had spent together. He was, he had found out, her 'invisible friend.' He was learning about humans from her, and he was teaching her about the Faerie Way; telling her of his people's plight, and introducing her to other nature spirits.

As he rounded the corner his heart leapt. Two burly goblins, with sharp fangs and stinking breath, had backed Dawn up against her fence and were snarling at her.

'Nice doggies...' she said thinly, her little voice shaking.

The Faerie King, although smaller and outnumbered by the burly goblins, pulled out his sword and rushed to her aid. 'Back I say,' he shouted at them. 'She is under my protection.' Dawn began to cry. 'Rest assured my lady, I am well versed in the use of this weapon and in the dispatching of goblins.' His sword was nothing more than a sharpened twig from a pine tree.

The first burly goblin lunged at him, but he danced aside, racking the goblin's behind with his sword and causing him to yelp in pain.

'Run along now, or to you I will be less kind,' the Faerie King said to the second goblin, his pine-twig sword slashing the air. The second one jumped at him, his claw raking down the Faerie King's left arm as the Faerie King's sword pierced the rolling fat of the goblin's belly.

One burly goblin held his behind, and the other held his belly, both grimacing in pain. 'Let it be known to you and yours that this girl-child is under the projection of me and mine. Now be gone!' The Faerie King leapt forward, his pine-twig sword coming near the burly goblins. They turned and ran, never to be seen again.

'You are hurt,' Dawn said.

'Oh this, it is but a scratch,' he replied, although it pained him greatly.

'You saved me!'

190

His cheeks blushed and he said, 'It 'twas nothing my lady.'

* * *

Some years later the Faerie King stood alone in the circle of irises, grieving. Dawn had outgrown her invisible friend and she no longer came to see to him.

The large beeping yellow monsters had arrived—more houses were coming—and he must finally yield more of his meadow and move his path.

* * *

Two decades later the Faerie King was headed down his path in a very foul mood. His last meadow was nearly full of houses and he was concerned for his people. What was a Faerie without a meadow?

Lost in thought, he was shocked to see them; a woman and a girl-child, both with yellow locks and blue eyes, sitting in a ring of wild irises in the middle of his path. 'I see him Mommy,' the girl-child cried, 'I see the funny looking squirrel!' The Faerie King's heart leapt; the girl-child looked so much like Dawn.

The woman spoke, 'Faerie King, it's me, Dawn, and this is my daughter Fay. I am so sorry that I can't see you anymore, but she can.'

The Faerie King, for once in his very long life, did not know what to say. 'He is just standing there Mommy,' Fay said.

Dawn smiled brightly, her blue eyes sparking, and said, 'I am sorry it took me so long to remember you, to remember that you are real, that you need help. We came here today to tell you that the houses will come no further into your meadow.' She then added in a formal tone, 'Let it be known that these faeries are now under the projection of me and mine.'

'You saved me,' said the Faerie King, which Fay relayed to Dawn.

''twas nothing my lord,' Dawn said with a giggle.

191

Patio Lights

By Joyce Meadows

The two boys rolled out of their seats and beelined for the patio door. Their parents watched them run out, then turned back to the wine. That was all fine with me. On such swampy, airless nights as these, no one ate on the patio, so the boys had it all to themselves. Despite the late hour, there was plenty of soft light: ropes of tiny white lights spiralled around the trees, snaked straight along the waist-high railing at the patio's edge, and even outlined the doors and windows. A million-bulb fairyland – the owner's favourite part of the restaurant.

I no longer even noticed the lights. Certainly not tonight, with both my co-workers out sick. I forgot about the boys in my haze of taking orders, shuttling food, pouring wine. When I delivered dinner to the boys' table, the parents dug into their plates, pausing only to ask if I would send the boys in.

It was easier to obey than to find a tactful way to tell the parents to do it themselves. I stepped outside, looking for the kids.

I saw a mess.

Both boys were at the far end of the patio, the end not easily seen from the windows. Small broken tree branches dangled by strips of bark, their strings of lights unlooped and limp. The lights along the railing now hung in long uneven curves. The plastic ties that usually held them in place were gone. One of the boys was trying to climb the side of the building by hauling himself up a vertical light string. It had already come loose from the clips holding it along the wall; only the top hook supported it now. He saw me, but didn't stop.

'Your food's ready.' Not quite what I wanted to say, but I needed to keep my job.

They trotted off, leaving me staring at the wrecked lights. No time to fix anything now, even if I could; headlights splashed into the parking lot, and I trudged inside to seat the newcomers.

My pasted-on smile never slipped as I opened the door for another family. Two parents and only one boy, younger than the light-pullers. He hopped with both feet as I led them to a table. As soon as he climbed into the chair, he picked up two forks, holding them together to compare sizes. While I described the evening's specials, he unfolded his origami napkin, then tried to refold it. His mother ordered him a soda. Sugar and caffeine – just what he needed. Right.

When I returned to take their order, he was twisted in his seat, cupping his hands to look out the window behind him. He asked his parents if he could go outside. I almost interrupted to say the patio was closed. But then I considered the candles, linens, and wine on the table, and decided it would be more dangerous to keep him cooped in here.

His father nodded, wineglass already in hand. 'I'll knock on the window when the food's here,' he said, and the kid scrambled away.

The evening slogged along. My other tables finished eating, paid, left. Each person out the door was a stone off my back. My smile was genuine as I closed the door behind the brothers of destruction and their yawning parents.

I brought steaming plates to Fidgety Boy's table. Before I set them all down, his father actually did turn to the window and rap on it.

The sound shot across the restaurant, cutting through the background music. He knocked again, harder now. The other remaining table stared at us over their coffee cups. 'I'll go get him,' I said.

I braced myself for further mayhem. How many more strings of lights would be wrecked? Did he break more branches, or maybe just tear off some leaves? Had he found new and exciting things to destroy?

He ran toward me, grinning. I held the door open and he rocketed inside. I had no time to go inspect the patio; my other table was waving for their check.

While the family ate, I dried silverware and restocked wine and tried to finish as much of my side work as possible. I wanted

193

to be home. They were my last table. I prayed they wouldn't order dessert. They didn't.

I stood at the door as they left. The boy stumbled a little on the welcome mat, and I heard his mom ask, 'Where are your shoelaces?' He shrugged and skipped down the sidewalk. After I cleared and cleaned their table, I went to the patio to survey the damage.

Something was wrong.

Or rather, something was not wrong anymore.

I moved closer. The vertical light string was now straight along the wall, pushed into its clips. Finding the broken branches took longer, but I finally saw that their lights had been re-looped to hold the limbs in place.

I hadn't seen anyone else go out onto the patio, but the cooks could get there through the back kitchen door. Maybe one of them had fixed the lights. Or maybe the dishwasher took care of it. I'd ask around.

Then I noticed the railing lights. They were once again strung along the rail, but not quite as tightly or straight as before. I leaned to look.

They'd been tied to the railing with pieces of shoelace.

Père Noël Pops the Question

By Kathleen McGurl

I'm half way down the mountain before it occurs to me that she might not say yes. My hat's slipping down over my eyes, and the beard keeps getting in my mouth. And why I thought I'd be able to ski with a pillow stuffed under my jacket and a sack on my back I'll never know. Suddenly, the whole idea of proposing on a ski slope, on Christmas Day while dressed as Santa, is beginning to seem a bit stupid.

I can see Janine further down the slope, waiting on the ledge just off the piste, as we arranged. Her hair is blowing in the breeze, and her purple ski jacket stands out against the pristine snow and bright blue sky. She looks stunning. The whole day is stunning.

She hasn't spotted me yet, but the ski school have.

'Père Noël! Père Noël!' A line of excited French children snake their way down the piste, performing perfect snowplough turns. I stop and give them a cheery wave. Might as well play the part!

'Vous avez des cadeaux, Père Noël?' Presents, they want presents. My French isn't quite up to saying, no, just one very special present for one very special lady, so I just attempt a Ho Ho Ho, a parallel turn and another wave of my ski pole, all at once.

Bad idea. My hat falls further over my eyes, and I hit some powder snow. My left ski tip digs in, my right ski goes over my left, and with my ski pole still completing its cheery wave above my head, there's no hope.

I tumble head over heels, and end up planting my face in a deep drift. I've bitten my tongue hard in the fall, and can feel a pool of warm blood collecting in my mouth.

It's not nice, but Père Noël has to do what he must do. The French children stand open-mouthed as I pull off my beard and spit a mouthful of blood onto the snow, then adjust my pillow-belly and re-attach a ski.

'Ho ho ho, Joyeux Noël,' I shout, as I gingerly set off again, somewhat slower this time. My words come out garbled – I've bitten my tongue so hard it hurts to talk.

Down the mountain, I see Janine has noticed me. Earlier, I'd told her to ski ahead to this point, while I visited the little boys' room at the top of the chair-lift. That's where I'd emptied the rucksack I'd been carrying (Janine thought it contained an extra jumper and a picnic for later) and togged up as Father Christmas.

I pat the pocket where I've tucked the ring. Thankfully it's still there, despite my tumble.

When I reach her, Janine's as open-mouthed as the children were.

'Nick? Is that you? What on earth...'

'Ho ho ho, Merry Chrithtmath,' I say.

Janine's not sure whether to laugh or look worried. 'Nick? It is you, isn't it? I saw you fall. Are you okay?'

'Yeth, it'th me. I'm fine!' I tell her. Time to get down on my knees and do the job properly.

I release the catches on my ski bindings, and in one smooth motion step off my skis and kneel in the snow. She'll guess what I'm up to now, I'm sure.

But she laughs. I'm a little disconcerted. Does that mean she'll say no?

'Nick, poor Nick, let me help you up,' she says, shuffling towards me on her skis. I get it, she thinks I've stepped into soft snow and disappeared up to my knees.

'No, no, I'm okay. I'm meant to be like thith,' I tell her. 'I'm on my kneeth.'

'Your what?'

'Kneeth. Thing ith, Janine. There'th thomething I'd like to athk you.'

Janine is still laughing. My tongue is swelling by the second. If I don't get this question out quickly I won't be able to ask it at all and I'll have to think of some other stunt. I draw a deep breath, take out the ring in its little box, and go for it.

'Janine, will you do me the enormouth honour of marrying me?'

She stops laughing. She fixes her eyes on mine, unclips her skis and kneels down in front of me. Her face is an inch from mine as she pulls down my beard, wipes a drop of blood from my lips with her fingers, and whispers, 'Yes, oh yes, Nick.'

We kiss then, a short, sore kiss owing to the state of my mouth, but a long and lingering embrace. We're on our knees in crisp white snow, half way down a French mountain on Christmas Day, under a blue sky and a bright sun. And I'm dressed as Father Christmas.

The French children snake past. Their instructor shouts to me: 'Oui, ou non?'

'Oui!' I shout back. She said yes. She said Yes! SHE SAID YES!

The children let out an enormous cheer. Janine turns and waves at them. She looks radiantly happy, and more beautiful than anything I've ever seen.

She's just given me the greatest Christmas present anyone could ever have.

Potifar Jones' Experiment with Time and Brains Beer

By Alun Williams

During my early college years I shared a room with a student called Russell Potifar Jones. To paraphrase Dickens, 'it was the best of times, it was the best of all times.'

'Pot', as he was known, was a ruddy faced, hairy Welsh speaking Welshman and it helped immensely that he was one sandwich short of a picnic. My subject, Law, was far removed from Pot's which was Astrophysics, but from the very first minute he breezed in like a Celtic Yeti carrying armfuls of books, we gelled.

'Potifar Jones,' he said in a lilting Welsh accent, 'from Cardigan. Lad down the corridor says you're from Brighton. Gay are you? No! That bastard said you're as bent as one of Uri Geller's teaspoons. He's a marked man, don't you worry. You got a spare cushion? For my haemorrhoids. Curse of the drinking classes it is.'

He dropped his bags on my bed and looked around. 'Shit,' he shouted picking up my toothbrush from the glass. 'Forgot to pack mine. No worries, I'll use yours.'

Before I could answer he threw me a can of Brains best bitter and slapped my back.

'All right, bud. I bet you're one of those geniuses aren't you? You've got a large head. Large cranium size, large IQ. Size is everything. Big dick too, I bet.'

I almost choked. I wasn't about to discuss the size of my penis with a total stranger, although Pot's carefree innocence made it difficult to argue. It was the start of a whirlwind period in my life which has yet to be equalled. Potifar Jones became my 'Bluto Blutarsky' and our room the hub of anything and everything that was mad, bad and dangerous on campus. Parties were wild and lasted two, even three, days and at least with Pot you were bound to end up in bed with one of his willing and very able retinue of girls.

Several months passed and we were in the throes of our first lot of exams when one day Pot stormed in, his rustic face blushed an angry shade of crimson.

'Fucking wanker!'

'Who? Me?'

'No, that Dr Reece. Gave him my essay on time travel. Ripped it to shreds. Told me I was a dreamer and blamed it on the Welsh mentality and my Methodist upbringing. I'll have him know I'm a Baptist!' He paced up and down the room like a man possessed. 'I know, I'll prove it. I'll build my own time machine. Hey, did you know there are parallel universes out there?'

'You mean to say there's another you out there!'

'Oh yes and other worlds. Imagine travelling back like Dr Who. Einstein knew it. It's finding the key see.'

'You're losing it, Pot, you really are,' I said.

I thought no more of it until the next day when I found our room filled with a myriad of paraphernalia.

'What's this crap?' I asked.

'That's not crap,' he replied, shaking his head from side to side. 'This is essential equipment. I'm building a time machine.'

'Still looks like crap,' I said, stepping over various metal artefacts as I made my way over to my bed. 'It'll never work, Pot. Time travel is an impossibility.'

He looked at me and threw over a can.

'You law students are all the same. You've got no imagination. Time travel is the final frontier...'

'That was Star Trek wasn't it?'

'...the final frontier. Just you wait, boyo, just you wait.'

His enthusiasm with time travel took over our lives. Wires criss-crossed the room. He experimented with the forces of nature, attaching my audio speaker wires to our obligatory house plant and running it to a lightning rod on the roof. A large cog wheel whirred, creaked and clicked all day long.

His frenzied obsession finally overtook our friendship and I moved out into digs of my own. I saw him occasionally over the next few weeks, then he suddenly vanished from campus and my life. It was rumoured that Pot had a nervous breakdown and had gone home to Wales. I felt guilty when I heard that and hoped that he would return when the new term started.

He didn't and life at university became predictable and tame.

Four months later, however, I received a parcel which contained a book on Twentieth Century History and a small note in Pot's familiar scrawl.

'See page 25 and 53.'

Curiosity got the better of me. Page 25 showed a picture of some passengers waving goodbye on the Titanic. An arrow pointed to a person in a straw hat. Pot! Page 53 showed the infamous scene in Dallas 1963. A man standing on the grassy knoll. Potifar bloody Jones!

The stupid bastard had done it!

I'm married now, but there's always a case of Brains beer in my fridge. My wife thinks I'm mad but Pot is getting closer to home. This morning I received a postcard from Chernobyl, dated 1986. I bet my life he pushed the wrong button. Guess they didn't know he was colour blind.

One day, Pot'll return. I can feel it.

It's just a matter of time.

Real Men

By Jan Wright

I was very young when I first saw that ad – you know the one where she knocks on her new neighbour's door and asks to borrow some coffee. She's sophisticated, he's gorgeous, and their eyes lock over a jar of instant. Well, it didn't give me a taste for coffee, but it did make me determined to one day buy my own apartment. Which is probably why, years later, I've emptied my bank account and taken on a large mortgage.

I picked up the keys late this afternoon, and my brother is helping me move in. Now the flat isn't like the one on the telly, but it's all mine and I'm pleased with it. Or I am until my brother discovers the problem with the loo. 'There's no water in it, Sarah,' he moans.

Which is odd because the taps are working. 'What do you think is wrong?' I ask.

'It's broken,' he mumbles.

'I've got a small toolkit in one of the boxes,' I say.

'Good, I'll leave you to it then.'

And before I can complain, he's off in his van leaving me stranded miles from the nearest public loo. Have you noticed there are no real men about anymore?

It's seven o'clock before I fling down the spanner and admit that I can't solve the problem. However, there is another problem I'm going to have to solve – and soon!

I'd been renting a fully furnished bed-sit, so I'm a bit short of things like buckets, but I do have a telephone directory. First I call a plumber, and then I call another one.

I'm near to tears by the time I hang up. I've always known I'll never find a rich, sexy man in this converted house miles from the city centre, but I guess the dream of the flat transforming me into a sophisticated woman with impeccable taste, is still alive – or it was. Now all I'm dreaming about is finding a friendly face on the top floor. I've already met the old man downstairs; he's

201

creepy and mutters to himself so there's no way I'm knocking on his door.

Things are now getting to the desperate stage, and I'm running out of options. I just pray there isn't some pervert upstairs, what I need is a female who'll find it amusing that the first thing I want to borrow is her loo.

I've spent the whole day lugging boxes around, and that was before I started fiddling with the plumbing, I must look a complete mess. But, as I haven't found my mirror yet, I can't be sure.

How typical, it's a fella who opens the door. But luckily he isn't sexy like the coffee man, or creepy like the man downstairs. Still, I feel myself blushing as I explain I'm his new neighbour and I have a problem with my plumbing. 'That's the plumbing to my loo,' I add. 'Look, I know it's a cheek, but I don't suppose I could...'

Perhaps it's the way I've been hopping from one foot to another, but he doesn't need me to say more. He simply grins and points to the second door on the left.

By the time I see him again I'm feeling much better... and much worse! It's obvious this is a bachelor pad and, having seen myself in his mirror, I now know just how dishevelled I look.

'Have you called a plumber?' he asks, after I've apologised again for interrupting his evening.

'I've called three firms,' I say. 'Have you any idea how much these bloodsucking sharks charge to look at a problem on a Friday evening? And waiting until tomorrow isn't an option, because weekend rates are just as extortionate. I can't afford it, not on top of all the other expenses. So I'm going to have to wait until Monday, when they've promised they'll only charge an arm and a leg.'

He smiles sympathetically. 'How about I take a look for you?'

'I couldn't put you to that trouble,' I say, before I realise he probably doesn't want me borrowing his loo all weekend.

'I'm Mark,' he says as we walk down the stairs.

'I'm Sarah, and I'm sorry, this isn't the best way to get to know your new neighbour is it.'

'Oh, I don't know,' he laughs. Which is when I notice how lovely his eyes are, especially compared to his rather crooked nose. He's about five years older than me, and has a soft Irish lilt that I find strangely comforting.

While Mark looks at my toilet I try to smarten myself up, which isn't easy without access to a bathroom. Then I finish unpacking and do some cleaning, all before he announces he's fixed it.

'You're a genius,' I cry, as I stare gratefully at my fully functioning loo.

He shakes his head and smiles. 'Not a genius, just a blood-sucking plumber.'

Ah!

Feeling dreadful, I mutter a grovelling apology.

Mark laughs. 'Don't worry, I didn't fancy going to the pub tonight anyway. And to prove we're not all sharks, Sarah, this lot will only cost you a coffee.'

How sweet of him. I guess there are some real men left in the world after all. 'I'd love to pay you in coffee, Mark, only I don't have any,' I admit. 'I could make some tea, but the milk's gone off.'

It's curdled along with my hopes of ever being a sophisticated hostess. There we are, me in desperate need of a shower and some make-up, him with his crooked nose and grease-covered hands. We're as far removed from the magic of the telly ad as you can get, but that doesn't mean there isn't a crackle of tension in the air as our eyes lock across my cistern.

Then he invites me back to his place, and of course I accept. Romantic dreams are all very well, but have you noticed they never rush to your rescue – not like a real man does.

Reshaping the Past

By Rosemary Gemmell

I slowly open the brown leather jewellery box. I've put this off for far too long. Now that my life is moving on, it's time to go through all these pieces I no longer wear. I wasn't sure what to do with them, but now I might have found the answer.

Staring at the contents, I wonder where to start. Thirty-odd years of my life are encapsulated in these pieces of jewellery; some expensive silver and gold, some cheap and cheerful costume paste. It's the silver and gold I need to sort out once and for all. It's going to be difficult, but it's necessary. Time to take a positive step forwards. Then I can get on with life as it's meant to be lived.

Picking up the childhood charm bracelet, I smile while examining each memory. The tiny silver horse for my birthday the year I was going through the 'My Little Pony' phase; the ballet shoes Mum gave me on the day of my first display; the delicate little heart that wasn't as fragile as Dad's real one. Every swinging charm is more precious than the next and reminds me how much I've been loved. Yet I don't need such tangible memories for they're all locked in my heart; just as the poor bracelet was locked away all these years. Anyway, I want to make new memories.

I pick up a gold and silver brooch inherited from my godmother. She was my parents' dearly loved friend, but I can live quite happily without the ugly beetle brooch which I've never worn. Its tiny, gleaming eyes seem to glare at me in accusation every time I open the box. How I wish it had been a delicate butterfly instead. It definitely has outstayed its welcome.

The ill-fated engagement ring is next. At least the engagement was ill-fated, not the ring which is a pretty gold circle topped by a tiny diamond. It was all Keith could afford at the time and I was ecstatic. In the end, the ring stood the test of time far longer than the engagement. We'd grown up and apart by the time we finished college. He didn't want it back and it's been buried at the bottom of the box along with the bitter-sweet memories of the relationship.

I finger the next item. Mark's solitaire completely replaced the diamond ring. I was so sure this ring, and the solid gold wedding band to match, would be as eternal as our love. They stayed on my wedding finger until the day he finally confessed he'd found someone to replace me. After ten years of a too-comfortable marriage.

I'd contemplated throwing the rings over the bridge in a ceremonious farewell to the past, but it seemed a bit sad to waste the jewellery. Besides, the memories don't disappear with the removal of the evidence.

I look at the gathering pile of jewellery and bite my lip, wondering if I'm being too impulsive. No... this is the right time to clear them out. I open the small compartment that holds Gran's rings. I'm the only granddaughter and I used to love the old-fashioned ruby ring and thin gold wedding band.

I'd always imagined I would wear them eventually, but they still haven't seen the light of modern day and I'm in my forties. It's a shame to leave them lingering unloved and I can't imagine ever selling them. On to the pile with them.

There's no room for sentiment today. I need to get through this by being practical, and ruthless if necessary, or I'll never let go.

There is one more expensive item. I look at it for a long time, wondering yet again if I'm doing the right thing. Wondering why I even kept it.

The small silver cross and chain was one of my favourites, since the day of my 30th birthday. Julie gave me it with the same love and affection that saw us through school, puberty and boyfriends. I hardly ever took it off, wearing it every time we went out together, secure in the knowledge this was the person who knew me best in the entire world.

So many years of friendship, so many joys and tears shared between us. This made it all the more devastating. That life-changing day when Mark, my husband, and career-girl Julie, my best and dearest friend, told me they had fallen in love and were going away together.

Even now, I can hardly bear to look at the cross. Yet, as with the rings, I could never quite bring myself to part with it. How could I just throw away our growing up years as though they hadn't existed?

It was the ultimate betrayal, but I've tried to understand why it happened, through these long and terrible years. And I'm finally able to recognise that Mark and I never had a passionate marriage; we'd been friends more than lovers. Maybe we both deserved more. If only it hadn't been with my childhood friend, for I lost them both that day.

I finally stand up, pushing the costume jewellery back into the almost empty box. I carefully place all the silver and gold items into a small bag, ready to take with me tomorrow. I'm going ahead with it.

You see, I've unexpectedly found my real soul-mate after all these years. So perhaps it's time to turn the memories of the past into a new beginning.

It was Alan's sister who gave me the idea when she showed me a beautiful, delicate silver and gold bracelet made from the melted down jewellery she no longer wore. It's the perfect solution.

The past is in everyone: on faces, in personality, in the wisdom gained through experience. As I think of my forthcoming wedding, I've decided I will proudly wear my memories on my wrist as I walk down the aisle. In reshaping the past, I can now look forward to the future.

The Ring of Truth

By Joanna Campbell

Marianne contemplated the ring for a moment. Turning away, she felt pangs of conscience. She slunk back to her room and pulled out a shirt from the heap on the floor. It was horrifically crumpled, but could hide under a jumper.

As she dressed, the usual slip of folded paper slid with a hiss under her door, forcing her to think about the ring again. She simply couldn't be bothered. There was no time anyway. She was already an hour late for work. She kicked a path through the magazines and foil cartons from last night's takeaway.

Tip-toeing downstairs, Marianne glanced behind, but she was lucky this morning. The bath taps were gushing and she could hear Gus whistling and scrubbing. Her relief was tinged with disappointment. Marianne was puzzled by this, because she didn't want to look at the ring again. Didn't want to discuss it.

So why had she slipped his note in her pocket? Why did she keep caressing it?

She slumped onto a bench in the park to read it, but buried her face in it first. She had no idea why, but it made her feel light inside. She felt sorry for the frowning men hurrying by, clutching cardboard coffee. There was a new sensation stirring and Marianne didn't recognise it at all. It made her sit straight and she smiled at how different it felt.

After she read the note, her smile withered like the unfortunate cactus living under her laundry pile. She slumped again, tears surging. Gus was about to give up on her. She wouldn't be able to see him again. It would be impossible to stay in her bed-sit. No other landlord would tolerate her laziness. Or her trumpet.

The church clock struck eleven, wrenching Marianne from her bench. The Boss wouldn't tolerate it either. She had received a written warning after he had found a stack of vital letters tucked inside her trumpet.

'What are they doing there? Playing 'The Last Post'?'

'No.' Marianne was bewildered. 'I was planning to take the trumpet to the repair shop, so I put the letters with it. And then I couldn't be...'

'...bothered. Yes I know. Always been your problem. I bet your mother did everything. Ironed your socks. Picked your hair out of the plug-hole.'

'Does hair get into plug-holes? I wondered why it took ages for the water to disappear.'

The Boss had shaken his head in despair as Marianne tried to recall whether she had ever had a close encounter with a plug-hole. Or an iron, come to that.

As the clock echoed across the valley, Marianne broke into a run. The first one since Primary Three's Sports Day. That had been three-legged with Susie Fitchett, the sprint star, and Marianne had sat down on the track. Susie had unbound their legs and whacked her with the school tie. This run took her to work. She put in overtime. The next run took her home in a torrential downpour. She battered on Gus' door. No response. She played 'You Are The Sunshine Of My Life' on her trumpet, still dripping from the rain, and he appeared. Beautifully unshaven and lean in his singlet and shorts.

'I was asleep.'

'Then it's time you woke up and smelt the coffee!'

'I'm on night shift this week, Marianne. And you don't make coffee. You wait for me to put the kettle on. But while you're...'

'I know. I know. The ring. Your note.'

'I've sent you hundreds of notes. About hundreds of rings.' He was wide awake now. Drinking in her damp red hair, cheeks rose-pink from exertion.

'I promise to clean the bath from now on, Gus.'

'Today's was like grey fur, Marianne. Half a tub of scourer it took.'

'I want to stay, Gus. No more rings. No more fur.'

'Good.'

'But you have to face facts. I was made with lazy bones.'

'Shall we have dinner on Friday? If you can be bothered of course.'

'I'll put a ring round the date on my calendar. If I can find it.'

Second Chances

By Ellie Garratt

Sarah paused at the door to her father's bungalow. She had gone over their conversation hundreds of times – what they would say to each other after all these years – and now she felt so uncertain.

Tom's voice echoed in her ears. 'Your father is alone now, Sarah. He needs you. More importantly, Emily needs a grandfather. Go and see him before it's too late.'

Checking her appearance in the window's reflection, Sarah pushed the doorbell and waited. She had chosen a simple blouse and modest skirt; her father disapproved of women in trousers. After a minute had passed, she pressed the bell a little harder and longer. This time she could see movement through the mottled glass and a shapeless figure approached.

The man who answered had aged; his tall frame was bowed and his face pale. Sarah felt her throat tighten; his eyes still held that dark rigid glare.

'Hello, father.'

'Come in,' he answered. No hello. No small talk. No, it's good to see you after all these years. This was the father Sarah remembered and expected.

She followed him in.

He started to walk away, and then turned towards her. 'You look well.'

Along the narrow hallway that led to the back of bungalow, he took Sarah past a selection of framed photographs – her parents on their wedding day; the Tipton Pigeon Club; Sarah as a young child – but none of herself after that summer.

'Would you like tea?' her father asked, pointing towards a door Sarah guessed led to the kitchen.

'Coffee would be nice.'

She entered a large room with pine cupboards and a dining table at one end.

'Just like your mother,' he said.

'Sorry?'

'Your mother drank coffee. Lots of it.'

'Yes. I know.'

'You used to meet your mother, didn't you?'

Sarah had always suspected he had known. 'Once a week since you...since...well I think we both know since when.' She could feel her face reddening. Why did she feel so ashamed? It had been his choice to exclude her.

'I told her that she could do as she wished. It wasn't my place to stop her.'

Sarah's father sat down on a tall grey pedestal that she remembered from childhood. He stared at her intently.

'That was in the past, father. I think enough time has gone by, don't you?'

'Aye. I guessed that's what you'd say.'

Sarah felt her anger building.

'I was young, father. I was in love. Can't any part of you understand that?'

'No. Not then.'

A small clock on the kitchen's rear-facing wall chimed midday, and Sarah saw another picture, Uncle Harry and her father as children clutching white rats that seemed almost as big as them. Tucked in the corner of the frame was a small battered picture of Sarah's graduation; the one her mother had kept in her purse.

'Maybe I was wrong,' her father said, unexpectedly.

Sarah felt her heart skip a beat, 'Perhaps we were both wrong.'

'Aye. Perhaps.'

Sarah wondered if he really meant it.

'I lost Albert last month,' her father said, changing the subject.

'Albert?'

'My dog.'

'You and mum had a dog?' Her mother had never mentioned that.

'We got him from a shelter. The little chap would follow me everywhere, scared silly we'd abandon him I suppose. I remember when you did that, following me around when you were a little 'un. You would sit with me in the garden, whilst I tended to the pigeons.'

Sarah smiled at the memory and realised for the first time how quiet her father's bungalow was – no pigeons cooing in a loft outside. 'You don't keep them anymore?'

'Pigeons are a lot of work, and I'm not as young as I used to be.'

'Couldn't Mike or some of the younger lads at the club help you?'

Her father looked puzzled and then headed to the kettle, which had finished boiling. 'Mike passed away a few years back and I don't belong to the club anymore. Your mother never mentioned it?'

'No. We didn't discuss you much. I'm sorry, I didn't know about Mike. So what do you...I mean...where do you go these days?'

'I prefer to be at home – nobody bothering me – and I used to walk Albert...until...well.'

Sarah wondered if he really minded being so alone. 'Will you get another dog?'

'Maybe.'

Her father sat back down and looked at her with a curious expression. 'Why now, Sarah? After all these years.'

'You have a grandchild. A little girl, Emily Rose.'

'A granddaughter?' He smiled momentarily.

'She'll be six months old this Sunday, and she needs a grandfather. Every child should have a grandfather, don't you think? Tom suggested...well insisted actually.'

'Tom insisted I knew?'

'He's not a bad person, father. I know it seemed that way when we eloped, but we wanted to be together. When you wouldn't give us your blessing, we did a stupid thing. Do we regret getting married? No. Do we wish it could have been different? Of course we do.'

Sarah felt a sense of relief pass over her, as she said the words that had gone through her mind countless times. This was her father, and no matter what might have passed between them, she wanted him to be a part of her life. Somehow, she was sure he felt the same way.

'I can see that now. I'm just sorry it took me so long to realise it,' her father confessed.

Sarah knew now what she needed to say. 'Tom and I were wondering if you'd like to meet Emily, father. Whether you'd like to have another little 'un to follow you around?'

He returned another intense stare. 'I'd like that very much, but I have a condition.'

'A condition?'

'You should all come to visit. You, Emily and Tom.'

Seedlings

By John Ravenscroft

It's early morning, the morning of Simon's eleventh birthday, and he's dreaming of Kanoni again, dreaming of the strange world she sometimes shares with him.

Kanoni straddles a tree branch that floats two metres above Simon's bed, her long legs dangling, her bare feet swinging close to his face. There's a cut on the underside of one of her toes, and he can see that her naked soles are lined with thickened, hardened skin.

Outside his bedroom window, London traffic rumbles by beneath grey clouds. A dog barks. A car alarm screams in the distance.

'Hello, little seedling,' says Kanoni. 'Happy birthday.'

Simon sees her lips move, hears her inside his head – but he knows her voice hasn't got into him in the usual way. Kanoni speaks her own language, her mouth forming strange, shifting shapes, yet the words he hears are always English words.

'Thank you, Kanoni,' he says.

He speaks quietly, for his parents are light sleepers and he doesn't want them to hear him talking to himself again.

Kanoni grins, her teeth a shock of white in the dark oval of her face. 'Come,' she says, reaching down.

He pushes back his quilt, takes her hand, and with one easy leap joins her on her African branch, the tree bark rough beneath his skinny thighs. He looks down the dry, deserted track that leads from the tree to the village and sees the sun, a huge, orange ball, coming up over a small group of dusty huts. The sky above is an inverted bowl of blue and gold.

When he turns his head just a little, he can still see his bedroom, the posters on his walls, his TV, his computer…

The car alarm stops, but the dog keeps on barking.

'This is strange,' he says, feeling poised on the cusp between two worlds.

'We are on a horse, riding towards Mombassa,' says Kanoni. 'A wooden tree-horse.' She laughs, and together they watch the African day dawn.

Simon is suddenly aware of his Spider-Man pyjamas. What must he look like, perched up here in this tree? He grins.

'Lean back, little seedling,' says Kanoni.

He does so, and she wraps her arms around him. He feels the warmth of her body, smells the good smell of her skin, and he feels safe. He feels like he belongs.

'Of course you belong,' says Kanoni, reading his thoughts. 'We belong together, you and I. My seed grows in you, your seed grows in me.'

Simon puts his hand in hers. She touches the bruises, the red, angry marks on his wrist. She traces them with a finger.

'Your father?' she whispers, kissing his ear.

Simon nods.

Kanoni sighs. He can tell she's looking around his bedroom.

'You have so much,' she says. 'And yet you have so little.'

Simon sees the dusty village, sees Kanoni's father emerge from a hut. He stands at the doorway, waving in the golden light.

'You have so little,' Simon says. 'And yet you have so much.'

Serenity Rules Okay!

By Kath Kilburn

'Ouch!'

I told myself the voice was just dirt in the engine and, ignoring the hazardous road conditions, I pressed harder on the accelerator.

'Ouch! Move your big foot. And slow down!'

Probably not dirt in the engine. I braked, pulled over and poured coffee from my flask.

'That smells disgusting. Howdy, mister. Just hitching a ride. Boy, are these little wings weary.'

There she was. Standing on the dashboard. A fairy. A fairy? A tiny red-headed fairy with lilac wings, a silver purse dangling from her slim wrist. For someone with such a cute face she wore a really querulous expression. And spoke with an odd, fake American drawl.

'But how did you...?'

'Slight miscalculation. I was aiming for your bonnet to chew the fat with the angel...'

'The angel?'

'...who rides with you 'til you reach 70 and then whoosh, there she goes, you're on your own!'

'Oh...'

'Anyway, something went awry...that really smells disgusting!'

Apart from this fairy lacking the sweet smile, the wand and the sparkly aura, why was that delicate letter P embroidered on her skimpy top?

Was this really happening? I was in a distressed state: I was going to see my grandmother, who was very ill. Was my state of mind responsible for this vision?

'You can't believe I'm real, can you?'

I jumped. 'What's your name?'

The arms folded tighter across the skinny chest.

'Serenity.' She paused briefly. 'Do you have a problem with that?'

'Absolutely not, Serenity. My name's James.'

I started the car and we drove a while in silence. Serenity folded her gossamer wings and napped. Waking later, she asked where we were headed.

'A Yorkshire village. My gran's poorly – dying probably – hey, maybe you could help? You're a fairy, right? You have some powers?'

Serenity managed to look bashful.

'Well ... not many. That P's for provisional.'

'So what can you do?'

'Turn milk sour. Or yoghurt back into milk.'

'So you're a dairy fairy?'

'Hilarious. They only give me a tiny amount of fairy dust. If I misuse it...well, I mustn't misuse it.'

'How would one misuse fairy dust?'

'Well, first thing, I'd make my stupid hair brown or blonde – anything but red! And believe me, making someone better if it's her time – well, that'd be equally wrong, against the natural order. Besides, I've no time. I'm on the fairy quest.'

'Which is?'

'Search me. Fairy tutors don't say much. We've to work it out for ourselves. Seems to me they like to make life difficult.'

We settled into a companionable silence, broken only by the wipers swishing the rain away. I couldn't help reminiscing about childhood holidays in Gran's tumbledown cottage. I'd promised at Grandad's funeral to visit, phone often, write occasionally, but back in London, I'd soon forgotten those reassurances. Since June had left with the children, I had little to tell Gran.

By the time Serenity stirred, I was wallowing in self-indulgence and guilt.

'Are you sure you couldn't help?'

She gazed into the silver purse.

'Have you been using my fairy dust? It's disappearing! It's not funny – I could be in real trouble...'

'Please, Serenity.'

She tapped her dainty foot a couple of times.

'Well, mister, seems like this dust is disappearing anyway. OK, I'll fly ahead and help your gran stay alive long enough for you to get there. Best I can offer, and that's assuming the rest of this dust doesn't vanish mid-air.'

I promised in return I'd colour Serenity's hair myself. That clinched it. Possibly a tasteful strawberry blonde, she thought, or honey highlights…

The nursing home manager was sympathetic.

'I'm glad you made it, James. Your gran so wanted to see you once more. She'll go peacefully now.'

Mrs Hope unplugged the kettle in her office.

'I'm sorry, I'd offer you a drink, but the milk's turned. I'll leave you with your grandmother for a while.'

I returned to where Gran lay, slipping away with quiet dignity.

There was no sign of Serenity. Who was I kidding? Fairies don't exist.

Weeks later I was back in Yorkshire, sorting Gran's belongings. I loved this old cottage, filled now with spring sunlight and memories. Maybe June would let me bring the children here in the next school holiday. We'd enjoy the walks I used to love; we could paddle in the stream under the bridge. June might even come along – a country bolthole might appeal. I started cutting lengths of string to tie the boxes.

'Ouch! Careful with those scissors!'

'Serenity?'

'Hi! So…impressed?'

She twirled around for me.

Gone the tetchy expression, gone the folded arms and tapping foot, gone the phoney American private eye accent. She'd grown a little, her fairy wings had changed from lilac to silver and her hair was a beautiful ash blonde.

'Serenity – you look stunning! What happened?'

'Well, I'm not a provisional fairy anymore. See? – no P? I'm a fully qualified 'special processes functioning operative' so I can be blonde. 'Course, it's not important now.'

'So how come you passed the quest? All your dust was disappearing, wasn't it?'

'Turns out I did the right thing, helping. The dust was disappearing because I wasn't using it. Then when I flew off to help you it started replenishing.

'You have to remember there's always enough fairy dust for the good stuff. It's not trying makes the magic disappear.'

She winked and skipped over to the basic black phone Gran had favoured.

'If I were you, I'd ring June right now. Put a bit of the magic back.'

The Show

By Victoria Biram

I want to put my hand up. I really do. I almost volunteer, but some unknown force freezes my hand somewhere around my shoulder. I end up scratching my neck instead, so that I don't look like a complete idiot.

'That's only six people wanting to perform,' Mr. Schul says. 'You can do anything – sing, dance, tell jokes. Remember, it's all in a good cause.' He shows us pictures of the floods and talks about why we should help.

It's not that I don't want to help. I really, really do. Sue's my best mate in the whole world and her family lost their whole house. Her mobile and television and laptop and the cute blue skirt like mine we got in the sales – all ruined. She's a social outcast having no mobile. It's not that I don't want to help.

I can't. Performing in a show is my worst nightmare, or second worst, after being naked in class or having to speak on live television. It's my third worst nightmare.

Sue has already put her hand up. The thing is, Sue isn't shy like me. I can't even answer a question in class when I know the answer's right. What if I stutter and everybody laughs? I go to answer, but my throat freezes up and all the blood rushes to my ears and it's so loud that I end up putting my hand down and not saying anything. Just like now with this fund-raising night. There are enough people who want to volunteer, surely. They don't need me. They'll do better without me. Someone else will put their hand up any second.

Nobody does.

'Anyone?' Mr. Schul says. He gives a big sigh. It's not cool, that's what it is, some school organised event.

It's not that I care about being cool, it's that I don't want to be laughed at. I won't perform anyway, I'd get up there and fall over, or lose my voice, and that will be that. It's a medical condition, shyness, I'm sure of it. Next time the careers person comes to talk to us about how choosing our options for G.C.S.E.s is important for our future, I'll tell her I want all sciences so I can cure shyness someday.

The bell rings for break. Sue is straight over to my desk, her cheeks all pink and her fists all scrunched up.

'Lucy, how...' Sue swallows. I see her swallow a couple of times. 'Lucy, it would be great if you'd perform with me. I'm going to sing, and your voice is ten times better than mine. We'd rock a duet.'

My voice is not better than Sue's. Sue sounds great, and she dances like she should be Beyonce's backing dancer, not like a block of wood who wishes she wasn't there.

'Sue...Sue you know I would if I could.'

'Don't give me that! You know how badly we've had it since these floods. If this night gets money for people like me, then I'm going to do it.' Sue's voice is getting so loud people outside peer in to see what's going on. 'I can't believe you won't help me. You're my best friend! This shy thing is getting really old.'

Sue turns and swans out, her bag hitting my side as she goes.

I hate falling out with Sue. I run after her. She's at her locker, banging books around like they've annoyed her. One of them falls to the floor. She doesn't pick it up. She sighs and stares at it like she doesn't know what to do with it.

'I'm sorry.' I pick the book up and hand it to her. 'If it were anything else, I'd do it.'

'You should do it anyway,' Sue says, without looking at me. 'Isn't helping me more important than this shy thing?'

My cheeks flame up. Tears prick my eyes. I dig my nails into my palms to keep the tears from falling. 'Of course it is,' I hear myself saying, and it sounds like somebody else is saying it. 'I'll do it.'

Sue lights up like the high street at Christmas, and I get the biggest hug.

I'm for it now. Why did I agree? I'm going to freeze and fall over and it'll all go wrong. Sue has worked out a routine she

221

thinks we can do to our favourite Girls Aloud song. We practice it all week. I'm okay doing it when there's just Sue around. I even manage to sing all the notes without being completely flat.

It's when I'm standing at the side of the stage that I know I can't do it. Sue strides onto the stage in front of me and I wobble after her, my feet barely walking me into position. My throat closes up. My palms are all wet and slippery, and my feet belong to somebody else.

The music starts and there's no way out now. I launch into the moves we've practised. Somehow my feet obey me and my arms don't hit Sue in the head. When it comes to sing I don't sound completely flat. We get to the big twirl at the end and Sue spins around, and does her point to signal it's my turn to spin. One of my feet hits the other and I stumble backwards onto my bum.

There's silence. I want to die. I knew this would happen. In a panic, I do the only thing I can think to; I stick one arm up in the air and kick both feet out in front of me.

By some miracle, people clap. A couple of people even let out a cheer. When Mr. Schul comes on at the end to say that between us we raised six thousand pounds, everybody cheers.

It doesn't feel so embarrassing now. I mean, I never want to perform onstage again, but six thousand pounds. That's pretty cool.

Sick Joke

By Charlie Taylor

No, ma'am, I'm sorry, I don't have a current tag. It ran out last March. Insurance? Yes, I have insurance but I don't have it with me. It's at home. Yes, ma'am, I do know that. I'm sorry. Yes, ma'am, I'll stay here...

Yes, ma'm, I understand. I'm sorry, truly I am but may I tell you something... yes, that's ok, ma'am, I'll sit with my hands in view on the steering wheel. Yes, ma'm. But can I tell you something. It won't take long. I'm sorry, ma'am, I can't help crying. Can I get my tissue? Thanks, ma'am. No, I have nothing else in the pocket. Thank you, ma'am. I'm sorry for crying but... yes... can I tell you now? Thanks, ma'am. Yes, I'll just blow my nose. Thanks ma'am...

See, I've been ill for the last few years... yes and I thank you for your sympathy, but can I tell you please? Thank you. I've been ill for a few years. I've got diabetes and I have a bad heart and I have one or two other things too, all of which meant... yes, ma'm, I'll hurry, I know you're busy... all of which meant I was under considerable strain and I had a breakdown and had to quit my job which meant that my insurance... yes, ma'am, my medical insurance... ran out and I'd spent all my savings on rent... yes, ma'am, all this is the gospel truth... and now I'm legally disabled which means I can get $601 dollars benefit each month, but that won't happen for about another six months because that's how long it takes, so I've been trying to make a little money waiting tables but I can't earn more'n $860 a month or I won't get the $601 benefits... yes, ma'am, that's correct... but my rent costs $650 a month so I got to earn some money to keep me going cause I got to eat... yes, ma'am, I do the best I can... and my prescriptions for the drugs I need... no, ma'am, that's drugs as in medication... come to $300 each month... so you can see that... yes ma'am I know that's no excuse for not getting a new tag for the car but, see, I was saving money by not running the car so I could pay my... yes. Ma'am, so I could pay my rent, but this morning... yes, ma'am, this morning, I got a call from a businessman across town who said he could give me some work... yes, I can give you his name if you want to call him... so I was between the devil and the deep blue sea so I drove over there and was on my way back when you stopped me and...

Yes, ma'am. Yes, ma'am. Yes, ma'am. I know it's still not right and I know you've already written the citation. Yes, ma'am. So I've got to appear at the court unless I pay these citations at the Sherriff's Office beforehand. Yes, ma'am, I understand. Yes, ma'am. And thanks for listening. Thank you. Yes and have a good day. Thank you.

Sixty Years Together

By Ryan Spier

They looked so sweet together; both of them must have been well into their eighties and they were holding hands across the table. The man had on his best suit and it looked well worn. She had on a long red dress that looked like it was fashionable during the war. There were red roses in a vase between them. The old lady kept looking round the vase at the man she had known for sixty years.

Seeing the two of them together made everyone else in the room feel relaxed and happy. No one guessed how long they had been together, but from the look on their faces they could have met at Primary School and been inseparable ever since. The waitresses argued over who should serve them; in the end they agreed they all would. Other people in the restaurant casually glanced round at them and looked back at each other and smiled.

They were both married.

They were booked in as Mr and Mrs Smith.

Skin Shed like Falling Stars

By Jennifer Pickup

They tell me that this is my skin, but I'm not sure I believe them. The moles are still the same, and in that strange twist of fate, I can still join the dots to make Cassiopoeia appear. The last time I did that, she confiscated the biro.

'Have you ever drawn on a slightly under-ripe banana with a biro?' I asked her, as she pried the orange plastic pen out from between my fingers. 'So smooth, the ink just runs so smooth,' I smiled wistfully. I remember because I was watching us in the mirror, but she didn't smile back, and my smile just hung there in the glass like an unwanted gift with no receipt.

I take a sniff, inhaling the strange scent of washing powder chosen by other people. In my mind's eye, I can see the glass shelf in the bathroom of our house, and its row of coloured bottles: a scent for every occasion, and more besides. It was my little addiction; I was almost a collector, and my smell altered with my mood. Perfume…mood.

'Why are you talking to yourself?' Emily sits down beside me and frowns at the blank lined pad of paper I hold firmly in both hands, resting it on my knees. There is a strong cardboard back, perfect to write on in the absence of a table, for there is no table in this room, only too many chairs.

'I'm making up a poem,' I tell her. 'I used to write a lot of poetry, until I wrote my first novel and found I had run out of words that rhymed.'

'So why aren't you writing it down?' she asks, picking at the chipped, black varnish on her nails.

'No pen.' I am blunt, in between my mutterings. 'It won't do me any good; I never could remember anything without writing it down, not even grocery lists, but the creative impulse is flowing now and I can't stop.'

'Here,' she offers, pulling the stub of a pencil out of her pocket. Only, it's not a stub, it's one of those short ones labelled

'IKEA'. I smile to think that the corporate world has intruded here.

'Thanks.' I take the pencil gratefully, wishing there was a stronger word for appreciation. And then the words come, flowing out like the river used to break its banks, swirling and gurgling, a great wave of milky tea, making all the steel boats creak and groan against the pontoon. So many words. Delicious, grey, shiny words, filling first one page, and then another. My hand is hungry; it bites the pencil into the paper, not neatly but quickly, and my brain finds the release it has been craving.

'I can't read it,' she leans in, squinting.

'My writing was always appalling,' I grimace.

She watches me, right hand scribbling frantically, left arm gripping the pad with white-knuckled fingers.

'Look,' she says, tracing my moles with a finger. 'Remember Cassiopoeia?'

And when I stop writing and burst into tears, she looks horrified, and recoils violently as if she's just hit me across the face.

I bite my lip. 'Come on.' I throw the pad back onto the chair as I rise, secreting the tiny pencil safely in the pocket of my hoodie. I take her reluctant hand and drag her up the stairs, right to the topmost window. Our faces shine in the glass as we gaze out at the endless, sparkling sky. 'What can you see?' I point at the heavens.

'Stars!' she gasps. 'A million of them.'

We are far enough from the city here to see them, winking in the velvet expanse above the trees. I try the lock and, with a small burst of exhilaration, push the sash upwards. We lean out into the night air, drawing great wafts of it into our lungs as if we haven't tasted it in months. The air is different here at the top of the building than it is in the garden. Up here, it tastes like freedom.

'One day, when I can't wait any longer, I will rise from my bed, drift along this corridor, and fly up out of this window.' I whisper. For a moment, I think she hasn't heard me, but after a few minutes she turns to smile at me, her hair blown back by a tiny breeze. She's smiling, but she's pressing her lips together slightly; fear or disapproval, I think.

'And then I will rise upwards,' I continue to whisper. 'Right up through the atmosphere, like a Mary Poppins kite, and as I burn through the ozone, out into the blackness of space beyond, I will shed my skin, and my light will shine out, brighter than day itself, and I will sit in the heavens for all eternity.'

'Do you think I'll see you?' she asks, clutching for my dangling fingers and gripping tightly onto my hand.

'Oh, yes,' I nod. 'You'll see everyone do it, one day. Skin shed like falling stars as we wriggle out of it and drop it behind us as we fly; you'll see it burn as it falls back to earth. Like those flakes of burning newspaper that fly up out of bonfires.'

'I think,' she starts, then sucks on her lip as she pauses to consider. 'I think...that humans are extraordinary creatures. Like you, with your skin and your stars and your poetry.'

'Imagination,' I nod at her, still whispering, even though there's no one near to hear. 'It's the most important thing. Letting go of reality and thinking outside the boxes they try to put you in.'

'Like writing on bananas?' She smiles, genuinely this time, no hint of darkness in it.

'Yes, like writing on bananas,' I reply. 'One day, we'll be able to write on bananas again without anyone sensible there to stop us.'

Snapdragons

By Alex Irvine

What happened next was … well, no …. The night before I was out on the front porch with a beer trying to look at the sky, one of those nights when the stars … the moon and Venus together looked like the Turkish flag. There was a garden tool of some kind, a trowel I remember thinking, on the steps, and it reminded me that I'd told her I would water the snapdragons. But the mint, the damn mint was growing everywhere, and the snapdragons had been dead for weeks.

I traded in the Buick for that truck, and four thousand bucks, all for a hundred thousand more miles and a ride like a hay wagon. But this was America, right, and if you can't throw away money on a truck … I loved that truck. It was blue except where it was rusty, and it pulled hard to the left when you hit the brakes, and the four-wheel drive ground like a nightmare, but I loved it. On the fire roads with her, ponderosa pines and sun-warmed granite. I thought it would be good luck.

The doctor appointment was at three o'clock. We got up early, and I looked up where the sliver of moon had crooked toward Venus. There were high cirrus clouds.

No, wait, the snapdragons weren't dead yet. That was when she asked me to water them. That morning. I was thinking which flag was it, the one with the moon and the star, or was it really Venus on the flag?

'Water the snapdragons, okay?' she said from inside. I was having coffee, and there were high cirrus clouds.

'Yeah,' I said, and stood there instead listening to her move around in the living room. She picked up this and that. Nervous. We'd been trying for a long time. I was optimistic about this doctor. We were optimistic.

No, I couldn't have remembered telling her I'd water the snapdragons. That was the night before. Later I went and looked up what the thing was, the garden tool on the steps. It wasn't a trowel. I had meant to ask her, but I forgot. So no, I hadn't told her I'd water the snapdragons. That was after I first saw the thing on the steps. But it was still there when she said, 'Water the snapdragons, okay?'

I think that's why I forgot to ask her what it was.

It was my idea to take the truck. *Good luck*, I thought.

The grinding was in the clutch, not the four-wheel drive, and if I'd paid attention when my dad told me about cars I'd have known. Anyway it kicked out of gear on Alameda and I jumped a little. We'd been trying for a long time. I was optimistic about this doctor. I was nervous, and I hit the brakes a little hard. We couldn't have crossed the centre line that much.

The snapdragons hung on for a long time. Longer than I would have thought.

Something Different

By Karen Milner

'There's definitely something different about him,' the head of my son's nursery school said.

I wasn't sure what she meant by different, but my heart quickened as we watched my two-year-old line up trains on the nursery floor.

'What do you mean?' I asked.

She didn't seem to notice the colour leave my face or the slight tremble of my lower lip as she replied.

'The hand-flapping, it's not normal, and he tends to only play with trains,' she said, as if she were commenting on the weather.

Not normal, my heart was banging. Jake was my first child, my only child. I'd just come to pick him up and had not expected, or prepared for, such revelations.

'Don't worry, we'll be keeping an eye on him to see how he progresses.' She smiled and retreated to her office.

'Don't worry, you're kidding!' I wanted to scream. How could I not worry? The hand movements were something I'd considered to be endearing, a trait my son would grow out of. I could feel the lines in my brow deepen as he got up from his trains and started to flap his hands in front of his slight body.

My furrow became deeper still as Jake grew older and his hand movements didn't stop. Instead they became more frequent and pronounced until it seemed, in-between every task, he was always flapping. He'd eat dinner and walk away from the table raising his fingers to eye level while frantically shaking his wrists. The noise sometimes reminded me of a trapped bird, beating its wings against some impediment.

Jake was seven when the head of his primary school called me in for a chat.

'His difference is setting him apart from the others,' he told me.

231

Difference, I knew was a euphemism for his flapping and my heart plummeted.

'He is detaching himself from his peers and going off on his own. We are concerned that his behaviour will isolate him.'

My worry thermometer reached a record high. 'Are the other children teasing him?' I had to ask.

'Not that I've seen but, if the behaviour continues, he will struggle through school life. Such a shame, he's a bright boy.'

I swallowed back the tears and looked out of the window in time to see the youngsters charging into the playground. Their shouts and laughter seemed to ricochet around the head's office. My eyes searched the blue and grey uniforms as the children played chase and kicked balls, but my son was not amongst them.

'Where is Jake?' I asked, unable to conceal my anxiety.

The headmaster looked at his watch. 'Year three will be having break.' He gestured to the mass outside.

'Do you mind if I go and look for him?'

'No, please do. Maybe you could have a chat about his behaviour.'

His behaviour, I felt my hackles rise. He made it sound like Jake was somehow misbehaving, something he'd never dream of doing.

'And don't worry, we'll be keeping a careful eye on him.' He opened the door for me.

I managed a shaky half smile and pushed back my prematurely greying hair before going in search of my son.

A quick scan of the main play area confirmed my fears and my forehead throbbed as I spun wildly, trying to locate him. I approached the young woman who stood shivering in the middle of the yard and asked if she'd seen Jake. She shrugged her shoulders. If this is what the head meant by keeping 'a careful eye', well God help my boy.

'Maybe he's still in his classroom,' Miss something-or-other offered. I was about to go inside when I spotted a group crouching at the far corner of the playground. I moved closer and saw they were looking through an archway to a small concrete area beyond. My breath caught in my throat as I realised they were watching my beautiful son, flapping for England. Jake was completely unaware of me or the boys that had gathered to spy and snigger. My eyes turned to ice as I focused on the gang and they scattered as if the bogeyman himself had landed. Jake continued to perform his complex hand movements, watching his fingers and skipping around in blissful ignorance. I realised then, I could not shield him and, like a shattered porcelain vase, my heart broke.

'Jake,' I called softly, but he remained locked in his world. I walked over and gently touched his shoulder. He looked up, bewilderment in his large brown eyes. 'Jake, we need to talk.'

How do you explain to a seven-year-old with a compulsive habit that he has to control it because the world is cruel? I did my best and slowly Jake began to manage his flapping at school.

On his 14th birthday, I was summoned to Jake's school. My son had been assessed and the headmaster had the results. However, this wasn't yet another of the numerous evaluations Jake had already endured; tests that said he had autistic spectrum disorder yet, beyond providing a label, proved of little use. This trial was to do with Jake's passion, rugby.

My hair had turned completely grey, but my heart beat steadily as I entered the head's office. He greeted me with a firm handshake and a beaming smile.

'Great news,' he said, 'Jake has been selected for the under-14 England squad.'

Tears stung my eyes again, but this time they were happy ones.

'The selectors say your son is different, special and they've never seen a more focused or talented player.'

That night, after suppressing the urge all day, Jake came home and flapped for his usual wind-down hour. Then we went out for a slap-up meal to celebrate my wonderful son's difference.

Sprawl

By Alasdair Stuart

'Play that back.' Three little words that changed everything. What she never told anyone, even her parents, even her girlfriend, was how close she'd come to writing it off. It was Monday morning, she was tired, she'd made a mistake. She had to have made a mistake.

On Alan's screen, the sprawl of Leeds leapt into view. For months now, they'd been patiently going through every single one of the locations in England again – the hundreds of thousands of photos from satellites and planes. On her first day, she'd been told that the technical term for aerial pictures was orthophotography and it had brought her up short. A beautiful word for an admirable job. She'd been proud of going to the office that day. Two years later, however, she was tired and hung-over and God, if she'd missed it…

'What is it?'

Streets, trees, fields and … streets. She had Alan dial the image back, pull the focus to take it all in. Then, she took a deep breath and told herself she was not going to be sick.

'Pull up the previous update, same coordinates. Don't say anything.'

Frowning, Alan did so. She watched, not the screen, but his face as the two images appeared side by side. Saw the blood drain. Saw the eyes widen. 'Bloody hell.'

'My sentiments exactly.'

'Bloody HELL. Jo, what are we-'

She held up a finger. 'Alan, you're looking ill. Why don't you come and sit down, in the lounge, with me. Now.'

* * *

Carolyn, from Rudloe Manor, was short and dumpy and smiled a lot. She had a maternal air to her and Jo suspected that was why she got this job. Go and talk to the crazies, calm them down, drink the tea, get them to sign the Official Secrets Act then run like hell. Carolyn stopped smiling when Alan showed her the pictures. The maternal air was replaced by something harder, sharper. 'Resolution on these?'

'15 metres.'

'Time between them?'

'Six months.'

'Told anyone else?'

'No ma'am.'

And the smile was back. 'Good.' She took two envelopes out of her suitcase. 'Sign these, then point me towards your boss's office. We're going for a ride.'

*   *   *

'Item one: six months ago this was an area of farmland just to the west of Leeds.'

Dressed in uniform, Carolyn stood unsmiling, the photograph projected beyond her onto a wall-sized screen.

'Item two: the same area, yesterday.'

The photo changed and suddenly Carolyn was covered in the dull greys of urban sprawl, her face a tapestry of rooftops.

'One hundred years of urban growth in six months. Why?'

Alan was generally a mouse in front of the Joint Intelligence Committee, but Jo had been proud of him that day. 'American Indians.'

Carolyn, the maternal smile back. 'Pardon?'

'American Indians. When Columbus first landed, the American Indians couldn't recognise his ships. They didn't have the mental vocabulary.'

'What relevance does this have here?'

Jo put it together first. 'It's camouflage. How do you blend in? You become what's around you, you become part of the landscape – you learn about somewhere by ... becoming somewhere.'

The phone rang, even though it shouldn't have. A web of electromagnetic fingers, nimble and quick and invisible, had tracked them down through the networks. The future had found their telephone number and was giving them a call.

'Play that back.'

'You learn about somewhere ... by being somewhere.'

Then, a cacophony of car horns and radios, dogs and cats, conversations and wind through trees and fried food and laughing children cycling down and down and down until they all spoke at once, each a fragment of a much, much larger whole. Each saying the only thing they could and the last thing anyone expected.

'Hello, my name is Sprawl. I wish to apply for citizenship.'

Stay

By Patti Jazanoski

The couple got into a fight and this time Rita decided to stay.

'It's your turn to stomp away mad,' she said, sitting on the couch and crossing her arms. She pulled the afghan around her even though it was mid-September and she was not that cold.

'Are you kidding?' Jacques wanted to sit down, but remained standing to defy her. He picked up the remote, touched the buttons, but didn't turn anything on. 'Besides, I wouldn't know what to do. Where would I go? This is my home.' He frowned, and then looked away. 'It's your job to leave.'

'Job,' she wanted to sniff, 'like I get paid for it.' But she didn't have the energy to say that. She didn't want to hear what he would say in reply.

After a couple of minutes, he turned to her. 'Where did you go, all those times?'

She caught her breath. All those times when she ran away and drove to bars and sat too close to other men and ordered scotch straight up – when she did those things just to have a ready answer –he'd never asked her once.

She looked across the room. He held the remote and rubbed it absentmindedly. He didn't know what to do. Neither did she. She pulled the afghan closer. 'Mostly I drove around,' she said. 'Wandered. I wanted to make you jealous.' She looked away. 'But you didn't care.'

'I never asked because I was afraid.'

Neither of them spoke again. After 15 minutes, Rita got up to wash her face. In this way, something in their lives had changed just a bit, something in their hearts had softened.

The Stories We Tell Ourselves

By Curtis C. Chen

Gerald sat and stirred his coffee, waiting to change the world.

The front door of the cafe swung open and the bell jingled. The balding man who walked in wore a thick overcoat, scarf, and gloves. His nervous, desperate eyes scanned the room.

Gerald waved to the man. He nodded and came over to the table in the corner.

'Gerald Mortman?' the man asked.

'That's me,' Gerald said.

The man sat down. 'Carl Point. Sorry I'm late. Thank you so much for meeting me. I know you don't take many appointments—'

Gerald held up his hand. 'You want some coffee? I ordered you a cup.'

He nodded at the table, where a second mug had appeared in front of Carl.

'That wasn't there before!' Carl said.

'Just a small demonstration,' Gerald said. 'I know you're a busy man, so I had them put in a go-cup.'

Carl looked down. Instead of a mug there was now a paper cup, with a cardboard ring around it and a plastic lid on top.

'That's incredible,' Carl whispered. He looked around the coffee shop. 'What happens if someone's watching? I mean, what if they're looking right at the mug when it changes?'

'Nothing changes, Mr. Point,' Gerald said. 'This is the way it's always been.'

'But I know,' Carl said. 'I remember the mug being here first. And so do you.'

'You'll forget soon enough,' Gerald said. 'Everyone does. Everyone except me.'

Carl picked up his cup and took a sip. 'That's good. Decaf?'

Gerald smiled. 'Sure.' He leaned forward. 'We don't have much time.'

'Okay,' Carl said. 'It's my daughter, Emily. She passed away recently. She had leukaemia. My wife and I—' He stopped, sucked in a breath, and paused before continuing. 'We did everything we could. We found the best doctors, the best facilities, but they couldn't save her.'

Gerald started pulling back. 'Mr. Point—'

Carl grabbed Gerald's arm. 'I need you to bring her back. Just do whatever it is you do, say that Emily didn't die, say that she's cured. I'm a very rich man. I can make it worth your while.'

'I don't want your money,' Gerald said. 'I think you've misunderstood what I do—'

'I know what you can do,' Carl said. 'Just four little words. 'Your daughter didn't die.' You say them, right now, and it'll be true. What could be simpler?'

'It's never simple, Mr. Point.'

Carl squeezed Gerald's arm harder. 'Why not? It's nothing to you. Just one simple sentence. I'll give you anything you want.'

'I can already get whatever I want,' Gerald said.

'What is wrong with you?' Carl said. 'What's the point of having this power if you don't use it? Why won't you help me?' His eyes lit up, and Gerald knew what was coming next. 'Why don't you just cure cancer? You can do that, can't you? Just say it, and it'll be true.'

'I can't do that,' Gerald said.

'You can't or you won't?' Carl snapped. 'Forget it. I've had enough of this.' He released Gerald's arm.

'You're free to leave,' Gerald said. 'I'm sorry.'

Carl reached under his coat and pulled out a revolver. 'Now I'm telling the story. Think you can talk faster than I can pull this trigger?'

Gerald shook his head slowly. He heard gasps and murmurs all around him. Patrons and employees moved away from the corner table.

'You're going to say my daughter's alive,' Carl said. 'You say anything else, and I'll shoot. Then I'll ask you again. It might

239

be harder to talk when you're bleeding out, and I can keep the paramedics away for as long as it takes.'

'Your daughter is alive, Mr. Point,' Gerald said. 'She's standing right behind you.'

Carl flinched, and for a moment, Gerald thought he might shoot anyway. Then Carl stood up and turned to the side, keeping the revolver trained on Gerald.

A teenage girl with long, curly, brown hair stood beside the next table. Her cheeks were wet with tears, and her delicate hands were shaking.

'Please, Daddy,' she said, 'put down the gun.'

Carl's head whipped back around to look at Gerald. 'What the hell is this? That's not my daughter.'

'This isn't my story,' Gerald said. 'This is your story.'

'I don't even know this girl.'

'Daddy!' the girl sobbed. 'It's me, Allie.'

Carl's face went pale. He turned back to the girl, who took a tiny step forward.

'Allison?' Carl said. 'My God. You're all grown up.'

'You have to stop this, Daddy,' Allie said.

'Look at your hair,' Carl said. 'Just like your mother's. God, we were both so young. We couldn't afford to raise a child...'

His arm fell just a little bit. As soon as Gerald was no longer staring down the barrel of the revolver, he spoke.

'I'm glad you didn't bring a gun, Mr. Point,' Gerald said. 'Some people get upset when they find out I can't help them. Thank you for being reasonable.'

Allie was gone, and so was the revolver. Carl looked down at Gerald, his expression blank, waiting for the rest of the story.

'I'm very sorry for your loss,' Gerald continued, 'but I'm glad you've finally come to accept your daughter's death.'

Carl sat down, wrapping both hands around his coffee cup. 'It's been very difficult.'

'Go home, Mr. Point. Spend some time with your family. If you ever need to talk, you know how to find me.'

240

He extended his hand, and Carl shook it. 'Thank you, Mr. Mortman. But I think I'm going to be okay.'

'I know you will be,' Gerald said.

They smiled at each other, and the bell rang as Carl walked back into the cold.

Gerald took out his notebook, and started writing. He had lied to Carl. If he didn't write down all the stories, he would forget them, too. And he wanted to remember.

Surf's Up

By Glynis Scrivens

I've been getting funny looks all day. And I've enjoyed every minute of it. Can't remember the last time so many good-looking surfers have stopped to give me a second look. A long puzzled look and sometimes a surprised shake of the head. As though they can't believe what they're seeing.

Not a bad effort for a 70-year-old girl. This birthday's turned out to be more fun than I expected.

I'm sitting on a grassy slope overlooking the sea. It's early evening. Pick-ups and camper-vans fill the car park. Among them my grandson's green estate car which I'm driving today. We've swapped cars so he can organise my birthday surprise.

When I parked here, I pulled up alongside an old white van. The driver was a bronzed sea god of about 40. About as close to physical perfection as our species can get. Tall, tanned, all muscle, with lovely black curls. Just the colour my hair used to be. He smiled and nodded, his eyes taking in the car.

My heart nearly missed a beat when he opened his car door and came over to my window and said, 'Can I ask you something?'

He touched the black rubber roof pads. 'How do you find these? Do they work okay or do they rattle in the wind when you're driving?'

'The only problem is they block your view a bit on the inside.' And I showed him the rubber rope that stretched across the inside of the car. It'd been getting in my way all day. But I'd put up with it. Julian relied on it to keep his surfboard attached to the car.

'Thanks. I've been thinking of getting some myself and wasn't sure. Maybe I should save up for something a bit better.' He took his surfboard from the back of his van and headed down the well-worn path to the beach.

That's when the penny dropped. It was the roof rack that was attracting the attention of all the surfers today. I finally

242

understood why they'd all looked puzzled and … well, impressed. Without realising it, I'd managed to convince these young sea gods that I was a seasoned surfer. Part of their culture.

I had all the right props. There was a surfboard on the roof rack and a wetsuit and beach towel in the back. And when I turned on the ignition, the car reverberated to the sounds of the Red Hot Chilli Peppers. I was still trying to work out how to turn the darned thing off. Julian had somehow hooked up a Discman to the car's cassette player. I was scared I'd wreck it if I fiddled too much.

I checked my watch. Time to head home. I had one last look at the sea then walked back to where I'd parked the car.

At home, Julian was waiting for me. He gave me a bear hug. 'Happy birthday, Grandma. What do you think of these?' And he showed me my new number plates. NAN – 070.

'They're a wonderful present. I love them.' And I did. But maybe my adventures today had gone to my head. I felt more like 007 than 070.

'How did you manage driving my car today? You're not used to an estate. And it's a manual.' His blue eyes took in the two vehicles, parked side by side. My small white Mini and his surf mobile.

'I raised a few eyebrows. Old ladies don't surf, do they?' And I smiled to myself at the memory of all the puzzled eyes that'd met mine today. No need to tell Julian how much I'd enjoyed the novelty of all this male attention.

He grinned. 'No. But apparently they can get away with careless parking.'

'What makes you say that?'

He told me how he'd parked at a bad angle at the shopping centre. 'I accidentally blocked someone in. I copped an earful when I got back and the other chap realised the driver wasn't an old lady.'

I realised my car had all the right props, too. I'd left my knitting bag on the seat. And I always keep a shady straw hat in the car. Not to mention the '70 is the new 50' bumper sticker.

I hoped it hadn't put him off. There was something important I needed to ask. 'Do you think I could borrow your car again next week, when I do the grocery shopping?'

He looked surprised.

'I need to buy a few bulky items,' I told him. 'The estate would be perfect.'

I've got the feeling I'll be borrowing Julian's car regularly from now on.

This is What You Must Do

By Kirsty Logan

First, walk through city streets congested with lightning-eyed boys and half-sleeping girls. Choose one if you like; take him home, make her coffee, talk all night.

Next, cut down the alley veiled with shredded billboard posters, dangling like torn silk. Choose your usual path if you like; the alley lit with fairy lights, crammed with teahouses and cafes.

Then, slip into the club, lights dyeing the fog of dry ice. Choose to stay here if you like; dance yourself into a bliss, sweat until you've washed away the city's dirt.

Finally, sidle through the bodies on the dance-floor, slick with sweet spilled liquids, until you reach the back door. Peek around you – quick now.

If no one is looking, you can go through.

Now exhale. Push out the smells of the city: smoke, exhaust, strange flesh. Breathe in the smells of the bar: cinnamon, pepper, polished wood.

Although the door that leads you in appears to be thin, pockmarked plywood, the bass-thump from the club will not penetrate. The only sounds here are the chink of glasses and the soft croon of the jukebox.

Before you look around the bar, you must prepare yourself. Outside – through that club, down those alleys, along those streets – people hide their deformities. They hack off their wings, file down their horns, saw off their tails. They think the scars are better.

Here, in this bar, they do things differently. Feathered wings unfurl, the twitching tips reaching to the ceiling as their owner ruminates over the jukebox. A unicorn horn – two feet long and gleaming white – knocks gently against the lights suspended over the pool table. Pointed teeth, as sharp as morning light, clink against the rims of glasses.

Not all the changes are so ornamental. There are hooves ticking against the bar's wooden floor, arms halfway to bird wings, a scaly tail fat as a tree branch curled around a table leg. You may stay a while, but not too long. You do not belong here yet.

Later, at home, you will look in the bathroom mirror and notice a bump on your forehead, hard and white as bone. You do not need to file it down this time; you know where to go. It's just a bar down an alley in the city, like a rainbow is just refracted light.

Three Drink Minimum

By Dr. Philip Edward Kaldon

The tall, thin naval officer slipped gracefully between the hardened spacers crowded in the bar – never once touching or disturbing another patron – until he reached the relative quiet by the brass railing. He raised three fingers to the barkeep, setting a small leather portfolio next to him. As the barkeep poured three shot glasses from a bottle of Jack Daniel's, the officer removed a small case from his inside jacket pocket, opened it and set exactly one perfect Oreo cookie atop each shot glass. The incongruity of the liquor, the starship officer and the cream-filled chocolate cookies caused a mild stir inside the spacer bar.

Mostly spacer bar patrons kept to themselves, watching their own drinks and swapping lies in the dim light. Some came to get drunk and pick a fight – especially with anyone in uniform. But those around this officer felt drawn first to his impeccably neat appearance: the not-too-short but perfectly trimmed black hair and razor thin moustache, then to the precise and even movements of his ritual. All the while, they couldn't tell if he was a youthful forty or an experienced thirty.

The tall, thin officer, however, chose not to notice. Instead, he ate half the first cookie and sipped the whiskey, then momentarily dunked the second half before finishing both the cookie and the shot. He paused, perhaps reading the headlines streaming on the newsie screen on the wall above, then proceeded to start with the next cookie.

'I seen 'im do this before,' a semi-retired tug captain whispered to his three equally aged friends at a nearby stand-up table.

'Who is he?' asked the second man.

'A lieutenant commander in the Unified Star Fleet,' said the third.

'I can see that,' the second man said. 'But what do you know of him?'

The fourth man said, 'They say he was in the Grilli Campaign. Made it look like the invasion was dropping every morning before breakfast, his job done for the day.'

'But he's not old enough,' the second man said.

'He's electronic countermeasures,' said the fourth man. 'See the lightning bolts inside the circled NO slash on his collars? Makes him important enough to get stashed in stasis between operations.'

The four old spacers found themselves staring at the officer and leaning closer towards him. When the officer polished off the third cookie, he finished the third shot and placed the glass hard on the counter. Turning toward his audience, he asked, 'May I join you gentlemen?'

'By all means,' the first man said, gesturing broadly to their little table in welcome.

The officer motioned to the barkeep and this time held up five fingers. Jack Daniel's wasn't the first spacer's preferred label, but he finished his own beer and set the mug aside to be polite.

When the drinks were poured, the officer opened his leather portfolio and extracted half a package of cookies. After placing one Oreo atop each shot glass, he picked up his own cookie and regarded it coolly for a moment.

'The secret,' the officer said, 'is to alternate between cookie and whiskey.'

'Ah-hhh,' said the four spacers, nodding sagely.

'But,' the officer added with a wicked twinkle in his eye, 'sometimes you have to enjoy the cookie – just like when you were a kid.' He twisted one chocolate wafer off the Oreo, exposing a perfect bed of sugary vanilla cream which he scraped off with his teeth before taking a sip of whiskey. Then he popped the cookie's top into his mouth.

With great solemnity, the four old spacers carefully twisted the tops off their own cookies, then scraped or licked part of the filling.

A dozen nearby spacers stood enraptured, some with jaws agape, watching the ritual of the Oreo cookies being passed on.

No one laughed – they were all too envious of the four old men and the officer.

Meanwhile the barkeep stood in the back, calling the black market dealers on the space station and trying to find even one package of Oreo cookies. When he finally made the deal, the barkeep wandered back to watch, grabbing a towel to look busy and polish a few glasses. He didn't mind losing the bet to the officer, because he believed him now. There'd be no fights in his bar tonight. And he'd make up the money quickly with this new revenue stream.

The tall, thin officer glanced back to the barkeep and winked. His job here was done.

Three Questions

By Dave Creek

Alice asked Dan, 'Why do you speak in questions all the time?' They were in Dan's small, messy apartment taking a break from studying for their gruelling college midterms.

'Why not?'

'Because sometimes it can be damn irritating.'

'Why would you think that?'

Alice sighed. 'Never mind.'

The devil picked that moment to appear, with a loud pop of displaced air. Dan's dirty shirts blew across the floor.

'Greetings, mortals,' he exclaimed, in all his crimson-skinned, brimstone-smelling glory. 'I have come for your souls. But in return, I can give you three wishes.'

What followed was the usual 20-30 minutes of disbelief, denial, demonstration, and finally, dumbfounded acceptance that this was the devil, and that his offer was valid. Actually, it was Alice who raised all the protests; Dan stood mute the whole time.

'I'm ready to accept your three wishes, which must be in the form of questions,' the devil said in his best Alex Trebek voice.

Now Dan finally spoke. 'Why would we want to ask you a question?'

The devil raised a smouldering eyebrow. 'You tell me. You have two more questions, then I own your souls.'

Alice put her hand over Dan's mouth. 'He can only speak in questions.'

'That's your misfortune. Ask another question.'

Alice's anger flared. 'Can't you just give us a minute?' Then she slapped her hand against her forehead as she realized she'd done it, too. The devil flashed a smouldering smile. 'I cannot. One more question, then you're both mine.'

Dan pried Alice's hand from his mouth. He spoke slowly, with clear effort. 'I believe I know exactly what to ask for.' Alice was amazed. A sentence! Afraid to speak aloud again herself, she motioned for him to go ahead. But Dan hesitated.

'Go ahead,' Alice said, her voice choking. 'Ask it.'

Dan, still uncertain, glanced first at the devil, then at Alice. 'You sure?'

Tom Jones Knew My Mother

By Barry Cooper

'It was long before he was famous, of course.' Mum was at it again. Like most teenage daughters, there were times when I thought the world of my mum, and there were times when I thought: Oh God.

One Oh God, situation was when she decided to tell one of her stories. I would never go so far as to say that she was a liar. It was just that there was no way I could see any one person having so many excitements in one lifetime.

This one was way over the top. The fact that she might have dated a singer in a band, I could live with. Even a band who'd made a record. But she said it was Tom Jones. No way; she was definitely off her trolley this time.

'It all started with a friendly argument,' she went on without even a hint of a blush. 'I was on holiday in Tenby at the time. I went into this little shop to buy an ice-cream. A boy had arrived just before me and, when I walked up to the counter, he stepped aside to let me go first. So I said no, you go first. Then we had a little to and fro. In the end he bought both ice-creams. We went out and sat on the sea wall to eat them.'

'So what was he like, then?' I demanded, with maybe a little too much enthusiasm.

'Oh, tall, a bit of a beanpole, actually. Dark, of course, and handsome. A boyish version of the legend.'

'So what about the date?' This time Mum had dangled the bait. I had taken it, hook, line and sinker.

'Well, he said his name was Tom Woodward and he was singing with a band at the cricket club dinner and dance that night. And would I like to go.'

'You said, yes, of course,' I anticipated.

Mum shook her head. 'I said I didn't think my Mum and Dad would let me. So he asked me where they were and I pointed them out. He marched straight up to them and asked. They were too surprised to refuse.'

She sighed and gazed at the ceiling. 'He had a beautiful voice, even then. The other thing about being in the band was that he had privileges at the hotel. He fixed it up for us to have a meal and a bottle of wine and I was only fifteen. The Gower Arms Hotel, it was. I felt really grown up. Afterwards, he asked to see me again but I was going back to England the next day.'

This was very good, even for Mum. Her face was beaming.

'I told him I'd meet him right there at the Gower Arms and he could buy me a drink in fifty years. Eight o'clock on the twentieth of July – which is this year.'

'Do you think he'll remember?'

'I doubt it. Mind you, he did carve the date onto the post holding the hotel sign, right under our initials. Anyway, he walked me back to our B and B and delivered me safe into mum and dad's hands. He kissed my forehead when he left and told me not to forget our date.'

*   *   *

It's a good job Dad's work brought him to Port Talbot. I didn't say anything to Mum about it, but I've come to Tenby today. It's the twentieth of July, and she doesn't know that I told Dad about her story. He said we should check it out.

Turning Things Around

By Paula Williams

'Are you okay?' Maggie asked, as Jane came into the Staff Room.

'I'm fine,' Jane lied, ignoring the voice inside her head that was screaming: No you're not. Tell her you've got a migraine. Anything as long as it gets you out of having to face that lot again.

'What class have you got next?' Maggie glanced up at the timetable on the wall and pulled a face. 'Poor you. No wonder you're looking peaky. They're a bit much, aren't they?'

'They're not so bad really,' Jane murmured. 'Just high spirited.'

High spirited? That isn't what you called them just now. The voice inside her head was screaming so loudly that her head was beginning to pound. Tell her, it went on, banging away at her taut nerves like a steam hammer, Tell her you made a right mess of it last week and you're scared witless at the thought of facing them again.

What a fool she'd been to think she could do this. A stupid, idealistic, over-ambitious fool. It had all seemed so easy at first. The fulfilment of a dream. Hard work, of course but she'd been carried along by her enthusiasm. She'd really believed she could make a difference. That she could change lives.

That had been during her training. Last week, her first time 'at the coalface', so to speak, came as a complete shock. There was so much to think about and the class so noisy and inattentive that, in spite of all her meticulous preparation, keeping one step ahead of them was far harder than she'd expected.

She'd almost lost it completely at one time as – for an awful, heart-stopping moment – she froze, her cheeks flaming, her mind a total blank, while from the back of the class came snorts of barely smothered laughter.

She didn't need to look to see where the laughter was coming from. The pair had been chattering and giggling from the start. Ruby had masses of wild hair in an improbable shade of red and far too tight clothes. Her friend Charlene had a permanent sneer and a thin, angular body with shoulder blades like pallet knives.

Jane had nothing against anyone having a laugh and a joke. In fact, it was good to hear them enjoying themselves, even if it was at her expense. She kept reminding herself what had been drummed into her during her training, 'They work better if you make it fun'.

But what really got her was the way they'd laughed when poor little Daisy Ford had got in a muddle and lost count. Her fragile confidence had shrivelled under their sniggers.

'Not having second thoughts are you?' Maggie asked, peering at her anxiously.

Jane shook her head. The second thoughts were long gone. She was well into third and fourth thoughts now. But she couldn't say that. Maggie, bless her, had gone out on a limb for her by offering her this job. All the other applicants had been better qualified, and considerably younger.

'It's tougher than I thought,' Jane admitted, feeling she owed it to Maggie to be honest. 'I wasn't quite prepared for the degree of resistance I encountered last week. I'd naively imagined they'd be more enthusiastic.'

Maggie snorted. 'That lot,' she said. 'The only thing they're enthusiastic about is who did what to whom in Eastenders. If there was an Olympics for couch potatoes, they'd scoop the pool.'

'The pity is, I think most of them would really get a lot out of it, if it wasn't for this pair of troublemakers who make no effort themselves and sneer at those who do. You know the sort I mean.'

'Indeed I do.' Maggie gave a weary sigh. 'It's a crying shame though. I thought if there was anyone who could turn that class around, it would be you, Jane. Don't give up on them yet, will you?'

'Give up on them?' Jane suddenly beamed at Maggie. 'No way. In fact, you've just given me a great idea. Thanks a million.'

There was a spring in her step as she went in to face her class. The nerves and self doubt had vanished and she was feeling quietly confident.

'Before we start,' she said, giving them her warmest smile, 'I'd like you all to turn around so you're facing the wall at the back.'

There was a buzz of murmuring and muttering as Jane walked to the back then turned around to face the puzzled class.

'Right now. Let's get started, shall we?'

She saw, with quiet satisfaction, that Ruby and Charlene weren't looking quite so sure of themselves now they were right under her nose, instead of lurking at the back.

'Are you ready for the warm up, ladies? On the count of four then. One and two and three and four—'

This time everything went right. Her timing was perfect. She never once put a foot wrong, and managed to stay one step ahead of them all the time.

There was no doubt, she thought proudly. Aerobics classes for the over-sixties taken by someone nearer their own age was one of her better ideas. She'd only taken up aerobics in her fifties and it had changed her life. Not only had her health and fitness improved dramatically, but it had given her the confidence to train as an aerobics instructor herself so that she could encourage older people to take more exercise.

As for dealing with Ruby and Charlene, turning the class around so they were at the front worked a treat. They were both working their abs far too hard to have the energy left to make a nuisance of themselves. And little Daisy was not so self conscious now, tucked at the back where she could work at her own pace.

It looked like it was working. After last week's faltering start, this week she really had, as Maggie hoped, turned the class around.

Updating Dora

By Linda Barrett

Dora sighed as the rock song on Clare's mobile sounded out yet again. 'You're welcome to give your friends my phone number, you know, if you want them to ring while you're here.'

'No, it's alright, Gran, everyone's got my mobile number. You should get one you know. A lot of people your age have them these days.'

Dora sniffed. 'I don't think so, one phone is quite enough, thank you.'

Clare looked heavenwards. 'Honestly Gran, you're so technophobic.'

'Well, when would I use it? I don't need a mobile phone.'

'Okay, you might be out shopping and need to ring someone. There aren't as many phone boxes around as there used to be. You're always complaining about them being vandalised. I don't know why you trek around town and the supermarket, anyway. Lots of people get their shopping online these days.'

'But I don't possess a computer, nor do I wish to. Secondly, I've been doing my shopping this way for the best part of 60 years and I'll carry on if it's all the same to you. Online, indeed.'

*   *   *

It was raining hard when Dora, laden with shopping bags, saw her bus pull in at the bus stop. Damn. If she missed it, she'd have to wait another half an hour and she'd be drenched. She hurried along the pavement, eyes locked on the bus. She was about a hundred yards away when she tripped. The next thing she knew she was sprawled on the pavement. She looked up to see the bus pull away and her heart sank. People started to gather around.

'Are you alright?' a kindly lady asked.

Dora didn't know if she was or not. She felt a searing pain in her ankle. A man offered to help her up but Dora couldn't put her weight on the sore foot. The man took out his mobile phone and called an ambulance.

* * *

'You haven't done much damage,' a young doctor informed her. 'You've sprained your ankle quite badly, but aside from a few bruises that seems to be it. I think we'll keep you in overnight, though, just to be on the safe side.'

The next morning Clare went to the hospital.

'Mum's coming later to take you to our house, Gran. She says you can't go home on your own, you wouldn't manage.'

'Nonsense, I'm perfectly all right.'

Just the same, Dora's youngest daughter, Sue, arrived late that afternoon and, after some consultation with the doctor, insisted on taking her home.

To Dora's surprise, she spent three very enjoyable days with Sue and Clare. On her first night there, her son, Jack, phoned from Australia to make sure she was okay. Dora was touched but afterwards chided Sue for telling him.

'There's no need for such a fuss,' she said, carefully lowering herself back onto the sofa. 'I've only had a bit of a fall.'

Sue grunted. 'Did you speak to the children?'

'Yes, I had a lovely chat with both of them.'

* * *

Eventually the older woman became restless to get home and back to her own bed. Sue relented and drove her there. Clare went with them for the ride.

'Now, you're sure you'll be all right, Mum?'

'I can stay for a few days if you want, Gran'

'Don't be so silly, get off the pair of you.' Reluctantly they left.

Six weeks after the accident, Dora and her granddaughter were sitting at the kitchen table, drinking hot chocolate, when the doorbell rang. 'That'll be my shopping,' said Dora getting up.

'What?'

The next thing a burly young man carried the shopping in. Clare gasped.

'I decided you were right,' Dora said. 'Don't get me wrong, I think there's a lot to be said for going out shopping. You get fresh air and exercise, not to mention the contact. On the other hand, there's not much to be said for having to go out in all weathers and carry back heavy bags. Sometimes it's nice to have someone deliver it.'

'But how did you order it?'

Dora went into the living room and came back carrying a laptop. She put it on the kitchen table and opened it.

'This is the latest technology, Gran. When did you get it?'

'I got it soon after the accident. The man at the shop said I should get the latest model because it's easier to use. Bob next door came in every evening for two weeks to show me what to do. He got me online and then I did a free internet course at the library. They taught me all about emails and surfing.'

'I'm really pleased you decided to move into the 21st century,' Clare said to Dora as she was putting on her coat.

'Are you coming next week?'

'Of course. Why?'

Dora opened a drawer in the hall table and took out a box.

'Gran, you've got a mobile phone.'

'Well, I thought that at least if I do have an accident when I'm out I can ring for help myself. Will you show me how it works next week?'

'Course I will. You have to be the coolest gran in the world,' she said, giving Dora an extra big hug.

After Clare had left, Dora headed straight for her laptop, sat down and switched it on. 'Bargain flights to Australia' she typed and clicked 'search'. Well, it was time she met the grandchildren. They wrote such lovely emails.

Voice in the Night

By Ian Rochford

Sarah hated the early morning. This was the time when the walls closed in, when the ceiling became overly familiar and the mind dredged up each small failure, problem and doubt and wove them into a soft chain mail that slowly compressed and smothered the mind. She had just decided to get up and turn on the computer, perhaps see if the morning blankness would help breathe some life into her stagnant novel, when she heard noises in the flat above. An agitated tapping sound, the rattling of a window and the creaking of the old lady's bed led Sarah to wonder if she'd have to call the ambulance again. At least that would wake everyone in the block, and they could join her in contemplating their mortality and failures until the dawn.

She heard the bed creak again. Two slight thumps as the old lady got up. Scraping sounds, then the thump-scuff, thump-scuff of slippers on lino. A shrill squealing as the window was opened. *Jesus, what are you doing?* Sarah thought. *It's bloody freezing out there.* Then there was a voice; just a few words, she couldn't make anything out. Her skin tightened and every hair stood up in alarm. The voice seemed to have gone right through the building, a deep distant hint of a power that no human throat could have summoned. Sarah sat upright. It was only three thirty. Another thump came from above; possibly the sound of someone falling, collapsing onto bare linoleum. Muttering a few tame profanities, Sarah threw back the blankets, climbed out of bed and slipped her feet into her sheepskin boots. 'Here we go again,' she said, under her breath, leaving her flat and groping her way up the dimly lit stairs.

She was still trying to tie her dressing gown when she reached the top step and knocked on the old lady's door.

'Mrs Dibney? Are you alright?' No answer. Two flats down a door opened and a shadowed face peered out.

'I think she's fallen,' said Sarah, 'Will you help me?'

The face disappeared back inside with a quiet, disgusted curse.

Sarah swore, and fished in her pocket for the key Mrs Dibney had given her after the last time.

Inside she found the old lady trying to get up. She was sprawled, half sitting on the bedsit floor. The window was open. Sarah helped her onto the bed, shut the window and sat beside her. She seemed to be stunned. Wisps of silver hair fell across her face as she looked blankly as Sarah draped a moth-holed blanket around her. Then, recognition.

'Sarah... I'm sorry. Did I wake you?'

'Never mind. Are you alright? Did you fall?'

'I think so. So strange. Did you hear him?' the goosebumps returned. Sarah had hoped that the voice had been imaginary, that it was some sort of waking dream.

'Do you want me to make you a cup of tea?' she didn't wait for an answer. It was always odd, being in this twin of her own room. They were tiny rooms, everything in almost the same position. The single bed, the table, the cupboard and the chair. Here they were just older and more battered, as if she were visiting some dismal future. Mrs Dibney's kitchenette was in a far worse state than hers; the floor was crusted with a dried green-brown scum. Sarah made two cups of tea, choosing to ignore the state of the cups, and returned to the bedside. Mrs Dibney was sitting up, clutching the blanket and staring at the window.

'Thank you dear, you're so kind,' she said, taking the cup. 'Tell me... do you believe in an afterlife?'

'Not really.' This wasn't a conversation Sarah ever enjoyed, let alone in the middle of a cruelly cold night. 'I'm not into that stuff. You know, not religious.'

'Neither am I' said Mrs Dibney. 'The voice was my husband.' She sipped her tea, a funny gleam in her eye. She pointed at a photo on the bedside table of a man in uniform. 'He said he will come for me, before the sun rises, that it was time.'

*   *   *

261

At five thirty, Sarah was still awake and trying to make some sense of the night's events, when she heard the window upstairs rattling again. She heard the bed springs and footsteps going across the tiny room, and the window opening. She heard the voice but it didn't chill her; there was a benevolent warmth in it that had her out of bed, out of her door and running up the stairs. A glowing golden light was shining out under the door. She could feel its warmth on her bare feet.

'Mrs Dibney! Wait!' As she fumbled with the key, the door two flats down opened again.

'I say,' said the neighbour. 'Some of us are trying to...'

'Oh, shut up already.' Sarah turned the key in the lock just as the radiance faded.

Inside, the room was warm, even though the window was wide open. Mrs Dibney's nightdress lay on the floor. Sarah leaned out of the window to see if she'd fallen, but the ground below was bare. A movement in the sky caught her eye. Two huge silver owls were circling the house in sweeping arcs. The smaller one peeled off and swooped by the window, brushing Sarah with its wing, then climbed the air currents back to its mate. They circled once more and disappeared behind the trees, wingtips touching.

Waiting for Sarah

By Elaine Everest

The wind whipped at my face as I walked slowly along the shoreline. Perhaps it wasn't such a good idea to meet on the beach. Springtime in Cornwall was still too early for sand castles and dips in the sea.

Hugging my coat close, I looked towards the horizon as clouds scudded across the sky and large waves crashed against the rocks. Tasting the salty spray, I exhilarated in the wildness of the weather and anticipation of our long-awaited meeting. When Sarah's letter suggested we meet on our favourite beach after so long, I couldn't resist replaying memories from our holidays together.

Our family used to meet each summer, renting the largest cottage at Tregellast Barton – an idyllic Cornish dairy farm. The long hot month of August was shared with partners, children, dogs and the occasional family friend; all lazing on the beach and messing around on the farm.

My niece and goddaughter, Sarah, always stayed by my side. At the time, her parents' marriage was winding quickly towards a bitter end. I did my best that summer to keep her away from the stony silences and recriminatory looks.

On one such day, we crept away and collected sticklebacks from the stream running by the cottage. We made a new home for them in a large bucket and decorated it with the black and grey pebbles predominant around the Lizard Peninsula. Then we went for ice cream, only to find on our return that the fish had vanished.

I told Sarah they'd gone home to their mummy because they missed her so much, but – if truth be told – they'd been a late lunch for a hungry crane. She'd sobbed in my arms, but the tears dried quickly when I suggested we go and search for crabs in the many rock pools close to our favourite beach.

It was the same beach I strode along now, only the sun didn't shine quite as brightly, and the sea, all choppy and grey, didn't seem quite so welcoming. Looking at my watch, I feared she wasn't coming. The car park closed in an hour and the afternoon was drawing to a close.

My mind went back to that long, hot summer when Sarah had impatiently hurried me to the beach to spend as much time as possible making sand castles. We discovered new and interesting things in the rock pools, and swam with the dogs in the warm sea. Concentrating hard on the large watch strapped to her thin wrist, she would report the time.

'It's one o'clock. The tide's going out. Let's have lunch.' Or, 'We haven't been into the caves yet and the sun will set in an hour.'

It amused me that small, shy Sarah never missed a thing. Sadly, that also included her parents' failing marriage.

'Do you think that when Daddy goes away, he'll still want to see me?' she asked as she poked about in a shallow rock pool with one of her sandals, her sad eyes glistening with tears.

I hugged her close, wanting to sob myself. 'Of course your daddy will want to see you. We all love you Sarah and no one will ever go away and leave you.'

'What if I go with Daddy? Will you come, too?'

'I couldn't Sarah. I have to stay here and look after the dogs. But I'll save all my pennies in a jam jar until I have enough to visit you.'

As it was, she did go away with her father at the end of that summer, to Canada. He started a new job and a new life, and before long he met someone else and Sarah had the brother and sister she'd always wished for.

My sister carried on with her high-powered city job, flying out to visit Sarah whenever she could. She met her new husband, an airline pilot, on one of the many overseas trips her luxurious lifestyle afforded her.

I never quite fitted with her new life. We slowly drifted apart, only exchanging Christmas cards and the occasional letter.

Sarah and I wrote often. I mastered a basic computer course, and emails across the world became a pleasurable hobby. I devoured every detail of her new home, watching television programmes and reading travel books, so that every time she mentioned a place in her adopted country I could picture her there.

We never managed to meet. Her father was always too busy to come back to England. And me? Money was always short. Despite saving hard, I'd not managed that promised visit to her new home. I'd not set eyes on my beautiful niece since that long ago hot summer.

As I gazed out to sea, deep in thought, I heard a voice on the wind.

'Auntie Jean, Auntie Jean, the sun's almost set. It's getting dark!'

An echo carried through the years on the wind, startled me from my reverie. Did I imagine the words? Was the age-old magic of Cornwall weaving its spell?

I turned to see a young girl running along the beach towards me, her long blonde hair streaming behind her in the wind, cheeks red with excitement. Coming to a halt in front of me she looked up shyly and asked, 'Is it you, Auntie Jean?'

With tears pouring down my face, I bent to hug her close. 'Yes, darling, it's me. Where's your mummy?'

'Here she comes now.' The little girl pointed with a chubby finger.

Looking along the beach I saw her mother walking towards me, the long blonde hair, so like her daughter's, blowing in the wind. I stood to greet her, arms outstretched.

'Hello Sarah, love. Welcome home.'

The Walk of Life

By Joanne Fox

Lacey thought that she could do without her mom's interrogation before she'd even emptied her schoolbag. Just because she'd banged the door and thudded through the house like an angry whirlwind. Had Myles upset her again, teasing her about her spots? Was it the maths teacher who'd told her off? As usual her mom was wrong. The only person who had upset Lacey was David Attenborough, talking on last night's nature programme about the pollution of the oceans. Lacey felt worried for those whales and dolphins. If only there were some way she could make a difference.

'Shouldn't we be more environmentally friendly?' she asked as her mom loaded the dishwasher after tea.

'Oooh, listen to her!' gibed her brother. 'Our Lacey's gone green.'

'Leave her alone Tom,' their mom cut in. 'Lacey's right. We'd use less electricity if you took turns washing up, instead of using the machine.'

Tom tutted loudly. 'Now look what you've started.'

Lacey pursed her lips. She didn't like washing up either. But it was no good having principles if you didn't stick to them.

'O.K. mom. I'll do the dishes.'

Her parents glanced at each other with raised eyebrows. 'So you won't want a lift to school any more either?' asked her dad. 'That'll save petrol.'

Lacey looked at her parents, waiting expectantly for her answer. And Tom, smirking like a Cheshire cat. 'No,' she said, trying not to imagine the long walk up Park Road. 'I won't want a lift to school.'

*   *   *

The next morning, it rained. Lacey trudged up the street, past the shops and down Park Road. *I wish I'd never mentioned the environment,* she thought. But then she remembered all the whales and dolphins swimming in the oceans. If walking to school meant the world was one tiny bit less polluted, surely it was worth it?

'Hey Lacey!'

She peered round the hood of her waterproof to see who was shouting at her. It was that stupid Myles again.

'Doing your drowned rat impression?' he grinned.

'Mind your own business.'

'Pardon me for breathing,' he snickered, and loped off ahead of her.

By the end of the week Lacey had grown more used to her daily hike, and she'd persuaded her parents to let her start a compost heap at the bottom of the garden. But it still wasn't enough. There must be something else she could do.

At morning assembly on Monday the geography teacher asked who wanted to help save the world. *I do*, thought Lacey. *Especially the whales and dolphins.* The teacher said that the school wanted more pupils to walk instead of being brought by car, in order to reduce congestion and traffic fumes. Then the P.E. teacher explained that walking was also good exercise. But apparently some parents didn't want their children to walk to school on their own. Would any of the older pupils volunteer to supervise a small group who lived in the same area as they did? Hands went up around the room, Lacey's among them.

To publicise the venture the teachers wanted as many pupils as possible to walk to school the following Friday. They'd even told the local newspaper what they had planned. 'But first we need a name for the scheme,' the teacher went on. 'Any ideas?'

Someone called out, 'School walk.'

'Walkabout,' suggested another.

Lacey's hand flew up. 'The Walk of Life.'

People murmured in agreement. It had a certain ring to it. So, the Walk of Life it became.

'Cool name,' said Myles, elbowing his way next to Lacey as she waited to add herself to the geography teacher's list. 'How about we take the Park Road stretch?'

Lacey wrinkled her nose. Walking to school with Myles was the last thing she wanted. Hadn't he teased her the whole year? But this was in a good cause. There was no room for quibbling over the details. She gave a resigned sigh. 'O.K.'

*   *   *

On Friday children appeared from all directions along Park Road. Myles and Lacey had a pair of twins to supervise plus three other youngsters. When they arrived at school, the teachers rallied them into a big group so the photographer could take their picture. As soon as it appeared in the local paper Lacey cut it out to stick on her dressing table mirror. Of course the picture had Myles in it too, standing right beside her with his lop-sided grin. But at least he hadn't teased her since the day of the assembly.

'Why don't you come to my house for tea,' he asked her one night when the Walk of Life had become a regular event. 'I could help you with your maths.' So Lacey went, and during their homework she discovered Myles wasn't as bad as she'd thought. In fact, he wanted to be a marine biologist. Boys. Who could ever understand them?

*   *   *

When Lacey got home she saw an envelope with her name on it propped up on the kitchen table. 'What's that?' she asked her mom.

'Open it and see.'

Lacey tore open the envelope and pulled out the contents. It was an adoption certificate, and a picture of a dolphin. She read it carefully. How amazing. Her mother had adopted her a dolphin. It was the perfect present – how could she have known? 'Thanks, mom.'

Her mom smiled. 'We're so proud of you, doing this Walk of Life.'

Lacey ran upstairs and stuck the photo of the dolphin on her mirror, alongside the one of her and Myles. She knew it wasn't really her dolphin. Dolphins were free and swam in the oceans.

No one could own them. But her mother had contributed to the charity in Lacey's name and that meant the world to her.

Lacey raced down the stairs to the telephone. She couldn't wait to tell Myles.

Walking for Water

By Gill James

Angela

Shouldn't have stopped at the Pit Stop, thought Angela, *never mind sat down.* She made the same mistake every year on this sponsored walk.

'Miss, me feet are hurting,' shouted Ben Thomson. 'Can't we give up?'

Angela smiled.

This was all as much about the getting the town kids into the fresh air as about raising money for the wells. Now her thighs were getting sore as they rubbed on the hem of her shorts. This slightly uphill stretch had only a relentless view of the grey sky.

Thia

Thia put Korran down. Her arms were aching. 'You'll have to walk a bit,,' she said. 'Look what a good girl Maite's being.' At least now they had got away from the smell of the decomposing bodies. But she was thirsty. She suspected her little brother and sister were too.

'You've got to get them fresh water,' the man who'd pulled them out from the rubble had said. 'They'll be ill if you don't.' They'd been told there was fresh water twenty-five kilometres away. They only had another five to go, but the sun was beating down relentlessly from the cloudless blue sky.

Angela

The ground levelled out.

'Only another two kilometres,' shouted the marshal handing them bottles of water.

The ground was easier to walk on now. There was woodland on one side and views of the hills on the other.

'Right then guys, let's go for it,' Angela called to her charges. She smiled as some of them started whooping and running. They were all going to make it. They'd probably come again next year. And this year, they'd' be bringing in £2000.

Thia

Korran spotted the river first. 'Look, Thia, a fat sliver snake,' he said.

Thia looked to where he pointed. Yes, it did look like a snake as it meandered below them, reflecting silver in the sun.

And Maite was the first to notice the people. 'Why have they got red crosses on their vets?' she asked.

Thia looked at all the families gathered there and she suddenly couldn't hold back the tears that had been threatening for days.

Korran slipped his hand into hers. Maite stuck her thumb in her mouth.

Thia took a deep breath and started walking slowly down the hill.

One of the men with a red cross on his vest came up to them when they were almost right by the river. 'On your own?' he asked slowly in English, which Thia could just about understand. 'No adults with you?'

Thia could only shake her head. How could she tell Korran and Maite that they would never see Momma and Poppa again?

The man had kind eyes. He seemed to understand.

'Go down there and join that line,' he said. 'They'll let you up to the front because of the little ones.'

Angela

'Here you go, I bet you're ready for this,' said David, handing her a large glass of red wine.

Oh yes, she was definitely ready for that.

The bath had been great. This was going to be even better. She took a sip.

The Merlot seemed to rush straight to her head, making her dizzy, but not at all in an unpleasant way. She felt her body relaxing. Then she needed another taste of its rich fruitiness. She took another gulp.

'Steady on,' said David. 'Don't drink it all at once.'

Angela shrugged. 'Plenty more where that came from,' she said.

Yet around the edges of her mind crept the thought that though they had walked well they might just fail to appear for the next day's maths exam.

Thia

They were almost at the front of the queue. A large man suddenly pushed in front of them knocking Korran to the ground.

'Please' shouted the man. 'My wife is pregnant. Please. You've got to let us have water now.'

Thia stepped aside and pulled Korran to his feet.

The lady filled two beakers and handed them to the man. Thia caught her eyes. The lady smiled and raised her eyebrows. She poured some more water and offered a beaker to Thia. Thia hesitated.

'Come on, take,' said the lady. She handed Thia a beaker. 'There is plenty more where that came from.'

Thia hesitated again.

The lady smiled. 'Drink,' she said. 'I'll see to your brother and your sister.'

Thia drank. The water was cool and fresh. Nothing had ever tasted so good before.

Angela

Angela was beginning to ache all over. She was tired from the walk, from the bath, from the wine. David had joined her in going to bed early, but he was snoring now. Her mind was buzzing. Would they turn up for the maths exam? They'd done so well today. She was proud of them. Would what they'd raised do any good? Would she be able to move tomorrow?

The phone rang.

Who the heck was calling this late? Well, no, it wasn't really late. She padded downstairs and unhooked the phone.

'Angela?' said the voice at the other end. 'You have done so well. I'll match whatever you get. Straight to the latest appeal.' It was Anthony Fletcher, chairman of the board of governors, and local business man. Amazing.

Thia

Thia couldn't sleep. There was so much to think about. Korran and Maite were snoring. Perhaps that was good. Would Momma and Poppa have been proud of her? She'd got them here. They were reasonably safe now. They were sharing a tent with a nice family. They were all snoring too.

Yes, at least her brother and sister were safe. Oh, she was so tired but she couldn't sleep. At some point she knew she would have to grieve properly for the loss of her Momma and her Poppa. But she had too much to think about for the moment.

A torch shone through the opening to the tent.

'Thia, can't you sleep?' It was Ingrid, an aid-worker she had met earlier. 'Don't you worry, my love. More help is coming soon.'

Thia smiled.

The Wonderful Thread

By Steve Moran

Mrs Snodgrass sewed all day and all night. She had nearly every colour of thread imaginable and her house was full with all the clothes she made. One thing she was very strict about, she would never, ever, use wrong-coloured thread.

One day she came to her husband and asked, 'Which of these two threads matches best, the pink or the red?'

The dress she was sewing was cerise so her husband told her to use the darker of the two.

'No, I'll leave it,' she said. 'It has to be perfect.'

That afternoon there was a knock at the front door. As usual, Mr Snodgrass answered because his wife was busy sewing. Standing outside was a peddler with a crooked smile and a canny look in his eyes.

'Will you be needing anything today?' asked the peddler.

'You don't happen to have a cerise thread, by any chance?'

'A cerise thread?' The peddler rummaged in a small suitcase balanced on his knee. 'Ah yes, the very thing. Here is a thread that will change to the colour of any material when it's sewn. It's called The Wonderful Thread.'

'Wait there,' said the husband, and he took a spool of the thread in for his wife to look at. 'Remember that thread you said had to be perfect?'

She looked at the spool her husband handed her. 'You stupid man, this thread has no colour at all!'

'No, but just wait and see. This is The Wonderful Thread; it becomes the colour of whatever it sews.'

'I'll try it then,' replied his wife, frowning as she threaded her needle.

'Wait,' said the husband. 'I'll check with the peddler first.' He went back to the front door. 'Is it okay if she tries some before we buy it?'

'Of course!' replied the peddler.

So, the husband went back inside and his wife sewed the dress with The Wonderful Thread. Sure enough, it turned into exactly the right colour of cerise to match the dress.

'Buy it! Buy all of his stock,' the wife cried. 'I won't ever have to change the thread because The Wonderful Thread will do for every material.'

'Okay,' said the husband to the peddler. 'How much is it?'

'A pound a yard,' replied the peddler.

'Nobody could afford that!' said the husband. 'Not even for The Wonderful Thread.'

'Then pay me for what you've used.'

The husband nodded. 'I will pay you one pound.'

'But how do I know she only used one yard?' said the peddler.

'Oh, for Heaven's sake, come and see my wife.'

He took the peddler into the room where his wife was sewing. The peddler was surprised to see the house full with garments of every shade and variety.

'Well, well,' he said. 'Look how much of The Wonderful Thread she's already used.'

'But these were not sewn with The Wonderful Thread,' said the husband.

'Of course they were,' said the peddler.

'Tell him, wife, tell him these were sewn with ordinary thread.'

'You can't trick me,' said the peddler. 'I can see the perfect colour of the stitches in every garment.'

The peddler's smile twisted in three different directions. 'You will pay,' he said, backing out and waving to his helpers waiting outside. 'I will leave the clothes you are wearing because they look ordinary.'

On the peddler's orders, the helpers marched into the house and carried out all of the clothes. There was nothing Mr and Mrs Snodgrass could do to stop them.

But very next day Mrs Snodgrass started sewing.

Wrong Direction

By Charlie Berridge

The must-have gift for Christmas was a satellite navigation system. Cynth gave Sid one. She bought it from Halfords, the one out on the edge of town next to the new ASDA. Sid was thrilled to bits. He sort of knew that Cynth would go for it and get him the sat-nav he wanted. He'd given enough hints.

'You're the worst bloody map reader in the world,' he'd told Cynth on many outings even though she wasn't that bad. 'What we need is one of those in-car satellite navigation systems. They're really affordable now and would save us a bundle on petrol.'

'How do you work that one out?'

'Well it figures doesn't it? The system will show us the shortest route to take so we'll save on fuel.'

'Hmm,' said Cynth, making a mental note to look out for one for Sid's present.

Sid knew that the box wrapped in funny reindeer paper under the tree contained his sat-nav.

'You may as well let me have it now.'

'You can jolly well wait until Christmas morning.' came the reply.

So Sid waited.

When Cynth and Sid emerged on Christmas morning, it didn't take them long to open the few presents under the tree. Sure enough, Sid found the sat-nav he had wanted and he gave Cynth a big hug and a squeeze.

'Thanks honey,' he said, and Cynth could see that her man was happy. 'We'll try it out when we go to Sal and Graham's for lunch.'

'But we know the way to Sal and Graham's.'

'We'll test it out all the same, see if it works.'

The mid morning journey to Sal and Graham's wasn't that far. As the crow flies it was about fifteen miles, and Sid's Ford Focus knew the route off by heart.

'The car knows the way without that,' said Cynth as Sid plugged the sat-nav into the cigarette lighter. He pressed the buttons and, with Cynth's help from the instruction booklet, the couple were soon being spoken to through the sat-nav.

'Oh err,' giggled Cynth. 'She's got a funny voice.'

Sid rather liked her tone. 'She sounds a bit like that Carol Vorderman,' he said, slipping the car into first gear and heading off in the direction he'd been told.

The instructions came thick and fast, and Sid obeyed even though he wouldn't normally have taken that route.

'We don't normally go this way,' said Cynth.

'I know luv. That's sat-nav for you. It'll be taking us the quickest way.' Sid was rather enjoying being told where to go by another woman. He nudged Cynth in the ribs. 'It makes a change from having you telling me where to go.' They both laughed.

'Take the next available turning on the left,' it said. When the next available left turn appeared, Sid swung the Ford Focus round the corner.

'This can't be right.' Cynth's voice contained a note of caution. 'Are you sure you've set the sat-nav up right?'

'I did everything the book told me to,' he said.

After nearly an hour of driving and following precisely the instructions from the sat-nav, Sid and Cynth were becoming tetchy with each other.

'All I said was, why don't we stop and look at the map.' Cynth was trying to be helpful.

'We don't need a bloody map.' Sid wasn't in the mood for Cynth's helpfulness.

'We're normally there in forty minutes at the most.' Cynth looked at her watch.

'I know we are,' shouted Sid drowning out the latest instruction from Carol Vorderman. 'Now you've made me miss the bloody turn.' Sid had missed the turning and was asked to do a legal U-turn as soon as possible by the unflustered guide.

'There's no need to shout at me like that.'

'Well you bought the bloody thing,' said Sid, firmly passing all the blame on to his wife.

'You were the one who had to have the bloody gadget in the first place. I want it. I want it. I want it.'

'Don't be such a pratt.'

'Pratt's are useful.'

'WELL YOU'RE BLOODY NOT.' Sid screamed with such rage that the car swerved in sympathy.

'WATCH YOUR BLOODY DRIVING.' Cynth screamed back.

'IF YOU DON'T BLOODY LIKE IT YOU CAN BLOODY WELL WALK.'

'RIGHT. I BLOODY WILL.'

Sid brought the car to a sudden halt and even before the tyres had finished their squealing Cynth had leapt out and slammed the door with the sort of force that could be heard several streets away.

Sid sped off not really giving the Ford Focus any time to think about being stationary at all.

'Take the next turning on the right' said the sat-nav and Sid did as he was told, at speed.

'In two hundred yards you will have reached your destination.'

Sid didn't recognise where he was. His blood pressure was as high as his engine's revs and he was very angry.

'You have arrived at your destination.' The sat-nav was quite clear as once again Sid applied the brakes with force, sliding alongside a covered bus shelter. The car behind only just managed to avoid running into the Ford Focus and hooted past as Sid jumped out.

'Where the hell are we?' Sid asked out aloud to no one but himself and the well dressed woman standing at the bus stop.

'Excuse me luv,' he said. 'I'm lost.'

'No you're not,' said Carol Vorderman in her unmistakable Countdown voice. 'You've found me. Happy Christmas.'

Your Voice

By Claudine Lazar

Totty, the first time I heard your voice – well, it was more or less the same as the last time. Loud – you had no idea about the concept of quiet did you? Screeching out the word 'darling'. Never mind the traffic noise, the builders working nearby with their drills – they all stopped to look at who was making such a racket – whenever you spotted someone you knew, it was always the same thing.

You worked at the playgroup – your son was a year older than mine, and they all loved you – you were like the pied piper there – as you were the whole of your life I think – followed around by a little trail of adoring children. It was the shy children you loved most I think – the ones who hid most of the time. There was something about you that made them trust you completely; something that made them feel braver.

As our children grew, I often saw you in the village, on your big old rusty bicycle. That was when they found the cancer – you must have been in your late thirties at the time, and then of course we all knew, because that's what it's like in a village. Life didn't stop though. You went off to Portugal. You and John didn't have much money, but it wasn't very expensive then, and you bought a ramshackle house in the middle of nowhere, and you restored it, and lived there in the sunshine.

Then your eccentric parents, who had the big house in the middle of the village – they were getting very frail, and you came home to look after them. You were the only one of your sisters who didn't have a big career – they all said they didn't have time. You came back all brown, with John, and Joe, and another boy too. Not your own – one you'd found, and taken in. I remember you telling me his parents were a bit hopeless – wrecked all day – and that was how he found you. He followed Joe one day after school and he never went home again. I don't think you actually ever adopted him formally, but by the time you came back he was as much a part of your family as Joe.

You all moved into the big house and, once again, we'd be stopped in our tracks by that loud voice, or passed in a whirr of bicycle wheels and a hurried wave. The cancer came back soon after, and you never really left the village again. You said your sisters were doing their bit for feminism, and you'd had enough of the BBC and globetrotting.

I think I only ever saw you get cross once, in all the time I knew you. Someone had been condescending about your parents, and you'd told them that your mother was not a 'poor old dear', actually – she'd done things that other people only dream about – been wild before it was fashionable – racketing around the country with Dylan Thomas thank you very much. The Queen of Bohemia. I expect that shut them up.

You carried on – your boys grew into lovely teenagers. They didn't always get it right – sometimes they got it spectacularly wrong, but you stood by them in everything – fiercely proud of them both – even after that party that went a bit wrong,

You carried on rescuing people – you had a special talent for it. That young girl – she had her baby when she was hardly grown up herself. We used to see her struggling along – trying to cope with a screaming toddler on her own. Sometimes I'd see them both in tears. You swept her up, took her under your wing, I think you'd be pleased to know she ended up with your startlingly handsome nephew in the end – the baby is at university now.

I moved away but still saw you from time to time, and people talked – they always talked about you. That's how I knew the cancer had come back again. The next time we met, the 'darling' was just as loud, but you were quite a bit smaller – you'd shrunk on the outside – on the inside you were just as big. I told you how sorry I was, and you brushed it off – said you hadn't finished yet. Then you told me about the puppy you'd bought John – 'to keep him company'. I think you knew then, despite what you said.

The last time I saw you, you were at the other end of a long street, and I was with my eldest son – he must have been about 16 and he was still so shy – he never really got over the bullying, and you stood still and flung your arms wide open, and you screeched his name at the top of your voice – and I remember thinking Totty, you might have overreached yourself this time – he is 16 now, not four – but as I watched his face, I saw the biggest smile appear, and I knew he still loved you just as much and that the love overcame the embarrassment factor. I think you were the only person who made him smile at that time – that was when his dad left home and everything fell apart for a bit.

At your funeral I've never seen so many people in one place before – most of the village came. All the 'important people' of course; the county people – because that's what they were supposed to do. But I think those you would have been happiest to see were the children – mostly awkward teenagers now, but some older than that; all the others you took under your wing too – all the misfits, the shy ones. None of them wore black, or even dressed formally, except a few of the boys who wore rather inappropriate clubbing shirts because they wanted to look their best for you Totts – they wanted to say a proper goodbye, as a thank you for everything that you'd given them.

So we don't see your bike anymore, and that's a shame, but you have left a little bit of yourself behind in all those people – a bit of hope. You didn't run a country, or wear a power suit, you were just an ordinary woman who did extraordinary things.

Haiti Before the Earthquake

By Susan Partovi

It was the day after Christmas, 2009. A Saturday. I was at a hotel in Haiti.

Four medical students, two translators and I had spent the previous week working at a rural clinic in Cazale, a small village nestled between mountains that lie about an hour from Port-au-Prince. We had come to implement a cervical cancer/STD screening protocol and experience international medicine. We knew it would be distressing and difficult. But no one could have prepared us for what we saw.

Lori, an RN, runs the clinic. Her sister, Licia, runs the rescue centre, where between 60 and 70 malnourished children are cared for.

The week before Christmas, Licia brought in a 16-month-old girl, Evangalene. She had been there for a month, suffering with Kwoshiorkor, a protein deficiency type of malnutrition causing the belly and legs to swell with fluid. She had responded to treatment, but began to deteriorate, refusing food. When I saw Evangalene, she was crying: 'Vle d'lo…I want water.'

We gave her fluids but she vomited. We had no option but to inset an IV in her scalp. While Lori and I were talking, I watched the baby peripherally and could tell her breathing was very slow. At one point we both looked at her to see if she was breathing (we had no monitors).

'Oh crap, did she just die?' Lori exclaimed.

I rushed over and put my stethoscope over her chest. Her heart was still beating. She was quickly put on oxygen and I ran to Lori's office and grabbed every book I could, trying to find the best way of helping this poor child. I was determined she should pull through.

We gave her Ampicillin, Gentamycin and Ceftriaxone IM. She had a World Health Organisation book about treating malnutrition, which I quickly read. 'Don't forget to check the blood sugar,' it recommended. Crap.

'Lori, let's check her sugar.'

'Undetectable,' she announced.

Oral Rehydration Solutions were administered, while the IV fluids continued.

That afternoon, another girl, Marlene, was brought in. She was 13 and also had Kwashiorkor. The weak teenager had been at the rescue centre a month and had been doing well. The puffiness was receding and she was eating food, including specially-formulated peanut butter made for children suffering protein deficiency malnutrition. But she'd had fevers for a week and had stopped eating the previous day. She was so weak, she could not walk. Her temperature was 103.7. She was pale and her hair had fallen out.

She had a cough but TB had been ruled out. She had been treated her for malaria and typhoid. She was complaining of chest pain and she had thrush (a fungal infection usually seen in AIDS patients) in her mouth. We did an HIV test and it was negative.

Luckily Lori, who has to run the centre without ICU monitors or lab tests, had good antifungal medicines, which I prescribed. I also put her on two other antibiotics in case she had pneumonia as well.

That afternoon, we finally got Evangalene's sugar up and about seven hours later she started asking for water again. She was looking good. We changed her feeds to every hour but at 1am, Lori was woken by the night shift team to report that Evangalene was grinding her teeth. Lori restarted the feeds every 15 minutes and gave her fluids and IV dextrose.

By the morning, she was unresponsive again. I emailed my cousin, who is a paediatrician, for help. She suggested an antibiotic. We looked at all the injectable antibiotics Lori had and chose something that looked like it could help and added that the regimen. Her temperature kept vacillating so we had to put an electric blanket on her.

It was Christmas Eve day and we were planning to leave 'early' to get to our resort before dark. Of course, there were tons of patients to be seen. There was a baby, about nine months old, called Nickenson, that the rescue centre were caring for. Such a big name for a little guy. He was the cutest little thing. He had HIV. His mother died two months after he was born and the father 'couldn't take care of him'. He had this huge mass in his axillae (armpit). No one was willing to take it out, so I said I would do it.

I had to question my judgment as I carried out the procedure. It took three hours to remove this mass. He was awake the whole time. He threw up about 1 ½ hours into the procedure.

'When did he eat?' I asked.

'An hour before the procedure.'

I'd forgotten to tell them not to feed him before the procedure.

Licia held him down. Lori, Sheila (a med student), and even her husband Mitchell (a translator) assisted. As I struggled through the procedure, students came in to present their patients to me.

Evangalene was in a bed next to us, so we were able to monitor her closely.

One of the students came in and said, 'A two-year-old has this white thing up her nose. What should we do?'

'Just take it out,' Lori and I chimed.

It was a balloon.

In the next room was a woman in labour. Lori was yelling across the room at the patient in Creole while Laura was trying to get her to push.

'She won't push,' Laura, one of the med students, lamented.

'Nothing I can really do right now,' I said as I continued to curse the mass.

Evangalene wasn't looking good. Her eyes started darting to the left. She was seizing. That's when I gave up.

Sheila looked at me, 'What else can we do for her?'

I just shook my head. 'She's dying.'

We both turned back to our little guy and kept working. Finally, I got this lime-sized mass out. Then one of the workers called me into the labouring woman's room to help her.

I manage to eat something and pack before going back down.

'The baby's out!' Laura and Sheila delivered the baby. It was a piece of good news. We needed that. Laura had already changed and was in her 'resort' gear.

Nickenson was done but looked tired. Evangalene was the same. Nine of us piled in the truck and took off at 4pm. I didn't get to say Merry Christmas to Lori.

On Saturday night, Sheila spoke to Lori. She told us the news: Evangalene, Nickenson and another child died on Christmas day. Marlene was eating and doing well. The little baby that Laura and Sheila delivered was alive and well.

By Tuesday we were back into the grind. Adoo came to the procedure room. We met Adoo on our first day at the clinic. His mother brought him to the clinic after walking ten hours. She had carried him every inch of the way. There was a twin but she couldn't carry both of them. This one was the worst. His eyes bugged out of his head; his skin looked as if it were tightly wrapped around his torso as every muscle between his ribs contracted with each breath. His belly was bloated; his legs and feet were swollen.

Adoo was looking poorly. His breathing was very laboured and his lungs sounded junky. We gave him fluids, put him on oxygen, started the IV dextrose right away and started the Meropenem – an expensive antibiotic that kills everything. I watched his breathing and temperature closely. He spiked a high temperature so we were right on it with acetaminophen and cooling measures. There was no way we could check his haemoglobin but I was sure he was very anaemic. A blood transfusion was probably warranted and might have helped him to not work so hard to pump blood and breathe but, alas, we didn't have it.

He perked up that evening. He raised his skinny, little arm and asked for someone to scratch it! He was peeing which meant his kidneys were working and he had no diarrhoea (yes!). He was more alert and started to speak. He would scratch his little foot. But his vitals were still worrisome. He was still breathing at 60 with a heart rate of 150. He also wasn't tolerating his NG tube feeds so we switched to Oral Rehydration Therapy...less amount but more often while continuing his IV fluids and four antibiotics.

The baby that Laura delivered last week came back on Monday. She was doing well although a little jaundiced and I suspected she had a little infection of her umbilicus. We gave her two shots of antibiotics, ensured her first-time mother knew how to breast feed and strongly recommended that she come back the following day.

Abscess-on-the-forehead-boy came back looking great. Amanda got to sew up a split lip. Victoria sewed up a scalp laceration on a boy who was very brave. Lori put in a scalp IV in one of the babies from the Rescue Centre after he fell into an open fire and burnt one-third of his body.

'He's not doing so good,' said Lori.

I'm surprised he survived, I thought.

We saw lots of fevers/belly pain/cough, diagnosing almost everyone with TB, malaria, typhoid or 'worms'. I'm sure there were other diseases I missed but those are basically the only tropical diseases I really know. Talk about feeling impotent.

Adoo was in the bed in the procedure room. I routinely checked his breathing, heart rate and temperature every 30 minutes but there was no change. I asked Lori what she thought about sending him to the paediatric ward at General Hospital. She had sent patients to the hospital before. They rarely survived. I've been duped once before. My ability to gauge 'badness' had been reset and was back on track.

'He'll be fine,' she assured me. I allowed myself to jump on Lori's 'fine' train.

The following morning I saw Marlene lying in bed at the Rescue Centre. 'Pa san bien...You don't feel well?'

She tells me that she had vomited three times, had diarrhoea, and chest pain. Her heart rate was 120. Just as I was about to panic, she grabbed my hand and with a little smile and she asked, 'Cola?'

'Vle Cola?...You want a cola?' I asked and ran upstairs, got a bottle of cold cola, opened it. and ran back down to give it to her. She can't feel that bad if she's asking for a Coke, I reassured myself.

When I arrived at the clinic, there was more bad news. Adoo had died. I didn't want to see his little body not living. Lori wrapped him in a blanket. Half an hour later, Lori delivers more bad news: the baby with burns didn't make it. I didn't know what to say. I hadn't expected so many deaths.

*   *   *

We left Cazale on the Wednesday at 4pm and I eventually returned home on January 1. Lori kept me updated on Marlene's status and the news wasn't good. She wasn't tolerating food and her breathing had become more laboured. She was on continuous oxygen, IV fluids and antibiotics.

I tried to get help. I called Dr Severe, a paediatrician at General Hospital in Port-au-Prince and the father of one of our translators but there was no answer. I called the medical director of General Hospital in Port-au-Prince and asked him which hospital had a ventilator.

He told me to give Lori his number. I called her, giving the details. But on Monday morning I received an email from Lori. Marlene had died Sunday night slightly before midnight. Despite offering to pay for the hospital fee and providing transportation, the family declined. She died 'comfortably with her family around'. She was 13 years old.

I don't know why she died.

*   *   *

Before Haiti's devastating earthquake, I believed the biggest health problem in the developing world wasn't AIDS, TB, or malaria, but that it was malnutrition which is caused by poverty and corruption. In Haiti, 13 per cent of children die before their fifth birthday. More than half the population in Haiti are under the age of 18.

HIV infection was down to two per cent of the population. Haiti finally had a handle on AIDS and TB. They had mobile

287

clinics that went to the mountains, educating people and testing them for HIV. The staff handed out condoms.

Most people with tuberculosis would get Direct Observational Treatment. I thought that we should get a mobile clinic that would educate people about prenatal care and nutrition. We could hand out eggs and peanut butter.

I thought, let's cure starvation. That's largely why so many children get so sick to begin with. Marlene didn't have thrush from HIV, she didn't have enough protein in her little body to make enough functioning white blood cells to kill off all the microbial agents that attack humans on a daily basis. A healthy body could fight it off.

That's what I thought before the earthquake.

Have I changed my opinion since this devastating event? No. I feel exactly the same.

This is a country without drinkable water, adequate sanitation, reliable electricity, sturdy housing, security or trustworthy medical care. While I am in awe at the international response to this disaster, I can't help but think what would have happened if the world had paid more attention to Haiti before the earthquake. Perhaps this is a wake up call on how we can respond to impoverished communities in the world before disaster hits. Perhaps we can commit to helping our brothers and sisters to overcome poverty and thus the sequelae of poverty before natural disasters hit and before children starve to death.

New Charity Book Coming May 2010

Gentle Footprints

Gentle Footprints is a wonderful collection of short stories about wild animals. The stories are fictional but each story gives a real sense of the wildness of the animal, true to the Born Free edict that animals should be born free and should live free. The animals range from the octopus to the elephant, each story beautifully written.

Gentle Footprints includes a new and highly original story by Richard Adams, author of *Watership Down*, and a foreword by the patron of Born Free, Virginia McKenna OBE.

£1 from the sale of each copy, plus a percentage of the author royalties, will be donated to The Born Free Foundation.

This special book will raise both awareness and much-needed funds for the animals. Check out the Gentle Footprints blog which includes links and information from Born Free about each of the featured animals. Find out how you can get involved in their conservation:
http://gentlefootprintsanimalanthology.blogspot.com

Official launch at the Hay-on-Wye Literary Festival June 2010.

The book will be available for pre-order from Bridge House Publishing:
www.bridgehousepublishing.co.uk

ISBN 978-1-907335-04-4

Bridge House

Do you have a short story in you?

Then why not have a go at one of our competitions or try your hand at a story for one of our anthologies? Check out:
http://bridgehousepublishing.co.uk/competition.aspx

* * *

Submissions

Bridge House publishes books which are a little bit different, such as *Making Changes*, *In the Shadow of the Red Queen* and *Alternative Renditions*.

We are particularly keen to promote new writers and believe that our approach is friendly and supportive to encourage those who may not have been published previously. We are also interested in published writers and welcome submissions from all authors who believe they have a story that would tie into one of our themed anthologies.

Full details about submissions process, and how to submit your work to us for consideration, can be found on our website
http://bridgehousepublishing.co.uk/newsubmissions.aspx